JAPANESE
GAME

JAPANESE GAME

RICHARD HOYT

A TOM DOHERTY ASSOCIATES BOOK
NEW YORK

JAPANESE GAME

Copyright © 1995 by Richard Hoyt

This book is printed on acid-free paper.

A Forge Book
Published by Tom Doherty Associates, Inc.
175 Fifth Avenue
New York, N.Y. 10010

Design by Lynn Newmark

ISBN 0-312-85553-2

First edition: February 1995

Printed in the United States of America

0 9 8 7 6 5 4 3 2 1

For Teresita Artes Hoyt

"The purpose of training is not health
but the forging of the soul, and a strong
soul is only born from strong practice."
—Suishu Tobita, the "god of Japanese baseball"

"Jangle gently to keep the juices flowing."
—American pitcher Satchel Paige

I

BESUBORU

ONE

In the morning, James Burlane caught two snook with his ultra-light spinning outfit in a big, deep pool of the Macal River that flowed into Belize from Guatemala. When the heat of the tropical morning began to build, Burlane put away his gear and headed for San Ignacio, waiting his turn to cross the single-lane Hawksworth bridge. When he proceeded across, the tires of his Plymouth Cherokee buzzed on the metal grid. Burlane imagined he was a World War II bomber pilot listening to the drone of the engines: *hhhhhhhhhhhhmmmmmmmmmmm*.

The eastern end of the bridge faced a turnaround that was the center of the town plaza. Community bigwigs had donated benches for the inside of the turnaround. The streaked, off-white police station, once white, boasting pillared colonial verandas, sat on a slight rise to the left of the turnaround; to the right, downhill, lay the entrance to Burns Street, the main drag of San Ignacio. Burlane parked his Cherokee, slung his daypack over his shoulder, and sauntered downhill past a popcorn stand, a barbershop, a hardware store, and a Chinese café.

On Burns, he stepped into a café, Eva's, and parked his jeans. He had been in Eva's when it was packed with customers; now he had peace, for which he was grateful.

Burlane had been in the jungles of Belize and Guatemala doing pen-and-ink sketches of Mayan ruins, but now his mind was on sports. At the public market in Belmopan, he had swapped a two-week-old *Newsweek* to a tomato-buying traveler for a current issue of *Sports Illustrated*. Since the *Newsweek* was dated, Burlane had offered to throw in a kilo of tomatoes, but the traveler declined; he understood the unaccountable craving for something current to read.

Burlane ordered beans and rice and a Beliken beer and proceeded to read *Sports Illustrated* from cover to cover. He even read the chatty little note to the readers, a regular feature by *SI*'s editor, Dutch Mandel. Mandel was excited about an unusual project by writer Darryl Lattimore. He said there were so many baseball metaphors in everyday language it was a joke.

Somebody or other struck out, or fouled out, or went for the fences. Outs, innings, bases advanced, runs scored; baseball, like life, was based both on subtraction and addition. Lattimore had this idea: In view of the current wrangling over trade issues between America and Asia, what if a writer compared baseball as played in the two hemispheres? Same rules. Different imaginations. Was the idea of fair play everywhere the same? Or were there elemental differences that had to be taken into account?

Lattimore would interview Americans who had played baseball in Japan, beginning with Bobby Carneseca, a nine-year veteran with the Hanshin Tigers, then go to Japan for a firsthand look at the action. While in Asia, he would research the simmering controversy about alleged cheating by Asian teams in the Little League World Series in Williamsport, Pennsylvania. This would be Balls and Strikes in Asia, from Little League to Sadaharu Oh.

TWO

Bobby Carneseca pushed the cocker spaniel's nose from his crotch. "Dammit, Harry." He grabbed a well-worn baseball glove from the floor beside his easy chair and used it to give the dog a swat. Carneseca, wearing sweat-stained gray cotton warm-up bottoms and a Lotte Orions tank top, obviously liked to be comfortable; his den was a litter of newspapers and magazines, and on the walls were photographs of him posing with various Japanese baseball players.

If Carneseca was aware of the tall, curly-haired photographer circling, Nikon in hand, click-clacking for the perfect shot of his rugged, lined face, he didn't show it.

He put the glove on his left hand and thumped it in the pocket with the fist of his right, then pulled the strap of his tank top. "A shirt like this is a collector's item. They're now called the Marines. The Lotte Marines." He eyed the tape recorder and said, "You say baseball is *besuboru*, right?"

Darryl Lattimore grinned. "Seems like a simple enough game. Simple and hard as hell at the same time."

The black cocker spaniel, nose twitching, made another try at Carneseca's crotch. "Get lost, will you, Harry." Carneseca pushed the dog away. "Marge, will you throw this dog outside so he can air himself out. He can't keep his nose to himself."

From the next room, a woman's voice called, "Harry!"

Harry ignored her.

"Harry!" she called louder. She rattled a plastic dish on the floor.

Harry went running.

"Jesus," Carneseca said.

He rubbed his blue eyes with his knuckles, thinking. He said, "Well, the bases are the same distance apart in the U.S. and Japan, I'll grant you that. The pitcher's mound is the same. Four balls and you take your base. Three strikes and you're out." He gave the mitt another whack and called out, "Come on, babe. Hon now! Hon now! Stand in there, babe! Hon now!"

As a young man Carneseca had made it to the top of the Baltimore Orioles farm system, but never made The Show, as the players called the bigs, and so had spent nearly a decade playing third base for the Orions. He had a wonderfully rugged, lined face; in Lattimore's opinion this was the way a storied old ball player ought to look.

Carneseca said, "I'll give you some examples. You have a man on first with nobody out or one out early in the game. You're the manager. What options do you have? What do you do?"

A door slammed next door. Harry yelped. Carneseca's wife said, "Now stay out for a while. It won't kill you. You're a dog, remember."

Lattimore thought about Carneseca's question for a moment. "It depends on the speed of the runner and the skills of the batter. I could call a hit and run. I might have the batter lay down a sacrifice bunt to move the runner into scoring position. If I had a left-handed long-ball hitter against a right-handed pitcher, I might let him swing away. The general advice is to go for big innings early on, and get more cautious later in the game."

"In Japan, you bunt."

"What?"

Carneseca said, "You bunt. Never anything else. The Japanese don't like things to be unpredictable. If the batter always bunts, the opposing manager always knows how to position his infielders. To go for a hit in a bunting situation would give one team an unfair advantage. The Japanese love their statistics. They collect numbers on everything, and there is much palavering to decide what to do next. You'd think the announcers had mainframe computers in the press box. The manager and his coaches huddle between pitches and swings of the bat so that a game ordinary lasts from three to four hours. In *besuboru* everything is by the book, just like flower arranging and jujitsu. Managers do not deviate. They talk and they talk and they talk, but in the end they do what the statistics tell them to do, or risk having to apologize to their fans for being boneheads."

"I see."

Carneseca said, "Say, can you guys use a cup of coffee?"

"I'd go for one," Lattimore said.

"How about you?" Carneseca said to the photographer.

The curly-haired photographer began packing his gear. "Thanks, but I think I got what I need here. I gotta plane to catch."

Carneseca called, "Marge, could we have a couple of cups of coffee in here, please?"

"Coming up," Marge said.

"Well, I'm out of here. I think I've gotten a couple of decent shots," the photographer said. "The dog is what did it." He grinned and slung his bag of gear over his shoulder, simultaneously extending his hand to Carneseca. "It's been a pleasure."

Carneseca said, "My big moment in *Sports Illustrated* and I'm pictured with a dog's nose rammed up my crotch. Wonderful!"

Grinning, the photographer headed for the door. "Later, then, Darryl."

When the photographer was gone, Carneseca said, "Okay, say you're Roger Clemens, pitching for the Red Sox. You're facing Ruben Sierra, a slugger from the Dominican Republic. You're playing Japanese-rules baseball. What do you do?"

"I'm careful not to put anything over the plate. I pitch to the corners. Maybe up and in, then down and away. It depends on the book. I'm a rightie. Sierra is what, a leftie? A rightie? I don't know. I'd need to know his strengths and weaknesses."

"You show him nothing but curve balls and junk, and you keep them well away from the plate."

"But I'm a fast-ball pitcher."

"It doesn't make any difference. Junk. He's a foreigner. You throw junk and nothing that he can really get his bat on. If he hits a home run, it's not your fault. You did the right thing. You can fuck up royally, but you have to follow correct form."

"I'd probably end up walking him."

"No, you try to strike him out throwing balls. A Japanese umpire expands the strike zone for foreign batters and reduces it for foreign pitchers. If the batter is a foreigner, you can bounce it in front of the plate or sail it into the stands and still have it called a strike. A friend of mine once struck out on a called strike that hit him in the small of the back."

"Well!"

Margez Carneseca, a rounded, pleasant-looking blond woman, came in with two cups of coffee on a tray with a small bowl of sugar and a creamer. As she set the tray down on a coffee table, she said, "They wouldn't throw Bobby anything but curve balls. Did he tell you that?"

Carneseca laughed. "Marge spent ten years of her life listening to me bitch about curve balls. Okay, Clemens, you start to lose your stuff and the batters jump on you in the fifth inning. The manager gives you the hook. What do you do?"

Lattimore gave his coffee a hit of cream and stirred it in. "I put my arm on ice so it doesn't start to swell on me. And when the trainer gives me the okay, I go take a shower."

"Wrong. You've disgraced yourself by getting tired. You go to the bullpen and throw fastballs as hard as you can for the rest of the game. One right after another, you smoke 'em."

Lattimore looked surprised. "Why, for heaven's sake? If I did that every game it would destroy my arm and shorten my career." He took a sip of coffee, clearly puzzled by Japanese training habits.

"That's thinking only of yourself. You do it to demonstrate

Fighting Spirit. You're not a quitter, see? You'll try harder next time. Americans play baseball. The Japanese work at it. Okay, you arrive at the park on the afternoon of a game. What do you do?"

Lattimore considered the question. "I loosen up so I don't pull a muscle in the game. I play a game of pepper or shag a few fly balls. I take batting practice, and maybe some infield practice."

Carneseca shook his head in mock reproof of Lattimore's answer. "That's American baseball, Darryl. In Japan, the first thing you do is run."

"I run?"

"You run and run and run. Hard. Then you do calisthenics. You do push-ups and sit-ups and squat-jumps and jumping jacks. Then you run some more. You do this to the point of near exhaustion."

"Why? I have a game to play."

"To demonstrate Fighting Spirit. Guts. The fans show up early to watch you punish yourself. Okay, assume you're playing third base. The batter drills a hard single in the gap between you and the shortstop. What do you do?"

"Huh?" Lattimore furrowed his brow.

"You throw yourself at the ball, even though you know you don't have a chance. You get your uniform dirty, a demonstration of *doryoku*, Fighting Spirit."

At the door of the den, there came a scratching. Scratch, scratch, scratch.

Carneseca glanced at the door. "Shit!"

Scratch, scratch, scratch.

Carneseca, trying to ignore the dog, said, "Say you're on first base with none out, Darryl. The batter hits a double-play ball to the second baseman. You're barreling down on the shortstop going full tilt. What do you do?"

"I get it. I show maximum Fighting Spirit and guts! I come in high and hard, Pete Rose-style, and slam into him to break up the double play. Pop a few ribs if I have to."

Carneseca shook his head. "No, no, no. You make a dramatic, hard slide. You get your uniform as dirty as possible, but you never actually touch the shortstop. That's not done."

"No?"

Scratch, scratch, scratch.

"Marge?"

"I hear him."

Carneseca gave Lattimore a reproachful look. "If you touched the shortstop, it would hurt his feelings."

"Ahhhh." Lattimore made another note.

"There is *tatemae*, truth that is stated, and *honne*, truth that is meant. You have to understand the difference. The idea of Fighting Spirit is enough to keep people happy. Real aggression is to be avoided. Harmony is the thing. In harmony is happiness."

Scratch, scratch, scratch.

"Aw, Marge."

"I hear him, just a second."

"Remember when the Philadelphia Phillies center fielder Len Dykstra and a friend got drunk at a party and ran off the road on their way back home? Dykstra got all banged up and spent time in the hospital. What do you suppose would have happened if he'd done that in Japan?"

"I don't know. Maybe a fine for missing games owing to stupidity. Those things happen."

Carneseca said, "It would have ended his career."

Lattimore looked startled. "What? Why?"

"For embarrassing his team."

"Dykstra didn't embarrass the Phillies. Himself maybe, but not the Phillies."

"He's a member of the team, so the team is embarrassed. What is important is the *wa*, the spirit of harmony. You do not break *wa*. Underline that if you want to understand Japanese baseball."

Marge Carneseca arrived, broom in hand. She opened the door and gave the dog a whack. "Now dammit, Harry, go play and leave your father alone. He's busy."

Carneseca said, "My father, she says. A dog."

Marge shut the door on the chastened Harry. She said, "He

might as well be." Shaking her head, she returned to the kitchen.

Lattimore scrawled and underlined *"spirit of wa."*

Carneseca, watching him, said, "And *giri.* Underline that too."

"Giri?"

"Sort of like loyalty. Loyalty to your family, your club, your country, whatever. Loyalty to a group. It's the glue of repression."

"Giri. Got it."

Carneseca said, "You get into a rhubarb with an umpire in the United States. What are the rules?"

"You can shout if you want. You can jump up and down like a monkey or Billy Martin. But you can't touch the umpire. That's a no-no."

Carneseca took a sip of coffee. "Correct. But in Japan, it depends on who you are; there are special rules for official heroes, and the legend-building never stops. For example, Masaichi Kaneda won more than four hundred games as a pitcher; as manager of the Orions, he became famous for kicking umpires in the ribs and stomach. When he was younger, people came to watch his curve ball; when he became a manager, they came to watch The Legend kick umpires. You're going to Japan and watch some games, I take it."

"Oh, sure," Lattimore said.

"You'll find that all cheering is organized in Japan. This is the system of *oyedan,* in which organized nonstop cheering and noisemaking is conducted, usually in the center-field bleachers. There are no individuals in the stands spontaneously heckling and razzing the players, no 'throw the bum out' or any of that nonsense. The fans in the *oyedan* follow instructions on how and when to cheer. They have these plastic gadgets they whack in unison."

Scratch, scratch, scratch.

"If you see Tokyo's Yomiuri Giants play, their uniforms are identical to the San Francisco Giants'. The Hiroshima Carp look like they're the Cincinnati Redlegs. The Japanese have Mickey Mantle bats and Frank Robinson gloves and Yogi Berra face masks. You think you're watching the same game as in the United States right down to the uniforms, but you're not. You're fooling yourself if you think otherwise. This is Japanese baseball. It's played by Japanese rules. They have ties. Did you know that?"

"Ties?" Lattimore looked surprised.

Scratch, scratch, scratch.

Carneseca got up and opened the door to let Harry back in. He sat back down, crossing his legs to foil the dog's nose. "Because of all the jawboning and conferring, they call a game a tie after twelve innings. If they didn't do that, a game might last five or six hours. Also, if the game ends in a tie, nobody has to lose. Everybody gets to demonstrate his Fighting Spirit, and *wa* is maintained."

THREE

It was sum-sum-summertimmmme, and all the trees and leaves were green along the Severn River on the western shore of the Chesapeake Bay. The air was humid. *Lethargic* was the word. Insects batted about in cobwebbed boughs leaning lazily over the water as they had since the time of George Washington.

The American vice president and Japanese foreign minister were at the riverside retreat of a wealthy admirer of the Harold Olofson administration. The admirer, who had made more than a fortune in the computer microchip business, was now ambassador to Sri Lanka. He consequently had fewer occasions to use his retreat, located only a few miles upstream from Annapolis, Maryland, where the United States Naval Academy was located, as well as St. John's College, where students yet studied the ancient Greeks.

Vice President Jack Shive, himself a graduate of the University of Virginia, felt confident in the presence of graduates of Harvard University or Yale or Stanford or the University of California at Berkeley. He felt truly humbled in the presence of a graduate of St. John's College or of the similar classics curriculum at the University of Chicago because he felt that at those schools students somehow emerged with an education that meant something in an age of intellectual mush.

The retreat was surrounded by rolling lawns that challenged a golf course in ambition, and dotted with cherry trees that were now in bloom. The two-story house built of stone in the eighteenth century, with a steep-pitched slate roof and gabled windows, mossy with age, was situated on top of a small bluff overlooking the river, well above the floodplain.

The back of the house featured a splendid veranda, once screened to repel the mosquitoes but now open—electronic insect zappers were now employed to combat them. Their host had a fifty-foot sailboat moored at a private dock at the bottom of the bluff which they could use for their talk if they wanted. Shive offered Yoshida his choice of veranda or sailboat; Foreign Minister Masayuki Yoshida chose the veranda. Would it be Wild Turkey or green tea? Green tea, Yoshida said. He was a veranda-and-green-tea kind of man. He was foreign minister, and this was serious business.

Shive was in a Wild Turkey mood, but he too ordered green tea. Whether he drank Kool-Aid or battery acid didn't make a whole lot of difference for what he had to do.

Yoshida eyed Shive calmly over his cup of tea, waiting for the vice president to get to the usual pleading and veiled threats. *You Americans are like senile old women, trying to gum us into submission.*

Shive said, "I will tell you honestly, Yoshida-*san*, if the President and I don't pay attention to the American voters, they'll take it out on us at the ballot box. All the polls say one thing: The voters are convinced that Japan is being allowed to play by an international double standard, and they're tired of that game. Our struggle with the Stalinists is over." *In short, we think it's time you gave up the tit.*

Yoshida sipped his tea.

Shive didn't know why he felt compelled to soften the little bastard up. Yes he did too; it was Shive's Western sense of squeamishness about being a total chickenshit. "Every year we go through the laborious, time-consuming drill of documenting our complaints under international trade agreements, only to have them ignored. You know the sentiment on Capitol Hill as well as I do, Yoshida-*san*. Fair is fair, is the way Americans look at it." *We paid for your goddamn defense. We let you screw us with your one-way trade policies. We thought when the old boys of the Liberal Democratic Party took their dive that things would change, but no. Business as usual. It's finally dawned on us that we're being played for suckers, and we don't like it one damn bit.*

"A beautiful view from up here. What a beautiful river, the Severn. The boats on the water, it's truly lovely."

Horseshit. "Now, Yoshida-*san*, you will note that the *New York Times* and even the *Wall Street Journal* have softened on the issue. In spite of what you may think, our voters can and do read. You apologize, you promise, then do nothing. They know that." *You've gone on a binge of apologizing for what you did in World War II. You've apologized for keeping women as sex slaves for your soldiers. You've apologized for using prisoners of war for slave labor. You've apologized for cannibalism committed by your soldiers. You think we longnoses want apologies, so you'll apologize. Your apologies mean nothing, and we both know it.*

Yoshida opened his mouth as though to speak, then closed it. *Can't you see that a man's word is a reflection of his giri? There's no point to telling the truth or keeping a promise if it gets in the way of giri.*

"We let you sell your cars in our market, but you effectively keep us out of yours. You add special 'luxury' taxes on almost everything we try to sell in your market. You cry 'luxury, luxury,' when you really mean 'foreign, foreign.' Your government stays out of competition in your market, and gives tax breaks and cheap financing to companies selling in ours. You have one price for your cars in Japan, another in the U.S. You know what that's called? That's called dumping. When you do assemble cars on our soil, you make sure we buy parts from Japanese companies." *You always have some little surprise for us, some little chisel or screw. Always. We thought a more expensive yen might do the trick. But no, you found a way around that as well. The Cold War is over, you little fucker. No more free rides.*

Yoshida said, softly, politely, "As you know, Mr. Shive, our government is fully aware of your complaints, and we sincerely apologize for any confusion there may have been in the past, but these things take time. We've had a political reformation in our government, and I'm sure nobody wants to go back to the old ways." *You might try building them with right-hand drive so they'll fit our highways. Idiots!*

Shive said, mildly, "Your patent laws are deliberately written to help your firms steal our ideas and inventions. Instead of reform, you change a comma once every five years." *We plead. You pretend to listen. You think we're beneath contempt, don't you? You'd bugger us forever if we didn't object.*

Yoshida looked grave. "We have our constituents just as you have yours, Mr. Shive. You're talking about the basic structure of our economy. But truly, we're making every effort to address your concerns. Every effort."

Shive said, "I regret to have to say, Yoshida-*san*, that President Olofson has authorized me to tell you, well in advance of his visit to Japan, that your government must actually do something to correct the dumping situation, or we'll be forced to even out the price at our ports of entry. For years, it was delay, delay as a matter of policy. Now it's delay, delay with a threat that if we don't support you you'll return to the bad old days of the LDP. Frankly we don't see any difference between the old LDP and the new LDP."

Yoshida looked alarmed. "Surely, Mr. Shive . . ."

"In addition, unless you publicly agree to rewrite your patent laws, President Olofson will instruct the Commerce Department to prohibit the sale of any product in the United States whose producer is accused of violating international patent or copyright laws. If an American company charges Mitsubishi with stealing the design of a windshield wiper, we will ban the entire model from our market until the issue is decided by the courts." *If you think your engineers and scientists are as creative as ours, Yoshida-san, we say let them show it. Let them prove it.*

Yoshida looked concerned. "As you know, Mr. Shive, we've been working on our patent laws. It remains a top priority." *Is there any confusion at all about who makes the best automobiles and television sets?*

Shive said, "The right to income from patents and copyrights is internationally recognized, Yoshida-*san*. Our creativity is a valuable resource, and we insist on being paid for it." *You're pretty quick at figuring out how other people's microchips work. If only you knew how to imitate fair play, eh, Yoshida-san?*

Yoshida sighed. "We too are weary of this cloud of suspicion and hostility, Mr. Shive. But it's extremely difficult to work under such pressure as you suggest. We have to take public opinion into account. You can understand that. Perhaps if we weren't facing such a harsh deadline . . ."

"We've been through this before. We both know that if we don't hold a pistol to your head, you won't do anything. President Olofson's advisers assure him that Congress will back his actions. He is too much of a friend and admirer of Japan to introduce them without warning, which is why I asked for this chat. We both know the importance of proceeding as friends rather than as adversaries."

"Worthwhile friendships have their ups and downs, Mr. Shive. We've always valued America's friendship, you know that." *Why don't you people try a little hard work for a change? It might work miracles.*

"I'll be visiting Japan again in advance of his visit. We can settle on the details then." *You still are an island nation, aren't you, dependent on foreign markets? Perhaps you'll be more comfortable staying in Asia.* Shive swirled the leaves in the bottom of his cup. "Say, isn't this tea good? I love your tea and your *sushi*, and my wife is quite fond of those pickled vegetables of yours."

FOUR

They sat at a bamboo table on the veranda of a sprawling bamboo clubhouse which had a thatched roof out of a tourist promotion. They smoked Marlboro cigarettes and drank Chivas Regal on the rocks. Their ashtray overflowed with butts. A slightly faded red-and-white checkered parasol kept the sun off them.

They wore Arnold Palmer golfing shoes and Gary Player slacks with a special crotch designed for an extra-smooth stroke. They had been golfing, and this was the nineteenth hole. They had paid off their gallery of a hundred Filipino college students whom they had hired for fifty pesos each, about two American dollars—never mind that they politely clapped for hooks and slices and missed sure-thing putts as well as decent shots. When the Filipino golf pro had first mentioned the possibility of hiring one's own gallery, they had been amazed. Their own gallery? Only fifty pesos a head? Of course, they had quickly agreed. They had never heard of the practice of hiring one's own gallery of supporters, but then there were few countries where labor was as cheap as in the Philippines.

A waiter in a sparkling white *polo barong* brought them another round of drinks and a clean ashtray. He wore polished leather shoes, which Shoji Kobayashi presumed was a fillip that would be added to their bill. It was a nice enough golf course, Kobayashi supposed, but there was something about the tropics that didn't match the feel of the gentleman's game that had originated in Scotland. A good turf ought to give a little for pleasant walking and so it could better stand the traffic. The courses in tropical countries inevitably looked like crabgrass struggling to grow on a field of old boards. Kobayashi found it difficult to imagine what happened in the hot season. There was little reason to believe that the Filipino groundskeepers had the energy or wherewithal to keep anything watered. Did tee shots bound *ka-boing-boing-boing* to absurd lengths on the rock-hard surface?

In Scotland, a greening mist rolled through the thrashy copses and o'er the mossy moors. In the Philippines, the water came in sporadic deluges accompanied by rips of white lightning and horrific booms and claps of thunder. Then, just as quickly, it was back to the searing heat. The water did not sink; it sat. This was not every groundskeeper's dream.

There were few proletarian courses in Japan where electric golf carts were not mandatory in order to hurry players through the course. Kobayashi had forked over the yen equivalent of a quarter of a million U.S. dollars to join a club outside Yokohama where he could play at a leisurely pace. But one would have to be a mad dog or an Australian to walk eighteen holes in the tropical heat of the Philippines.

The course where Kobayashi played had been designed by the American supergolfer, Jack Nicklaus. It was craftily studded with lakes and sandtraps that looked like twisted boomerangs. The sand in the bunkers, said to be the whitest in the world, was imported from Ata Iti, a remote Pacific island. Both fairways and greens, despite their appearance, were planted with the same grass as the famous Pebble Beach golf course in California.

There was a good reason why golf had become wildly popular in Japan. It was a game in which form mattered. Details counted. One learned by concentration and perseverance. One mastered the rules and eliminated dysfunctional tics that impaired the quest for a perfect swing. One endlessly repeated the same correct swing for each situation.

Kobayashi was not surprised when the Japanese national basketball team got thrashed by Africans. But golf, like archery and baseball, was a Japanese kind of sport. Volleyball, too. The Japanese didn't mind sacrificing their knees and elbows for the good of the side and so were superlative diggers. The taller long-noses could wear their arms out delivering vicious spikes, but the Japanese, pumped full of fighting spirit, would return the ball every time.

Kobayashi's companion, Tsutomu Kamina, said, "What are they going to do?"

Kobayashi, who had been thinking about golf and games, said, "Who?"

"What you told me back there. The story about Yoshida and Shive. Is it true, *oyabun-san?*"

"Oh, that. I don't know. There're all kinds of rumors. But it's all nonsense. One would think they would act with their country's best interest at heart, but they won't."

"They have to do something."

Kobayashi made a farting sound with his tongue.

"They'll politely sit and think and talk and grunt and train mightily for consensus and then . . ." He repeated the sound.

"Did you call him to find out if the rumors were true?"

"Call who, Kamina-*san?*"

"Your influential friend."

"Ahh. Yoshida. I called him."

"And?"

"We either dance to the American tune on the dumping charges or they'll level the prices with taxes, and unless we rewrite our patent laws, their customs inspectors will go over our cars like monkeys after fleas looking for anything an American company claims is stolen." Kobayashi let smoke from his cigarette trail out of his nose. He mopped his forehead with his handkerchief. The tip of his left little finger was missing to the joint.

Kamina chewed on a piece of tobacco.

Kobayashi said, "They tell me if the Americans follow through with their threat, it will cost us trillions of yen. It will cost us all. You. Me. Everybody. It's business expense accounts that support the *japayuki* trade, face it. We're all in this together."

Kamina took a drag and talked through clenched teeth as he inhaled. "I suppose they have to have somebody to quarrel with. They lost the Soviets."

"You never know about longnoses. They're different, let's face it. They're impulsive, for one thing. And they're short-sighted."

"They're barbarians, *oyabun-san*." Kamina snubbed out the butt of his Marlboro and lit another.

"We've known that all along."

"But they do consume, you have to give them that."

"The government says if we've learned anything at all from the past, it's the need to be patient. Ignore the Americans long enough and they'll go on to other concerns. But I don't know."

Kamina said, "They're like excitable dogs that way. They hop up and down barking and baring their teeth until they wear themselves out. When they finish drooling, they go to sleep."

"The government feels if we can make it past the Olofson administration, there's a good chance they'll calm down and come to their senses. The question is how to do that. It doesn't look like my influential friend did his job, does it?"

"Yoshida probably did his best, *oyabun-san*. Maybe it had to come to this sooner or later."

Kobayashi started peeling the cellophane from another package of Marlboros. "Not good."

Kamina sighed. "No, it isn't."

"In any event there's nothing we can do about it down here. Kao will have his wisdom teeth pulled and the orders from Fukuoka and Kyushu taken care of and meet us at Cebu. We've got plenty of time to get to Yokohama before the series. It was down here someplace—Cotabato, was it?—that Miki snagged that little Angie with the tits. Hard as coconuts. Remember her?"

"How could I forget? You're definitely not going to watch

the playoffs, then. Remember, Miki says there are several airports along the coast here, assuming the wrong Muslims don't try to jump us. All we have to do is put in and buy tickets out of here."

"If I don't watch them in the stretch, maybe they'll hold on to their lead. I'll watch them play the Lions in the series. If I watch them in the series, we'll bring home the *sashimi*, you watch."

"If our pitching holds up."

Kobayashi gave Kamina a look of mild reproof. "Of course our pitching will hold up. You've been reading too many newspapers, Kamina-*san*. I've ordered extra work to build up their arms. Sitting around playing with themselves might be fun, but it won't do a whole lot for their arms. Rest, give us rest, they say. More work is what they need. You always need to remember, Kamina-*san*, *besuboru* is a form of combat. Players must realize the importance of training and maintaining their fighting spirit."

"It would be nice if we had Ozawa's heat available in the late innings."

"Ozawa will be ready, you'll see. There's little in life that dedication and hard work won't cure, including an athlete's arm. If we get the series, we'll take it all. We've got Kama, Sugimoto, and Billy Radford in the heart of our lineup. You watch."

"Seibu'll be tough."

"Their pitchers still have to get past Kama, Sugimoto, and Radford. Radford may be a *gaijin* playing over his head, but he's *our gaijin* playing over his head."

FIVE

Beth Anne and Leanne wanted to be travelers, not tourists. Rainer Wiethoff had listed the *MV Santo Niño* among the hundreds of vessels catalogued in his *Tramping*, an international guide to traveling on steamers, freighters, and whatever. In a cover blurb, the *London Daily-Telegraph* said the guide was "straightforward, impeccably researched poop on everything from Developed World cruise liners to Third World barges."

On his rating system of one to five stars, Wiethoff had given the *MV Santo Niño* two stars, which meant Third World barge. He said the food was "adequate," which meant that one of his researchers had made the trip without a violent bout of diarrhea.

Their guidebooks to Southeast Asia, while not saying so directly, suggested that female vagabonds traveling solo might consider an alternate trip, and that women traveling in pairs should exercise care.

When they got to Davao, at the head of Davao Gulf, on southeastern Mindanao, Beth Anne and Leanne found that, sure enough, Jas. Cunningham Lines did exist. The ticket counter was by the market as it was supposed to be. And it was open. Behind the wire cage, the clerk, a young woman in a white blouse and blue jeans, read a horoscope comic book in Tagalog.

When they inquired about the *MV Santo Niño,* the clerk blinked. She said she had imagined they were interested in taking the ferry to Digos farther down the gulf. Digos was at the foot of Mount Apo, a favorite destination of visitors. The trip to Digos was a six-hour day trip. Would they like tickets to Digos?

They said no, they wanted to take the *MV Santo Niño* to Zamboanga, which was listed in their guide as a two-day trip with a stopover in General Santos.

"Is the *MV Santo Niño* still in business?" Beth Anne asked.

The clerk said yes, it was, and yes, they did accept passengers on the trip to Zamboanga. The *MV Santo Niño* was a cargo boat with several cabins aft that could be booked to passengers. There was a cabin available.

"What kind of cargo?" Beth Anne asked.

The clerk smiled. "Just about anything. In this case, I think it's corrugated tin to General Santos, and cement from General Santos to Zamboanga."

Leanne asked who "Santo Niño" was.

The clerk said, "The brown one, Baby Jesus. He's the patron saint of Visayans."

Beth Anne said, "Santo Niño delivereth. We ought to be safe enough. We'll book a cabin, then."

The clerk started filling out the ticket form. She said they should report to Captain Jun Peylado at least an hour before the two P.M. departure so he would have time to make sure that their trip would be a pleasant one. "If you have sensitive stomachs, you might want to bring some bottled water."

"This is not the commuter special to Manhattan, then," Linda said.

"To be honest, Captain Peylado doesn't carry very many passengers. An occasional pair of adventurous travelers like yourselves, but that's about it."

SIX

The *MV Santo Niño* was what Beth Anne and Leanne had come to learn was Third World standard, a decrepit, rusting hulk. And Captain Jun Peylado was not a reassuring, take-charge type of ship's captain. He was more like Reiner Wiethoff's description of the food—adequate—than Charlton Heston.

Captain Peylado had a quick, broad grin. Although he scrambled the genders of pronouns like most Visayan speakers—whose language did not distinguish between sexes—he spoke reasonable English. After he got over the surprise of having two good-looking longnose girls book passage aboard his vessel, he did his best to be a gracious host.

He showed them to their coffin of a room, and to a spot on the bow, under a canvas overhang, where they might enjoy the breeze and the view. Mindanao would be off the starboard bow.

Peylado was full of questions. Where were they from? What were they doing on Mindanao? They learned that he was married, that his daughter was an art student, and that his twenty-two-year-old son was engaged to be married. Unfortunately, the impossible in-laws-to-be had an instinct for wretched excess, and had demanded, for the reception, a carabao and four *lechon*—roasted suckling pigs.

Where was Peylado going to come up with the money for a carabao and four pigs? Oy!

Speaking of pigs, he said, the ship's cook was a Muslim who could do wonders with pork for the Christian Filipinos he had to feed. The cook had once worked for Indonesians on an oil rig and knew how to make good, spicy food if Ms. Holden and Ms. Tompkins were interested.

He said, "You should ask her to make you her special fish curry."

"A lady cook!" Beth Anne was surprised.

"Yes, she is a man."

The question of the cook's gender was left unresolved as they went ashore and bought some plastic jugs of water, plus some cans of corned beef, tuna, and pork and beans—just in case—and stowed their gear in their cabin.

As the *MV Santo Niño* pushed off, riding deep under its heavy load of tin, they followed Peylado's advice and took their seats on the bow under the overhang. The tropical air over the water was balmy.

This was what they had dreamed about and talked about in the library back in New Haven. Books, books, books. History, history, history. They wanted to see and feel and smell the here and now.

This was how they had imagined it would be.

The sun sank slowly over Mindanao, with thatched bamboo nipa huts tucked into tropical thickets. An occasional row of coconut palms towered overhead, and here and there Beth Anne and Leanne could see a tiny house with a rusting galvanized tin roof.

Except for the tin roofs and a few power lines, the coast of Mindanao looked much the same as it must have for hundreds of years. They understood intuitively that this was a primal sort of island, an archetypal tropical place: out there, largely forgotten; hot and humid except when it was being drenched by rainstorms or whipped by monsoon winds or buffeted by typhoons; infested with every damnable bug and hungry insect one could imagine; and forever subject to the unrelenting march of weeds and brush.

Their guidebook used indirect language, but the author managed to clearly warn the reader about one of history's unfortunate screws. Owing to the circumstances of its settlement and evolution, Mindanao had arrived on its present tack beset by seemingly endless guerrilla warfare between Christian and Muslim factions on the island; numerous treaties and deals had been signed with the government in Manila, but the Muslims were still not satisfied with their lot in life, and the Christians didn't like the Muslims one damn bit.

The sorehead Muslims inhabited the interior of the island and its southern and western coasts, both of which were beset by pirates. This was precisely where Beth Anne and Leanne were headed. The Muslims didn't warm to the idea of being governed by Christians; they wanted their own place. Besides that, the author suggested, they apparently fancied the business of kidnapping, banditry, and extortion; ambushing people and throwing bombs into movie theaters was a form of entertainment that pushed back the tropical monotony.

Equally tenacious and combative Roman Catholics, their religion scrambled with a congenial mix of indigenous spirits and spookie-wooks, lived on the northern and eastern coasts of Mindanao, and they tended to regard the Muslims as murderous oinkers.

As it slowly turned dark, the bright green tropical undergrowth washed yellowish under the unrelenting sun. The sun seemed to rest momentarily on the tops of the palms, reddening, as though contemplating the coming of the purple, with the palms backlit by the fading ember.

When darkness set in and the shoreline was a brooding shadow, they followed Peylado's advice and tried the cook's fish curry. "She," it turned out, was a he, and his curry was delicious.

They were on their way. Adventure!

Shortly after dark, a hulk appeared out of the darkness and a man shouted something across the water at the *MV Santo Niño*. Captain Peylado killed his engines and the anchor hit the water with a splash.

Astonished, Beth Anne and Leanne watched the hulk lower two small boats and eight Filipinos load themselves into them. They bore M-16s and had bandoliers of ammunition draped casually across their shoulders. Hand grenades were clipped to their belts. They did not look like the deacon and the church ladies come calling.

Even more astonished, they watched Captain Peylado greet the bandits, or pirates, like old pals, buddies, calling them by their first names, Muslim names; they were Muhammads, Abduls, and Husseins. They were Filipinos, not Semitics, but they were Muslims nevertheless.

Just to make sure everybody knew he was no Christian worshiper of pagan idols, their leader—a baggy-eyed, droopy-faced Abdul Somebody—wore an Arab *kefiya*, making him look like a Filipino Yasser Arafat.

On their way to the canteen, the accommodating Peylado and his first officer led Abdul and his group single-file past Beth Anne and Leanne. Blonds. And such long legs! They were all smiles as they trooped by. *La illah il Allah.* There is no God but Allah.

In the canteen, Peylado and the first officer opened bottles of San Miguel; Abdul produced a brass hashish pipe and lit up.

Above the babble of palaver, Beth Anne and Leanne could hear an occasional burst of laughter from Peylado, who seemed to have momentarily forgotten the onerous demand of a carabao and four pigs. Was he just trying to bluff his way past the pirates? Or was he trying to charm them, or buy them off with some tin? If Peylado was concerned for the safety of his ship or crew, it was impossible to tell.

Whatever Abdul's business was, he seemed in no hurry to conduct it. As the white moon rose in the tropical sky, Peylado and Abdul and their companions drank more beer and smoked more hashish.

Then, the near-rotten, pungent smell of dried fish being fried in palm oil joined the odor of hash in the balmy night air. The cook was preparing snacks so that the gracious Captain Peylado and his gentleman guests might better enjoy their various pleasures.

SEVEN

Eric Tennyson at the State Department, undersecretary for Asian affairs and Jack Shive's former administrative assistant in the Senate, was the one who had arranged for a false passport for Linda Elaine Shive, twenty-one, blond hair, green eyes, of Boulder, Colorado, under the name of Beth Anne Holden, twenty-one, blond hair, green eyes, of Lincoln, Nebraska.

When Linda and her college chum had popped into the American Embassy in Tokyo on the first leg of their Asian adventure, Tennyson had quickly called the vice president.

Did Shive know his daughter and a friend were traveling unescorted in Japan?

"Jesus fucking Christ no," Shive said.

The independent-minded Linda had declined to even discuss the matter with her father. What was he going to do, have the CIA kidnap her? No. She would go where she pleased.

Tennyson gently suggested that the State Department might cut fake passports for Ms. Shive and her friend.

Linda was not a political offspring who sought media attention; instead, following the lead of the many Kennedy children and Harold Olofson's two daughters, she shunned it assiduously. It didn't make squat to her whether or not her father was the vice president. She valued her privacy.

Now she had a hankering for an Asian adventure. She was an emancipated woman. She would go where she pleased, when she pleased. If her father wanted her to use another passport, fine, she would do that, but come home she would not.

Thus the compromise, which was no compromise at all as far as Shive was concerned. He remained furious. A rafting trip on the Colorado River or wind surfing on the Columbia River was one thing: He'd been able to have his adventurous daughter watched covertly. Of course she knew this, and resented it. If her father wanted to live in a gilded cage of the public, fine. That was his business. She had her own life.

Now, when Jack Shive talked to Tennyson, Linda's mother, Gloria, listened from another phone. She and Tennyson's wife were good friends.

Shive said, "Linda agreed to call us once a week. She's always been good about keeping her word. If she says she'll call, then she'll call. We've never had to worry. It's been twelve days now. She's five days late."

"We're just worried sick," Gloria Shive said.

"Where was she when she last called?"

"Davao City in the Philippines. That's southeastern Mindanao."

"And they were headed where?"

"She said General Santos, which is on the southern coast, then on to Zamboanga on the southwest."

"How were they going?"

"Five days! Five days late!" Gloria said.

"By boat," Shive said.

"Mmmmmmm. What kind of boat?" Tennyson was taking notes.

"She said they had booked a cabin on a vessel carrying corrugated tin."

"And the name of the vessel?"

"The *Santo Niño,* something like that."

"Something like that? You don't know for sure?"

"It was a long-distance call from halfway around the world, and we could barely hear her. You know how these things go. Questions don't get asked. She seemed to think it wasn't much more than a day trip."

Gloria said, "What do you think, Eric?"

"I think I should ask our people in Manila to run down the *Santo Niño* so you two can get a good night's sleep. It won't hurt them to help us out."

"You think she's okay, then, Eric?" Gloria said.

"Until we know otherwise, I think we should assume the best. They could still be at sea, or maybe it was difficult to make a phone connection. Communications are especially difficult in that part of the world. Mail can take weeks, and phone service is a dicey proposition at best. Sometimes you can call, sometimes you can't."

"That has to be it," Gloria said.

"That's what adventure is all about, isn't it? The unknown and all that."

"Of course that's it," Shive said.

"Is she having a good time? That's the important thing. I'll call Vice President Estrada's office in Manila. We'll find out where she is."

"Mr. Crime Buster of the Philippines," Shive said sarcastically.

"Estrada likes to call press conferences, but he's serious about his job, from what our people in Manila tell us."

"He's a nationalist, isn't he?"

"Yes, but he's not a knee-jerk American-hater. He's reasonable. If we tell him our problem, he'll see to it that our inquiry doesn't take forever. Who knows, maybe we'll be able to patch through a call for you on the ship's radio, and you can talk to Linda from your living room. Then this will all seem like a bad dream."

Jack Shive said thanks and hung up, biting his lip. "I knew it, I just knew it. God, why won't that child listen once in a while!"

"Just like you."

"Shit too!"

Gloria Shive said, "Surely there must be something else we can do. Everybody knows how the police are in those tropical countries, *mañana, mañana.*"

"If I dispatched the CIA and the Republicans found out, they'd have my ass, the bastards." Shive started punching another number.

"Who you calling now?"

"Someone in Langley who can put me in touch with Sid Khartoum's partner. Find the partner, find Khartoum."

"And Sid Khartoum is?"

"Major M. Sidarius Khartoum, something like that, but that's a pseudonym. I don't know his real name. He was the one the Senate drug committee sent to Latin America and Miami a couple of years ago, remember? Remember the FIFA investigator who shot down the Red Card terrorist and casually walked away before anybody could talk to him?"

"Khartoum?"

"Same guy."

"Reporters are like bloodhounds. If they couldn't lay their hands on him, how do you propose to find him?"

"His partner, a man named Schott, is a former director of counterintelligence at the Company. He lives somewhere here in the Washington area. Hello? Ara? Listen . . ."

EIGHT

By agreement with the Philippine National Police—at Vice President Joseph Estrada's insistence—the President's Anti-Crime Commission received a copy of all missing-person notices from INTERPOL and from foreign governments.

Winston Monzon, executive secretary to Vice President Estrada, chief of the Anti-Crime Commission, studied the vice president's copy of a request, marked urgent, from the U.S. State Department, asking for information as to the current whereabouts of Beth Anne Holden, twenty-one, of Lincoln, Nebraska, and Leanne Heather Tompkins, twenty-one, of Boulder, Colorado. Ms. Holden, a blond, was 5'7" tall and weighed 122 pounds. Ms. Tompkins, also a blond, was 5'8" tall and weighed 119 pounds. They were last seen in Davao City two weeks earlier.

Monzon wondered who Beth Anne Holden and Leanne Heather Tompkins were to merit an urgent dispatch from the American State Department. "Urgent" meant that the young women in question were Somebody, as opposed to Nobody or Anybody.

Holden? Tompkins? Monzon didn't recognize either name.

NINE

Darryl Lattimore had no sooner retrieved his check-on bag from the PAL flight than a tall, middle-aged man with a large mustache and an Einsteinian tangle of silver hair approached him, hand extended. "Are you Darryl Lattimore of *Sports Illustrated*?"

Lattimore blinked. "Well, yes, I am."

"Sid Khartoum. By golly, isn't this place something? Hotter than the sheriff's pistol!" James Burlane mopped his forehead with the back of his arm. "You know, I read this copy of *Sports Illustrated* a couple of weeks ago where this editor was saying how you were going to be doing an article about baseball and Asia. I took a flier and called Dutch Mandel to find out where you were. Bingo!"

"Bingo?"

"Davao City. Zamboanga. Bingo!"

"I see. No, I take that back. I don't see at all."

"I've got a car rented. What do you say we go for a drive and talk?"

"Oh? Talk about what?"

"About two missing young women who may have gotten themselves in trouble down here, one of them the daughter of a prominent American political figure, and about me doing your legwork for you here and in Zamboanga City. I was a journalism major at the University of Oregon. I can fake it.''

Lattimore blinked.

"All I ask is for you to listen to my story while we go for a drive. Then you can say yes or no. Fair enough? I'm not a pushy kind of guy. Here, let me help you with your stuff.'' Burlane grabbed the heaviest of Lattimore's bags and was off, leaving the writer no option but to follow.

They stashed Lattimore's bags in the trunk of Burlane's Toyota, and climbed in. Burlane, eye on the rearview mirror, pulled into the traffic, saying, "My guidebook says if you go by area incorporated, Davao might be the largest city in the Philippines. But it's only third in population, behind Manila and Cebu.''

"What prominent American political figure?''

"There's no need for you to know. The young woman and her friend were supposed to have taken a boat that was going from here to Zamboanga via General Santos with a cargo of corrugated tin. Only the captain maintains that his passengers didn't show up. The company that owns it is as stumped as we are. There are all kinds of things that could have gone wrong. The captain might have been lying, but they won't admit it. You've got Moros down here. You've got the New People's Army. You've got pirates. The love of M-sixteens and Kalashnikovs is pronounced in the tropical world. The sun does something to 'em, I think. Plus that you've got screwballs and psychopaths and nitwits of the sort you find in all cultures.'' Burlane reached over the seat and grabbed a folder from the back which he flopped on Lattimore's lap.

Lattimore opened the folder and flipped through copies of his articles, some with Burlane's photo where his had been. The folder also contained a much-stamped passport with Burlane's photo and Lattimore's identification.

"Where'd you get this done?''

"In Virginia.''

"The CIA promised Congress not to use journalists as a cover."

"Hey, hey! I'm not Company. I'm working directly for the family. Maybe this man's daughter is okay. Maybe she isn't. This is a touchy business."

"Yes, touchy for me."

Burlane said, "Look, under ordinary circumstances, I wouldn't ask you to do anything like this. Truly. But the deal is, what with screwballs under every rock, it's downright dangerous for a longnose to be poking around here without a reason. The Filipinos won't fancy an American asking questions about the Little League fiasco, but they understand it. And don't tell me Time-Life or Time-Warner or whatever it is these days has never used gofers to do research for their writers. Come on."

"I won't do it. No."

"Aw, shit! Are you sure?"

"Of course I'm sure. The answer is no."

Burlane's shoulders slumped. "Figgers." He handed Lattimore a card with a telephone number on it. "I'll take you to an office of the Philippine Long Distance Telephone Company, and I want you to use this number to call Jack Shive."

"*The* Jack Shive?"

"I told him you likely wouldn't go for it. Now he gets to make his pitch."

"Vice President Jack Shive?"

"If Linda Shive is kidnapped, and her kidnappers think she's nobody college student Beth Anne Holden, of Lincoln, Nebraska, which is on the passport she's carrying, we may have a shot at getting her back. If they find out who she really is, that's something else again."

"You're serious!"

"If he puts Gloria Shive on the line, and she starts blubbering, believe me, you'll knuckle immediately. Sometimes, you know, you have to bend the rules a little bit, and I think this might be one of those times."

TEN

Davao City, on the southeastern shore of Mindanao at the equatorial end of the Philippine archipelago, was far, far from the workaday world of shifts and shopping malls where longnose lives were measured by yards advanced in commuter traffic.

It was in this place, famous for a smelly fruit called durian, that Tony Valenzona, disgraced coach of the Zamboanga City Little Leaguers, had opened a bar after his team's World Series title had been yanked for cheating in 1992. Valenzona was disgraced not because he was responsible for the embarrassment—he had in fact been replaced by a Tagalog, along with most of his Zamboangueno players—but because he had later told the truth. Relatives of several of the players had threatened to kill him, so Valenzona was forced to seek refuge in Davao City, fink hell.

Valenzona had told Lattimore to look for the bar where it was okay to eat durians.

Burlane had read about the smelly durians—they were in all the Philippines guidebooks—but really didn't believe their reputation until he saw signs over several bars and eateries banning their presence. The Men Seng Hotel, where Burlane had a room, banned them.

The air was as wet as sweat soup as Burlane walked down

ELEVEN

Tony Valenzona's was empty except for a round-faced, round-bodied Filipino sitting on one side of a double bar with a bottle of San Miguel and what James Burlane assumed was a durian—a yellowish-green fruit the size of a softball and covered with villainous-looking spikes. He was watching a Philippine Basketball Association game on a television set mounted on the wall. The Purefoods Tender Juicy Hot Dogs were playing the San Miguel Beermen.

Burlane was relieved at the sight of overhead fans.

Chewing, watching Burlane yet not taking his eyes off the basketball game, the durian eater said, *"Day!"* This was pronounced "die," and was short for *inday,* "in-die," the polite Visayan word for *lady,* a proper way to address a clerk or waitress. The polite word for a male was *dong,* pronounced "dohng."

A Filipina in blue jeans and a Chicago Bulls T-shirt appeared from the back room.

Suddenly Burlane smelled something awful. He grimaced. "Shit!"

The man shook his head. "Durian. They say shit smells sweeter."

broad San Pedro street in what Davaoans called city town, that is, downtown, looking for Valenzona's bar. Sweat welled up from every pore on his body. His ass was as oily as his forehead. Sweat passed through his eyebrows and burned his eyes. A rivulet of sweat ran down the valley of his sternum. Sweat slid in gathering beads down his ribs. Sweat trickled down the insides of his thighs. His body was leached by sweat, enervating him, he supposed, in much the same manner as the soil in a rain forest was leached of minerals. He kept his head tilted to keep his vulnerable beak out of the sun. He was sure his brains were coddling in the fluids of his skull.

In Indiana Jones's movie tropics, the armpits of Harrison Ford's shirt were correctly soaked, and—in keeping with Steven Spielberg's pursuit of verisimilitude—the back was properly plastered to his spine. But the sweaty sheen on Ford's rugged forehead was put there by a prop girl with a plastic spray bottle, and not by the high gloss of suffering.

Ford could grimace and mop his forehead dramatically with his arm, but no amount of skillful pretend could make the audience understand the debilitating heat longnoses suffered in the deep tropics. Compared to Mindanao, Miami was Finland. If the producers did it right, Burlane reasoned, they could run the temperature in the theater to ninety degrees Farenheit and jack the relative humidity up to a wonderful ninety-five percent; theater owners could issue salt tablets together with tickets.

Truly, longnoses were better off staying in the climates where their stupid white skin had evolved.

As far as Burlane was concerned, the chief reward of adventure—which in fact was voluntary isolation and deprivation—was the delayed satisfaction of remembering; in most cases, the experience itself sucked. It was far more sensible to buy a ticket and a bag of popcorn and watch Harrison Ford pretend to suffer.

Burlane needed a bottle of San Miguel to replace his body fluids. Maybe several bottles.

He spotted Tony Valenzona's watering hole. A sign above the door said, BEWARE, DURIANS EATEN IN THIS ESTABLISHMENT.

Burlane opened the door and stepped inside.

Burlane settled onto a stool opposite the fruit eater. "Tony Valenzona?"

"Me."

"I'm the guy from *Sports Illustrated*."

"Hah, Darryl Lattimore." Valenzona extended his hand. "Mind if we put the talk off until the game's over?"

"Big game?"

"Playoffs."

"No problem. I'm too pooped from the heat to think now, anyway."

The stench of the durian was odious. "San Miguel, please," Burlane said to Chicago Bulls.

Valenzona said, "You have to get past the smell."

Burlane regarded the eater with amazement.

Valenzona grinned. "Tastes like heaven. You tried? *Day*, get the gentleman a durian, will you? First one's on the house."

"Seems like every other place in town won't let them inside."

Valenzona laughed. "That's why we welcome them. They say it's an acquired taste, I admit. Some say they taste like one part pineapple juice, one part pussy juice. Others say they taste like a sweet *otot*." He pronounced this "oh-toht."

"What's an *otot*?"

"That's Visayan for *fart*. I'm a Leyteno originally. Had to get used to durians myself."

Ms. Chicago Bulls arrived with Burlane's beer and a durian, split open, revealing seeds shaped like grapefruit sections and covered by a yellowish, cottony-looking pulp. Burlane dug out a section and gnawed at the slippery pulp around the seed. Not only did it smell terrible, but it wasn't the easiest fruit to eat.

"Well?"

Burlane pushed the fruit toward Valenzona. "Sweet *otot* with maybe a hint of vanilla. I think you better finish it. I don't suppose you have peanuts."

Valenzona, his eye on the television, laughed. "It's an acquired taste. *Day! Day!* Peanuts for the gentleman."

Burlane understood how a fan could get behind a team that

represented a city or region, but Purefoods Tender Juicy Hot Dogs didn't seem to cut it. He was glad Valenzona's mind was on Alvin Patrimonio's performance, held to be crucial to Purefoods, and whether or not the Tender Juicy Hot Dogs could slow down the high-flying Beerman, Samboy Lim. All Burlane wanted to do was veg out on the barstool and replace his lost body fluids with San Miguel. He fingered his handlebars, wishing he were back in longnose land, on a couch with his feet up, watching the White Sox on television. Carlton Fisk had retired, but the Sox were still his team, had been since he was a kid. Sweet memories.

The door opened and in stepped an odd duo:

The woman was a short-haired, light-skinned Filipina, wearing a form-hugging, thigh-length white tube dress. She had a spine like a willow, and her hips moved her sweet butt to and fro in a form of undulating hormonal man trap.

The man was wide and broad-faced, a Japanese suit. Obsessive suit-wearers were uncomfortable without the tit of a half-Windsor knot and the solace of sharply creased trousers. This one was erect and serious-faced. He walked like his bearings needed grease. Burlane thought they were more likely friends or coworkers than lovers or spouses.

The woman, getting a whiff of durian, bunched her face. She put a hand over her mouth and without a word pivoted and strode out of Tony Valenzona's.

The broad-faced man gave Burlane and Valenzona a look that, for a Japanese, was positively demonstrative: What's wrong with you idiots, putting up with that stench?

Not taking his eyes off the television, Valenzona said, "They don't like durians."

"Didn't see your warning. Do you know who they are?"

"They say *yakuza*. In town recruiting *japayuki*. The woman's been around before."

TWELVE

Tony Valenzona chewed thoughtfully on a peanut, then washed it down with a San Miguel. "The way I see it, we Filipinos are Hispanized Malayans pretending to be Americans. The Malay in us saw nothing wrong with a little cheating if that's what it took to win the title, but the American in us was furious."

This cultural schizophrenia was apparent in the Filipino newspaper articles Lattimore had given Burlane. Some papers pretended nothing untoward had happened, while others spared no effort at digging out the truth.

Valenzona said, "You want chiselers, go to Taiwan. You going to Taiwan?"

Burlane nodded yes.

"But you won't find—what is it you Americans call it? Doo doo?"

" 'Doo doo' covers it."

"The Nationalist Chinese are the world masters at pirating tapes and records and books and copying everybody else's electronics gear. They won fifteen Little League World Series titles beginning in 1969, sometimes by embarrassing scores. Now how do you suppose that happened, Mr. Lattimore? Were the Chinese kids eating their bok choy and rice while the Americans and Canadians loaded up on Mars bars and Big Macs? Is that what happened?''

''I could make a few guesses, but that's all they'd be.''

''They did it by counterfeiting birth certificates, by fielding all-star teams rather than district champions, and by training all year round. The people in Williamsport took their word for everything. We Asians all knew the Chinese were cheating. It was obvious. Only you Americans seemed not to know, or pretended not to know. It was a giggle, it really was.''

Burlane said, ''I suppose even if the Williamsport people had sent an investigator to Taiwan, he wouldn't have learned much.''

''Of course not. We're talking Chinese rules here. The Chinese help one another out. You only learn what they want you to learn. You said you were going to write about baseball in Japan. Well, the Japanese are Chinese cubed. In China, you owe your loyalty to your family; in Japan, you owe it to your race—all outsiders exist to be screwed. We Filipinos have family loyalty, not racial loyalty. We got busted because we've got a Western-style press and fools like me with flapping mouths.

''Yes, my team won the Philippine championship, but money for overseas travel came from league headquarters in Manila. Everything is done by Manila rules in the Philippines, so the Tagalogs pulled all but six of my Zamboanguenos, and replaced them with overage kids from Luzon. Then they yanked me. If a Manila team had won, they'd have just faked the ages and everything would have been okay. As it was, they got caught by the district rule.''

''But you didn't say anything until after they won the series and the charges surfaced?''

Valenzona looked at Burlane like he was crazy. ''It was bad enough as it was, people threatening to kill me. Can you imagine what would have happened if I'd pulled the plug on my own? The *Inquirer* reporter asked me what happened; I told her the truth.''

"But you didn't mind it when the reporters pinned the Manila crowd?"

Valenzona grinned. "Foolish question. I loved every second of it, of course." He finished his beer. *"Day, day!* Another round over here, please."

Burlane said, "I suppose they saw what Taiwan had been doing and figured why not go for broke?"

"Of course! The officials in Williamsport were so easy it was unreal. There are no lessons here. What it all comes down to is that we Filipinos got caught. That and nothing more."

Burlane was unable to purge from his system the idea of fair play that he had been taught as a child. The way he saw it, a person would have to be lower than buffalo chips to cheat at cards or lie about a Little Leaguer's age. He knew that this was an elemental cultural difference between longnoses like himself and those Asians to whom a lie that worked was a tactic and not a question of morals or ethics. To them, the longnose fixation with truth was a curious if not outright amusing mental quirk.

Burlane admired the Filipinos, because in spite of all their problems and poverty they had the courage to expose the scumbags in their midst. If some Little League hotshots in Manila had dishonored themselves by cheating, the *Philippine Daily Inquirer* had honored itself by blowing the whistle in detail. Also, Filipinos knew how to kick back and laugh, and they counted among their numbers straight-shooting durian-eaters like Tony Valenzona.

Valenzona said, "What do you think?"

"Me? I think the biggest shits in the whole business are the longnose promoters in Williamsport who had to know the Taiwanese were cheating, yet for decades pretended everything was on the up-and-up."

Burlane, affecting the tone of a good-natured rube, said, *"How old are they this year, Mr. Chang?"*

Burlane, the earnest Chinese, replied, *"Why, Mr. Smith, they're all twelve or under, of course!"*

The rube said, *Okey-doke, Coach, just sign this affidavit. This'll take care of everything. Say, you people must mature early out there, eh?"*

Valenzona said, "See no evil. Hear no evil. No evil exists."

"My guess is that an international World Series was originally promoted as a way of hyping the gate; the U.S. versus Taiwan is a far bigger draw than Butte versus Galveston. But the Williamsport longnoses had the imaginations of Rotarians and Jaycees. Early on it was obvious the Chinese were systematically lying to them, but they couldn't stop the crapola without admitting they'd been had. So they continued, all liberal and righteous, rubes pretending everything was hunky-dory."

"And maybe the Chinese used a little of their pirating and patent-stealing money to ensure their continued cooperation, eh, Darryl? Is that out of the question for a Pennsylvania longnose?"

"That might be true too, I admit. You can't overlook that possibility."

"See, just like us Asians." Tony Valenzona rolled his eyes in amazement and disbelief. "You Americans!"

James Burlane grinned. "We mask our greed with a gloss of piety and naïvete and pretend it's gilt. The truth is, they wrap Juicy Fruit in fancier stuff than that. It's fool's gold, but you gotta admit, it's what makes us such a distinctive and exasperating pain in the butt."

THIRTEEN

Maria Reyes had rice and *pancit guisado*—noodles with bits of shrimp and pork—as she waited in a Zamboanga City *carenderia*, where customers browsed the aluminum pots, lifting the lid of each in turn to see what the cook had to offer that day.

Maria was a pure Filipina, that is, racially a full-blooded Malay. She had rich, copper-colored skin and big, almond-shaped black eyes. Her mane of curly black hair fell to her shoulder blades. Although she was just four eleven and ninety-five pounds, she had an extraordinary, shapely body. She was unselfconsciously sexy. She was, in fact, doll-like.

She was waiting to talk to Miki Cruz, who had arrived on the large white yacht anchored in Zamboanga harbor. Locally, the word was the yacht belonged to the *yakuza*, but Maria didn't know whether to believe that or not.

Yes, Maria knew what the *yakuza* was. Japanese gangsters. That she pronounced the word "ya-kuza," rather than "yak-uza," with the accent on the first syllable, was no matter. It was difficult to believe the *yakuza* could be any deadlier than the Muslim guerrillas in Zamboanga, the Moros, whose name was no problem at all to pronounce.

And yes, she knew all about *japayuki*. At least something

about them. She had heard about all the rip-offs, yes. Her *tio* was a cop. But then . . . the money!

Maria was the oldest of the eight children of Carlito Reyes, who ran another man's pumpboat in return for a share of the catch. A pumpboat was an outrigger powered by a dependable, easy-to-fix Briggs and Stratton engine designed to pump water. If necessary, the motor could be pulled to move water from one rice paddy or field to the next.

By any name, Carlito Reyes's share of the outrigger's catch did not produce enough income to feed his family. A half hour after Maria finished her rice and noodles, Miki arrived, a sleek Filipina *mestiza*—that is, racially mixed. Miki had lighter skin than did Maria. Her cheekbones were more prominent than Maria's, and she had a slightly more prominent Mongoloid eyefold. Her short-cut, jet-black hair was thin and lank, whereas Maria's was thick and slightly curly. Miki was half Japanese.

Miki wore an impeccably tailored, double-breasted navy blue blazer with gold buttons. She wore this beautiful, summerweight jacket over a flowing black silk skirt with abstract bronze-colored flowers. A red silk scarf was tied loosely around her throat. Her earrings featured neat rubies that complemented the scarf, and she had four gold bracelets around each wrist. All this spoke of money, and lots of it. Maria had seen wealthy Chinese women dressed this well, but such stylish clothes were less seldom worn by Filipinas of Malay descent. And her earrings! Rubies. Real rubies.

Maria told Miki she needed to earn money because her family was desperate. She was willing to go overseas to work, but she'd heard terrible stories about Filipinas who went to Japan to work as entertainers.

Miki looked surprised. "Have you heard anything to match the stories about what happens to Filipinas who work as maids and *yayas* for Arabs?" A *yaya* was a nanny.

"Well, no, that sounds pretty bad too," Maria said. The Arabs had a fondness for anal sex, she had been told, and were given to beating Filipina maids and *yayas*. On one occasion ninety-nine maids and *yayas* had shown up en masse at the Philippine Embassy in Kuwait, pleading for passage home so they could be liberated from their nightmare.

Miki showed Maria photographs of the Harvard Club in Yokohama. The Harvard Club was sort of an imitation longnose men's club, all woody and expensive looking, if not truly exclusive, with marlin, swordfish, elk, moose, and other fish and big-game heads mounted on the walls over shelves of old books. A ripping fire crackled in a huge stone fireplace. Smiling Filipinas in sexy outfits served drinks to prosperous-looking Japanese males in business suits.

Miki said, "The waitresses in the Harvard Club are legendary in Japan for being sexy and good-looking. All they have to do is look cute and serve overpriced drinks. Nothing to it."

Maria, looking at the photographs a second time, said, "Who are they? The customers, I mean."

Miki laughed. "Oh, the peeping Tanakas. They're executives in the Yokohama financial district. They pay the yen equivalent of thirty U.S. dollars for a bottle of beer and the kick of being served by Filipina beauties like you."

Maria blinked. "That's seven hundred fifty pesos! For one bottle of beer?"

"That's also why we can afford to pay you eight hundred U.S. dollars a month plus a small apartment. We have a special apartment building where you'll live with the other Filipinas who work at the Harvard Club. Since you'll have your own kitchen, you and your friends can cook the kind of food you like."

"That's all I have to do, wear an outfit and serve drinks?"

Miki looked surprised. "That's it. That's all there is to it. If the customers thought the girls were for sale on the side, they wouldn't spend all that money just to watch them walk back and forth. So you can rest assured that's all you'll have to do, serve drinks."

Maria shook her head. "I just don't know."

"I can offer this job only to the very hottest Filipinas, and there are other girls who would love to have a job at the Harvard Club, believe me. You'll have to make a decision."

Maria sighed. "I've heard so many stories . . ."

"Maria, Maria, of course you have, but the truth is a lot of that has been overblown by Japan-bashing media. In this case you can truly relax. I'd recommend the Harvard Club to my sister."

FOURTEEN

In addition to giving James Burlane the names of coaches, fathers, and players associated with the ill-fated 1992 World Series squad, Tony Valenzona had drawn maps directing him to the fields where the Zamboanga Little Leaguers practiced and played their games.

Zamboanga del Sur was the jumping-off place for the Sulu archipelago, dominated by Tausug Muslims and by animist sea gypsies, the Badjao, thus putting it beyond the ken of the law. Zamboanga City was infested with Moros, Muslim guerrillas given to kidnapping Christians, foreigners, and the Chinese-Filipinos.

It wasn't cool for longnoses to linger too long watching infield practice, but Zamboanga was Burlane's best bet for getting a lead on the whereabouts of the missing girls. Besides, he had promised Darryl Lattimore he would do his Zamboanga research for him. Do it he would.

After he had checked in at the Jumawon Hotel and stashed his belongings in his room, Burlane, his stomach growling after a three-hour delay in the flight from Davao, set off to find a *carenderia* with some interesting-looking seafood in its pots.

He chose one on the ocean end of Corcuera Street that offered a good view of the harbor. It had a large bunch of tamarind beans hanging from a nail, a tip-off to the cook's preference in making fish soup, called *sinigang* in Tagalog, *tinola* in Visayan. The Chabacano-speaking woman who ran the Corcuera Street *carenderia* offered *sop' pescad'* featuring simmered chunks of fish, a few hunks of tomato, a couple of slices of onion, one or two small, dark-green hot peppers, and a leaf or two of cabbage. It was sometimes flavored with slivers of ginger and sometimes by tamarind beans, which gave it a pleasant, sourish taste.

Most of Mindanao spoke Visayan, which was also the language of the islands in the central part of the Philippines— eastern Negros, Cebu, Bohol, and Leyte. The people of western Negros and Panay spoke Ilongo, while it was Tagalog in Manila and central Luzon and Ilocano in northern Luzon.

There was a movement by the culturally dominant Manila to pass off Tagalog as Pilipino, or Filipino, and this was the language of Filipino movies made in Manila, but the rest of the country largely resented this form of cultural imperialism. English, a legacy of the American colonialists, remained the language of the courts and the most influential newspapers.

The language spoken in Zamboanga was Chabacano, said to be seventy percent Spanish, mostly unconjugated verbs, and thirty percent indigenous languages—the result being a Creole Spanish of sorts. Burlane knew enough Spanish to understand respectable stretches of Chabacano.

As he settled down to enjoy his tamarind-flavored *tinola*, he saw a sleek white yacht anchored in Zamboanga harbor. The *Sagawa Maru*, eighty feet or longer, looked splendid in the company of pumpboats and rusting freighters. Such an ostentatious vessel represented maximum bucks and expansive ego on someone's part; he wondered who owned it.

A few minutes later, his mind still on the yacht, he saw an unusual duo walking down the opposite side of the street toward the water. It was the same pair that had bolted from Tony Valenzona's bar at the first whiff of durian. They were *yakuza*, Valenzona had said.

After a few minutes a man came down the sidewalk who

looked like a Filipino version of the late American movie actor, Richard Boone. Or at least Burlane thought so; he conceded to himself that nobody else probably would. The Filipino paused at a sidewalk vendor selling mangoes, but Burlane didn't think he was interested in fruit. Was he watching the unusual duo that had passed by Burlane's *carenderia*?

Burlane was curious. He paid his bill and abandoned his remaining *tinola* to follow the man who looked like Richard Boone.

Yes, Boone was following the two Japanese, if that's what they were. As Burlane observed him from down the crowded sidewalk, the Filipino watched the two take a small boat to the *Sagawa Maru*.

FIFTEEN

That night James Burlane sat on the veranda of his aged hotel enjoying a Tanduay rum and coke as he looked out over Zamboanga harbor toward the *Sagawa Maru*. Burlane called Filipino rum and cokes Cebu Libres, after the town where he had first tried one. The *kalamansi*, or *lemoncito*, on the rim of the glass was a marble-sized, lime-colored citrus with a distinctive lemonlike flavor.

Three Filipinos at the next table were talking in Chabacano about the *Sagawa Maru*. Burlane heard *yakuza* mentioned. Then he heard them say two young women had been on a boat that was hijacked by Abdul al-Jabar, a Muslim pirate in the Sulu Sea.

Burlane, wondering how word of pirate activities spread from the Sulu Sea to Zamboanga, heard the word *rubio*. *Rubio* meant blond in Spanish. The Shives said their daughter had changed her hair to blond for the trip; her friend Leanne Tompkins was a natural blond.

He said, "Excuse me, I couldn't help overhearing your story. What was the boat that was hijacked carrying?"

"Corrugated tin." The Filipinos looked mildly surprised that Burlane could figure out their Chabacano.

Burlane said, *"Hablo un poquito español.* What will happen to those young women, do you think?"

The oldest of the three Filipinos looked grave. They had been talking about longnose women, and Burlane was a concerned longnose. "Not much that's good, I don't imagine."

Burlane, reading the reluctance in his face, said, "How much that's not good?"

"You know them?"

"I may have met them in Davao City."

"You should have told them to go home. After al-Jabar and his pirates get bored with fucking them, he'll likely sell them to the *yakuza,* if he hasn't already."

"The *yakuza?* Sell them for what?"

"For *japayuki.* They recruit some. They buy some. They take some. Down here they do all three."

Burlane, knowing the answer, said, "And *japayuki* are?"

"Officially, entertainers."

"And unofficially?"

The Filipino said, *"Si uste' conocer* those *rubios,* you might not want to know."

"Did you say that yacht out there belongs to the *yakuza?"*

The Filipino shrugged. "That's the word. Of course, they didn't publish an announcement in the newspapers."

SIXTEEN

Joe!"

"Hey, Joe!"

"Joe! Joe!"

The sweat was starting to roll the next morning as James Burlane, wearing his British tropical hat and a multipocketed photographer's vest over his short-sleeved shirt, set off in the miserable heat and humidity to find the police department. A longnose would have to be nuts, just freaking crazy, to voluntarily live in heat like this. Keeping his eye on the next awning or overhang, Burlane walked as fast as he could without risking heat prostration.

"Joe!"

Burlane had gotten used to the Joe business which dated to G.I. Joe and World War II. Manilenos rarely called "Joe" to Europeans; they were used to longnose visitors. Longnoses avoided Zamboanga because of the Moros, and so, it seemed, nearly everybody felt compelled to call, "Hey, Joe!" when they saw Burlane walking down the street. It was mostly innocent, he knew, but there was always the possibility that a bored Muslim would translate it as, "Hey, Abdul, there goes a longnose to kidnap."

At first, Burlane had responded to the Joe hooters. He

wanted to be polite. Then he saw that it was impossible, and he really wasn't expected to reply. If the Joe caller was a child, that was different. At least there was a history behind calling Americans Joe; he pitied the poor German and Australian visitors to the Philippines.

Burlane had nothing at all to do with those who tried to open a conversation with "my friend," just as he avoided Latin Americans who attempted "mi amigo" openers. More often than not, these "friends" had their hearts set on his wallet. Burlane never carried a wallet in the Third World. He stashed a few bucks in a money belt, but this was a decoy; he kept his real money and his laptop in a safe deposit box and spread his walk-around money in several pockets and in the bottoms of his Saucony running shoes.

Burlane stepped into the Zamboanga police department, mopping his sweaty brow with a handkerchief. The sergeant on duty sat behind an aged, cluttered desk. He was a small man with a high forehead, large, intelligent eyes, and a substantial black mustache. An automatic pistol on the desk kept a pile of forms and reports from being blown away by an overhead fan. The sergeant had "Canizares, B." on the plastic ID tag pinned to the chest of his brown uniform.

"Joe!" Canizares said.

Burlane grinned. "Lattimore. Darryl Lattimore."

He checked out the wall of wanted posters. Several of the criminals were Japanese with full-body tattoos, marking them as *yakuza* soldiers. There were a few longnoses.

"Don't get many Joes in this part of *el mundo*, Mr. Lattimore. *Estar* Americano or German?"

"American born, country raised."

"Where are you staying, Mr. Lattimore?"

"At the Jumawon Hotel."

"Room six. Private bath. They've fixed the lock on the door and plugged the hole in the wall between five and six. Gave you six out of respect." Canizares grinned. "See, down here we keep track of foreigners. It's for your own good, what with the Moros and all. What can I help you with?"

"I'm looking for *dos muchachas.*"

Canizares looked relieved. "I thought maybe you'd been robbed. What kind of young women? Filipinas?"

Burlane shook his head. "Two American blonds I met in Davao City."

"*Do' rubios?*"

"They were hippie-looking, with sweatbands around their foreheads, and they shouldered backpacks. They were supposed to be taking a boat carrying tin from Davao to here via General Santos. The boat showed up, but they weren't on it. The captain's story to the boat's owners is that the girls may have bought tickets at Davao, but they didn't show. Last night I overheard some Filipinos saying some pirates hijacked a boat just short of General Santos and made off with two blonds."

Canizares didn't look surprised. "Abdul al-Jabar. I heard that story too."

Burlane felt better. Maybe he was getting somewhere. "More likely the captain sold them to the *yakuza,* they said."

Canizares nodded in agreement. "Probably. Unfortunately, there's not a whole lot we can do."

"No?"

"No *barcos* outside of a harbor boat and a patrol boat that belongs to the customs people. Nobody to man them if we had them. No budget."

"Big ocean too, I suppose."

"*Grande!* Lots of islands for al-Jabar to hide out on. *Mucho* dangerous. Even if we had boats, where would we begin?"

Burlane sighed. The overhead fan felt good, but the stench of sweat wafted up from his soaked shirt.

"May I see your passport?"

"Sure." Burlane unfastened the safety pin on the zipper tab of an inside pocket of his vest. He retrieved his passport and gave it to Canizares.

Canizares flipped through the pages, studying the border chops. "I understand your concern, Mr. Lattimore, I really do."

"These young women are halfway around the world from

their families and friends. There must be someone I can talk to about something like this. Some way to help them."

Canizares gave the passport back. "You've been around. All those chops."

"I'm a writer. A professional. Or at least that's what I tell myself. If you looked at my tax returns you might wonder." Burlane looked rueful.

"Do you know what I would do, if I were you? I'd take the next flight to Manila and see if I couldn't talk to Joseph Estrada."

"Vice President Estrada?"

"His movie name was Erap. He's now chief of the President's Anti-Crime Commission. If there's anybody in the Philippines with the budget and the clout to help you, it'd be Joseph Estrada. You have to believe me, I understand your concern, and I would help you if I could, but . . ." He shrugged his shoulders.

"Tell me, that ridiculous yacht out there, the *Sagawa Maru*. Does that thing belong to the *yakuza*?"

Canizares turned the palms of his hands up and looked chagrined, his body language saying, of course it's *yakuza*, but what are we supposed to do about it? He said, "They checked in with customs like they're required to."

"And its home port is where?"

"I'm police, not customs."

"I see." Burlane pretended to have an afterthought. "Say, I sure do appreciate your help. Are you allowed to accept tips in this part of the world?" He hooked his thumb over the zippered front pocket of his vest.

Canizares paused, studying Burlane. Then he said, "They put Yokohama on the form."

"Thank you." Burlane unzipped the pocket.

"But you didn't hear it from me."

Burlane retrieved a five-hundred-peso bill, about twenty bucks American, and gave it to Canizares, whose salary, he knew, was maybe twenty-five hundred pesos a month, thirty-five hundred tops. "Anything more?"

"Don't they have to list a registered owner?"

"Sagawa Rice and Sugar Limited, of Yokohama."

"Do you think Sagawa actually deals with rice and sugar?"

"No."

"Did the customs people actually board the *Sagawa Maru* and take a look around?"

Canizares grinned and rolled his eyes. The captain of a boat like the *Sagawa Maru* obviously had lots of five-hundred-peso notes to pass around.

SEVENTEEN

The pumpboat was to be piloted by Ninoy, a weathered, dark-skinned, Chinky-eyed old man in thongs, cut-off jeans, and Dunkin' Donuts T-shirt. Maria Reyes, herself dressed in jeans and T-shirt, was apprehensive and quiet as she stepped aboard. The startling white *Sagawa Maru*, a dazzling star among the more pedestrian vessels moored in Zamboanga harbor, looked both grand and slightly malevolent. Was Maria to be taken all the way to Japan on a yacht?

As the pumpboat slid through the water, its Briggs and Stratton going *pop-pop-pop-pop*, Maria thought of her family and felt a twist of anxiety in her stomach. She had never been off Mindanao, much less to Japan. She had left a note to be delivered to her parents. She knew they would object to her going, but she had hungry brothers and sisters; somebody had to put food on the table. If her father couldn't come up with the necessary pesos and she could, she had to do it. She had no choice.

She had a change of underwear in a plastic bag from a Gaisano department store. Miki had said not to bring extra clothes. They would outfit her with everything she needed. She was no longer a girl from the provinces; she was a Harvard Club girl and had to look the part.

Maria thought of the chunks of squash, *malunggay* leaves, and pieces of *bareles*—tuna no more than six or eight inches long—in her mother's *otan*. It was unlikely they would have soup like that in Japan. Still, Miki had said Maria and her fellow Harvard Club waitresses would have their own kitchen. Even if little tuna were not to be found in Japanese markets, they could surely come up with something that approximated *otan*.

Maria hoped there would be other Filipinas on board so she would have somebody to talk to. If there were no Chabacano speakers, she hoped they spoke Visayan. She felt more comfortable in Visayan than Tagalog, or Pilipino, which Manila promoted as the national language—Manilenos being Tagalog speakers.

The man in the Dunkin' Donuts T-shirt idled the pump boat close to the *Sagawa Maru* and cut the Briggs and Stratton. The bow of the pumpboat drifted to the bottom of a folding stairway that led up an open gate in the yacht's rails. There Miki stood in a form-fitting bright yellow pantsuit.

She was in a buoyant mood. "Welcome, welcome, Maria. Welcome aboard."

Dunkin' Donuts helped her climb from the bow to the bottom of the stairs. As she took the first step upward, Dunkin' Donuts pushed off behind her, *pop-pop-popping* his way back to shore. It was done, then. She was on her way. There was no turning back. Heart pounding, she continued climbing the white metal stairs to whatever lay beyond.

When she reached the rail, Miki welcomed her aboard with an embrace. Miki's pantsuit, it turned out, was translucent, revealing long, dark nipples and a shaved mons veneris. This wasn't the way Miki had described a Harvard Club woman.

Maria's mouth turned dry.

Behind her, the *pop-pop-pop* of the Briggs and Stratton grew dimmer. Like many Filipinas, Maria Reyes didn't know how to swim. She had no escape.

She was aware of the hum of an electric engine. The anchor was being reeled in.

The yacht's diesel engine rumbled to life.

Beneath her, the deck began to vibrate.

Miki, taking her by the elbow, said, "Come, Kobayashi-*san* wishes to meet you."

"Who is he?" Maria glanced back at the lights of Zamboanga.

"The gentleman who owns this boat." Miki took Maria down a narrow companionway to the splendid main cabin, paneled in cherrywood, where a Japanese man wearing a blue blazer, white trousers, and white shoes was enjoying a Scotch on the rocks. The man, in his late fifties, studied Maria through his spectacles and seemed pleased at what he saw. He motioned with his hand for her to turn around.

She did.

The man said something in Japanese.

Miki said, "Show him your tits."

Maria was stunned.

"Do it," Miki said.

Maria peeled off her T-shirt and unfastened her bra. Staring at the floor, she took the bra off.

"Turn to the side. Do it."

Maria did that too.

Kobayashi took a sip of Scotch. He looked pleased.

"Now the rest of it."

"What?"

"Everything off."

Maria did as she was told. As she slipped off her underpants, she saw that Miki was now holding a thick leather strap.

Miki said, "Kobayashi-*san* wishes you to know he expects you to earn the salary you are being paid. He wishes for you to know the consequences of not doing as you are told. I want you on your elbows and knees in front of him. Sideways so he can see your profile. Legs wide. Turn your face so he can enjoy your suffering. Do it now."

Maria got down on her elbows and knees.

"You have beautiful hair, but he can't see through it. Put it on the other side so he can enjoy your face when you take the strokes."

Maria adjusted her hair.

"I'm going to give you twenty. You will count each stroke. You will count backwards, twenty, nineteen, and so on. If you miss a count, you'll earn an extra swat. Do you understand?"

Maria nodded yes, she understood. The *japayuki* stories she had heard about the *yakuza* were true. What had she done? She closed her eyes.

The man said something in Japanese.

Miki said, "He wants you to keep your eyes open."

EIGHTEEN

Miki followed her aft.

Miki had her clothes. She obviously liked seeing Maria naked and so left her that way, requiring her to lead the way.

Maria's rear end was on fire.

The lights of Zamboanga were gone. The sky was overcast. There were no stars. She was in a black void, sliding into the darkness of her future.

She felt ashamed. Humiliated.

She preceded Miki down the narrow stairs.

Gingerly, she touched her inflamed rump with her fingertips, couldn't stop herself. Ouch!

As she turned down a narrow companionway, the sound of the engine grew louder and louder.

Miki stopped at the brass knob of a cabin door, and returned Maria's clothes. "Your bunk is on the right in the middle. I've given you a good one. It has a porthole so you can see out. Your cabinmates can explain the routine in the morning."

With that, Miki rapped on the door and departed.

Maria opened the door. She stepped into the cabin, where three Filipinas waited, having been alerted by Miki's knock. They hugged as they introduced themselves. Two of them, Evelyn Fernandez and Marnie Toledo, were Visayan speakers from Davao. The third, Iris Rodriguez, was from Zamboanga and spoke Visayan and Chabacano. Iris, it turned out, was Maria's third cousin, although they had never met. Maria, at nineteen, was the oldest.

The six-feet-long by five-feet-wide cabin was designed to accommodate six tiny Malayan females. The three bunks on each side folded into recesses in the bulkhead when they weren't being used. There were two portholes just above the middle bunk on the seaward side that Miki had said was to be hers.

Maria joined them squat-legged on the floor. They talked about where they were from and how they had come here. From their eyes, Maria knew that they too had received an initiatory strapping. Nobody mentioned the subject. It was a private humiliation, not something to be talked about.

Later that night, as Maria lay in her bunk wide awake, unable to sleep, the *Sagawa Maru*'s engines fell silent. She felt the boat glide to a stop.

Her cabinmates had awakened. They folded the bunks on the seaward side so they could see outside. The cloud cover was gone, and in its place was a starry skin. In the distance was the profile of coconut trees on an island.

A pumpboat, containing two longnose women, blonds, passed by their portholes on the way to the lowered aluminum stairway.

II
WASLIKS

When the Japanese succeeded in capturing thirty percent of the U.S. car market, many were convinced that their achievement was an enduring triumph of culture. Watanabe was shocked that the American govenment let the figure get that high without doing something about it, and where his colleagues were pleased to celebrate the superiority of organization and hard work over the slothful Americans, Watanabe was cautious. He said the twentieth century was a century of struggle against authoritarians. To ensure a stable market economy on the frontier of Maoist China, the Americans had given the Japanese market concessions that Japan had unrealistically come to regard as its due.

Watanabe said it was foolhardy to expect these concessions to continue. The twenty-first century would be one of a struggle for markets. The Americans were simply sending the message that they expected the Japanese to play by the same rules as everybody else. Barring any bellicose moves by China, the Americans could be expected to stick with that policy.

He said that just as Detroit learned that the fifties and sixties couldn't last forever, the Japanese had to put the successes of the seventies and eighties behind them.

This was not what the Japanese wanted to hear, any more than the fat-cat Detroit executives had twenty years earlier, when they kissed off their critics as deranged. Watanabe was widely quoted in Japan, but not listened to. He was popular with the Americans because they liked what he was saying.

At the bottom of the nineties recession, Detroit, faced with virtually going out of business, had revamped itself by copying Japan's faster, computer-aided design and production models.

A group of Japanese investors, concerned about the restlessness in Washington and bent on overtaking Nissan and Toyota, formed Sapporo Ltd. out of several smaller companies and named Watanabe CEO.

Now Prime Minister Jomo Konobe dispatched Koji Watanabe to Washington to have a heart-to-heart with Vice President

ONE

As manager of team Japan, Prime Minister Jomo Konobe knew he had to send a pinch hitter to the plate. The strategy of politics was the reverse of baseball. In baseball, a manager wanted a rightie at the plate against a leftie and vice versa, but Japan sent rightie special emissaries to bat against Republican righties, and southpaw special emissaries to bat against Democratic lefties.

Political-like thinking encouraged a soothing *wa* between the two countries, and forced American trade representatives to fight their way through time-consuming nonissues, political junk balls, to get at the good stuff, the trade issues.

Harold Olofson and Jack Shive were Democrats. Konobe decided to send an all-star leftie to bat, Koji Watanabe, a man who wore eyeglasses with thick, pale green lenses that looked like the bottoms of Coke bottles. Watanabe was said to be the best leftie on the Japanese roster.

The wide-bodied, scowling Watanabe was unusual in the Japanese automobile industry. His reputation for most of his career was that of an intellectual or gadfly rather than an engineer or manager. In corporate meetings, where self-effacement and modesty were thought essential to executives with a future, Watanabe was indifferent to *wa* if it got in the way of logic.

Jack Shive. Watanabe was a stylish rationalist. Maybe he could make the Americans come to their senses.

"We're in trouble," Konobe said. "The game's in your hands, Watanabe-*san*."

TWO

Whereas the Japanese foreign minister, Masayuki Yoshida, had been content to sip green tea on the veranda, Koji Watanabe had wanted to go down on the dock so he could see the lights along the shoreline of the Severn River. And yes, he was game for a little bourbon.

Watanabe had an interest in fish in general—he himself was a breeder of exotic goldfish. As they strolled down the curving, graveled path to the dock, he was full of questions about the weakfish, flounder, perch, and other kinds of fish that were found in the Severn.

Foreign Minister Yoshida talked in stilted textbook English; Shive had been told that English was a formidable challenge for most Japanese, and Yoshida could no doubt be counted among them. Watanable was one of the few truly fluent Japanese English-speakers Shive had ever met. Watanabe was known for his love of singing "On, Wisconsin" when he was loaded, and, owing to his education in Madison, could swear with a midwestern accent if the occasion called for it.

Watanabe obviously liked sitting in the darkness on the Severn. When his cocktail glass was empty, he didn't have to be told what to do next. He simply grabbed some fresh cubes with the ice tongs and poured himself another shot of Jack Daniels followed by a hit of soda.

The river was a slow and dark and ancient gloom, come from the hinterlands of Maryland and Pennsylvania, sliding softly toward its exit in Chesapeake Bay. Both upriver and downstream, there were house lights tucked back in the trees. It was a warm night and the water was calm. The dock had an electronic zapper to nip the mosquitoes that strayed their way.

Shive felt that Watanabe, almost alone among Japanese executives, actually listened to what he said. Looking Watanabe in the eye, liking him because he had a reasonably open mind, Shive said, "It's true, I grant you, Watanabe-*san*, we got ourselves into a jam because of the avarice and essential stupidity of our executives. I don't think there's any denying that. The evidence is in, and it's persuasive in that regard. Greed and arrogance, bottom line."

Watanabe grimaced.

Shive said, "We insisted on building sloppy barges. If Detroit had built cars to last, their customers would have had no reason to trade them for new barges in three years. That was their logic. They deliberately built disposables. Drive a car for two years and trade it in. It was a policy that was doomed to failure."

Watanabe said, "We slap a 'safety inspection' fee of twenty-four hundred dollars on a car that's two years old, and another twenty-four hundred annually from the fourth year on. You built heaps that wouldn't last, while we forced our consumers to trade theirs in. Also building fuel-efficient cars wasn't especially brilliant on our part. We've always had to import all our gas. We had no choice."

Shive slapped at a bug on his forehead. "We had all the resources we needed. Cheap steel. Power. Everything. The danger signs were clear early on, but we ignored them. We should have changed after the Arabs jerked us around in 1972, but we didn't. We clung to the old ways of doing business like a dog chewing a worn-out bone. The ragheads pushed us around again in 1978. Still we refused to change. Our automobile executives didn't want to screw up a good thing."

Watanabe said, "That about sums it up. What can I say? To paraphrase your Mr. Bob Dylan, when you're not busy growing, you're busy going out of business."

Shive slapped at another bug. "The truth is the truth. It was never the case that our engineers weren't talented or creative enough, but that they weren't listened to. Our executives were overpaid and literally had to see their companies on the brink of extinction by recession before they started to change. Also, long after it became apparent that the automobile workers weren't earning what they were being paid, the workers insisted on more money. They wanted more time off. More benefits. More of this. More of that. More of everything you care to name. But they weren't producing enough to cover all that. Rather than argue the point, the executives simply passed the costs on to the consumers. It was a game that couldn't last forever."

Watanabe looked grave. "We have our problems too. When you make a lifetime commitment to your workers, it's hard to reduce your labor costs in a recession. Also, where is the incentive for innovation when you have a guaranteed lifetime job and decisions are made by consensus? Everybody wants to please everybody else, especially the boss."

"I suppose the strengths of one are the weaknesses of the other."

"Exactly." Watanabe poured himself another whiskey.

"Our future depends on gaining and holding markets, same as yours, Watanabe-*san*. But as I told Foreign Minister Yoshida, our voters know how to read newspapers."

"We understand that."

"Voters are smarter than most people think."

Watanabe said, "We also know we have to face facts or risk going out of business." He too slapped at a bug, this one a mosquito on the back of his left hand.

"The way our voters see it, the Cold War is over, Watanabe-*san*. They don't see why the policies of the past should continue forever. They want fairness in the present, and they're tired of what they see as eternal delay by the Japanese government. The auto companies wanted us to take you to court for violating

GATT agreements, but we backed them off. Now we're obliged to do something or hand the Republicans an issue that could haunt us if the economy turns sour again. George Bush made the mistake of standing pat when he had numerous opportunities to do something about the recession. We can't afford to repeat his error. You're smart enough to know that."

"But surely you can understand the consequences of this proposal of yours, Mr. Shive. We're just coming off a major recession ourselves. We need time to plan the necessary adjustments to our economy."

"All we want is to play ball with the same rules for everybody. The same strike zone. Same everything." It was Shive's turn to freshen his drink.

Watanabe sighed. "Now, you act."

"You learned from our engineers after the war, Watanabe-*san*, and now, finally, belatedly, we have had the good sense, if not humility, to learn from yours. It cost us dearly, but we made the necessary adjustments."

"Will you agree that there was more to it than foot-dragging on our part, Mr. Shive?" Watanabe asked mildly.

Shive smiled. "You're suggesting that we couldn't act earlier because our consumers wouldn't let us."

Watanabe nodded yes. "You see the irony." He swirled the ice cubes in his drink.

"I don't think there's any doubt you're right. Also, Japan could have had better news than the end of the Cold War. Our having to fight Joe Stalin's boys made you a lot of money. Now the competition is for markets. We tell our people they need to compete in order to produce jobs. Well, they're ready to go. All they require is the same rules for both sides."

Watanabe sighed. "For us, it is an economic Pearl Harbor. Why can't you look at it this way, Mr. Vice President? Instead of complaining about our dumping on your market, look at the deal your consumers get—automobiles and electrical entertainment gadgets of a quality and a price they couldn't otherwise obtain. Their good deal was paid for by a willingness of Japanese workers to turn themselves into workaholics. We grind our fingers to the nub and save every possible yen we can. While you Americans live it up, we live repressed lives. The hours our managers work are legendary. The routine of work has become so ingrained in our lives we feel uncomfortable not working. We don't use up our vacations."

"Most Americans wouldn't want to do that, I agree." Shive began digging for more ice.

"We both know there is no free lunch. For every benefit there is a cost, and for us it has been the quality of our lives. We have lived stunted lives so others could have fun in Hondas and Toyotas that perform and don't fall apart, face it." Watanabe wiped his forehead with a handkerchief.

"Try selling that pitch to an automobile worker who has lost his job." Shive mopped his forehead with the back of his arm.

"You have to weigh both costs and benefits, Mr. Vice President. You say we make far more money off your market than you do ours. So what? I say again, we sacrifice ourselves so you Americans can have a good time. This truly is a case where insisting on some righteous ideal is not in your best interest."

"Watanabe-*san*, please, we both know that argument is just politically impossible for us to make. We may be wrongheaded as a country, but we are what we are. We worry about fair play; it's in our blood. It's at the heart of our culture. For whatever mix of reasons, the Japanese are popularly regarded as one-way parasites, and people want it stopped." Shive dug at a mosquito bite on his neck.

"So what if we have made some money off you? We have to spend it somewhere, right? We don't hear you or your stockbrokers complain when we buy your bonds."

"And our real estate and movie companies and whatever. Watanabe-*san*, please."

Watanabe looked chagrined.

"They sent you here to soften me up, didn't they, Watanabe-*san*? Hoping for a miracle."

Watanabe didn't say anything, which was the same as saying yes. He poured himself yet another drink. He was getting drunk.

"We can't back off this time, you understand that, don't you?

Especially not with the obvious dodges of GATT agreements. It is very likely a basic cultural difference, but the way the game is played truly does matter to us, no matter what the outcome. You have obviously taken the time to understand how we think. You know what the score is."

"I know that I've struck out," Watanabe said.

THREE

The embarrassing chartered sex flights—in which the *yakuza* had gone so far as to lease banks of airport lockers so husbands going "golfing" could stash their clubs on the way to Manila—were halted in 1981 on the eve of a tour of Asian capitals by the Japanese prime minister. But despite the ban on sex flights, groups of Japanese men still found reason to visit the karaoke bars in Manila.

In karaokes, which were popular all over Asia, drunks, using a device that amplified their voices over recorded music, pretended to be pop singers. Every Woo, Chan, or Tanaka his own Elvis Presley. In Manila, the girls who sipped high-priced "lady's" drinks of Coke or 7-Up in a cocktail glass and listened to the sodden crooning were for sale.

The current mayor of Manila, an owner of massage parlors, was trying to limit the competition for the hormonal buck by busting places too small to afford a nick high enough to please His Honor's ego. The mayor, who had paid fifty pesos a vote for much of his support, promised the undecided—that is, unpaid-for—voters that he was going to clean up Manila. He was going to do for Manila what Lee Kwan Yew had done for Singapore. So, with the exception of Teddy's and a couple of other *yakuza-*

owned bars, he put the Ermita area out of the sex trade business. But this did not by any means halt the sex trade or the alarming spread of AIDS. Metropolitan Manila did not have a single city administration; it was split into a crazy-quilt of towns—Makati here, Quezon City there—each a political fiefdom with its own mayor and city council. The Ermita sex trade simply moved south to Pasay City, which stretched from Manila Bay to the airport.

In allowing select *yakuza* clubs to continue doing business in Ermita, the mayor demonstrated that he understood the virtue of discretion as well as political image-building. The *yakuza* expected to have to pay a nick to cops and politicians—in Japan there were tithes to be paid at every turn—but one did not flat work over Japanese gangsters and get away with it.

The mayor's men occasionally tut-tutted over the goings-on in Teddy's, but they did nothing about it. Teddy's dancers continued to flash their pussies in the most imaginative and satisfying manner possible. Such activity was the perquisite of Takeshita-*kai*, the Yokohama-based *yakuza* organization that owned Teddy's. Takeshita-*kai* literally meant Takeshita's gang, a man named Takeshita being the founder.

An engineer from Fukushima or a manager from Nagoya didn't fly to Manila to imitate Julio Iglesia or watch dancers with bikinis covering the fun spots. Once they got an eyeful of bare pussy, price was the last thing on their minds. They dug for plastic and worried about the silly pesos later; men of the world didn't waste time calculating the yen-to-peso exchange rate.

For reasons that were culturally impossible for Winston Monzon to fathom, the Japanese were embarrassed to ask how much something cost, so the prices in Teddy's and several other *yakuza*-owned karaoke bars rivaled their counterparts in Japan. This was the cost of maintaining cultural enclaves or reservations so they could enjoy Filipinas without having to deal with anything Filipino.

Nobito Kao had once told Winston Monzon that the Japanese believe they get what they pay for; buy cheap, get cheap. They didn't think they were getting a good deal unless they got screwed. Kao said he wanted to be a good host; he charged them outrageous prices so they could have fun.

Kao was the biggest bird in the Manila pit. Winston Monzon liked big chickens, especially when the big chicken was the godfather of Takeshita-*kai*'s Manila operation, and owner of Teddy's. Kao liked Monzon to give his reports in Teddy's, which was more than okay by Monzon.

FOUR

As Nobito Kao and Winston Monzon settled in at a table below one of Teddy's glitzy dance ramps, Monzon could hardly keep his eyes off the pussy of the Filipina dancing just above his head. The ramp was elevated so that the pussies of the Filipinas, most of whom were about five feet tall, were just about eye-level to an Asian.

The angle wasn't as good for the occasional taller longnose customers. While longnoses liked bare pussies the same as everybody else, they didn't linger in Teddy's. Teddy's was a Japanese place; there was no mistaking that. Also, the prices were ridiculous.

Monzon knew that the Japanese had a thing about pussies, and he had to agree, a pussy had a primal beauty about it that was nothing short of wonderful. He found it difficult to keep his attention on the conversation, as the waitress, Ellie, a favorite of Kao's, delivered sweating bottles of San Miguel.

Monzon said, "You told me that if anything passed through that you would be interested in, I should let you know. Well, last week I got a query in from the Americans about two missing young women, both blonds, who were last known be in Davao. They sent a copy of their passport photos. I thought I'd seen one of them before, but I couldn't remember where. I know a young secretary in the Philippine Embassy in Washington, so I sent her a copy of the pictures and asked her if she recognized either one of them."

Kao had had his wisdom teeth pulled two days earlier and touched his jaw with his fingertips. "What happened?"

"She sent me some photocopies of newspaper articles. The one I thought I'd seen before really isn't blond. She has brown hair. And she isn't Beth Anne Holden of Lincoln, Nebraska, like they said in the query."

"Oh?"

Monzon said, "She's Linda Shive."

"No relation to the American vice president, I take it."

"She's Jack Shive's daughter."

Kao blinked. "Shive's daughter?"

"Yes, Jack Shive."

"Did you tell anyone about this?"

"No."

"You're sure."

"Absolutely." Monzon gave Kao the newspaper articles.

Kao studied the pictures.

"How about the woman who faxed you these articles? What did you tell her?"

"I didn't tell her anything. I'm Joseph Estrada's executive secretary."

"You're sure you didn't tell anybody else."

"Positive. Nobody."

"Not even Estrada?"

"When I found out it was Shive's daughter, I knew it behooved me to keep my mouth shut. How about it, boss, did I do okay or what?"

Kao tucked a wad of thousand-peso notes into Monzon's pocket. "I'm willing to spring for a fourteenth month if this information is exclusively ours."

In the Philippines it was common practice for companies to give their employees a Christmas bonus equal to one month's pay. This was referred to as the thirteenth month.

Monzon looked pleased. "Sure!"

Nobito Kao hissed at the waitress and waggled two fingers for more San Miguel.

A fourteenth month from Takeshita-*kai*. Okay. Winston Monzon kicked back to enjoy the view.

FIVE

James Burlane regarded most Third World cab drivers as licensed bandits, but none were more rapacious than at Manila's International Airport, where outside sharks received inside descriptions of travelers dumb enough to list large sums of hard currency on Philippine declaration forms. The cabbies were just as bad at the domestic airport, a half mile away, only there were fewer of them.

The drivers liked to see longnose heads floating above the black-haired glut of arriving passengers, but they loved the Japanese even better. Longnoses were often frugal, and experienced Aussies, Americans, and Germans, on the alert for hustles, sometimes bargained hard-core, holding their ground whatever pitch was thrown at them. The Japanese, being more civilized and polite, nearly begged to be ripped off. Why else would they flash fist-sized rolls of greenbacks as though the yen and dollar sold at the same rate? It was said the Filipinas in Manila preferred them as customers; little dicks, big tippers.

Unfortunately, the solo pigeons were almost always longnoses; the Japanese preferred traveling in groups so they could be more efficiently relieved of their money in Japanese-owned hotels and *yakuza*-owned karaokes. Burlane was one of those determined longnoses who counted every peso. He pulled back the hidden straps of his travel bag, turning it into a backpack. Then he safety-pinned the zipper tabs on the pockets of his photographer's vest. Thus prepared, hands free, alert for razor artists, he pushed forward, using his height advantage to survey the confusion of bodies in front of him. He ignored peddlers, fast-talkers, and scam artists until he found what he wanted—a metered air-conditioned cab.

The driver said, "Six bucks U.S. to Ermita."

Burlane said, "Meter doesn't work?"

"Out of order. This is a better deal."

"Ahh." Thinking *like fuck too*, Burlane went to the next cab, also air-conditioned and metered.

The driver of the second cab, having observed the failure of the first, said, "Where will it be?"

"Meter work?"

"Japanese made. Tamperproof."

"Banilad Pension in Ermita." Burlane slid onto the back seat for his sixty-peso ride, saying, "Guy in that other cab thought I was a damn fool."

"Maybe he didn't see the safety pins on your vest pockets. You've been in places like this before."

"A Filipino Sherlock Holmes!"

The driver grinned. "I don't know why people think Filipinos wear shirts with stupid flowers on them. A *bakla* might wear one."

"And CIA agents," Burlane said.

The driver laughed. "Right, change that. *Baklas* and CIA agents." Bakla was Tagalog for homosexual.

The rule of bargaining that Burlane had encountered in Thailand, Malaysia, and the Philippines was that the seller, or vendor, felt compelled, if not honor-bound, to nick the maximum profit from any stranger or outsider. One could either bargain or go elsewhere, as Burlane had chosen to do. Either way, there were no hard feelings. Any experienced foreigner understood this. It was foolish to lecture or get uptight about ad hoc rules of fair play. When in Asia, one played by Asian rules.

Burlane had stayed in the Banilad Pension on his way through Manila going to Mindanao; his room had been small but clean, and the price was fair enough. As before, the young man who escorted Burlane to his room asked him if he wanted a girl for the night.

"No, I don't believe so," Burlane said. "Not tonight."

"Short time?" A short time was three hours max.

"I think I'll eat and go to bed early, thanks." Later, as Burlane lay in bed reading a paperback, the phone rang. He fumbled for a moment, then found the receiver.

A dulcet-voiced Filipina said, "Are you sure you can't use a good blow job?"

"Thanks, but I'll pass. I just want to get a good night's sleep."

"You'll sleep like a baby after I get through with you. Guaranteed."

"Ahhh, no," Burlane said.

Laughing at his hesitation, the Filipina gave him an edible okay—dipped in hormonal chocolate, rolled in womanly walnuts, and topped with a maraschino cherry of sensual promise—and hung up.

SIX

The next morning, James Burlane took a cab to the headquarters of the President's Anti-Crime Commission in posh Makati, the financial and business district of the urban sprawl of Manila. Trying to score an audience with Vice President Estrada might be tough, but he had to try.

Burlane had dealt with government officials long enough to know that wangling an audience with Estrada might take days, if not weeks. The more powerful the bureaucrat or politician, the more complicated and humbling was the drill. Estrada was vice president of the Philippines. The cooling of Burlane's heels in the reception room was just the first step. If Darryl Lattimore had been a reporter for the *New York Times* or a producer from *CNN*, it would have been different. As it was, Burlane found it tough to estimate his chances.

Bearing a folder containing photographs of show-off Lattimore articles that had been published in *Sports Illustrated* and other biggie magazines—a few impressive extras had been faked by Ara Shott's Company friends—he took a deep breath and began his chore. He started with a lowly receptionist, a gorgeous Filipina who, judging from her smart outfit and jewelry, was a rich man's side action.

She listened to his story and said, "If you'll just take a seat, please."

Burlane grabbed a *Philippine Daily Inquirer* from the display of newspapers and magazines on a mahogany table and took a seat in a leather easy chair.

On the eve of Vice President Shive's visit to Japan, Reuters reported there was fear in Tokyo that the Americans had come to the end of their patience and no longer cared whether the Japanese lost face or not.

Reuters reported a "high American official," speaking off the record, as saying, "To hell with saving their face. I don't give a squat. If they want to sell to us, they're gonna have to buy from us, and they're going to have to sell their stuff for the same price on both sides of the Pacific. And they're gonna have to deal with us now, not later. No more horsebleep stalling."

The way the story was written, "high official" could have been the vice president himself, who once had been charged with working his mouth like William F. Bonney fanning a six-shooter. Burlane, an admirer of his current employer's impolitic cheek, was certain the "I don't give a squat" was Shiveian. The use of "bleep," as in "horsebleep," was definitely a Shive favorite. Burlane had grown up on a farm and so appreciated a straightforward scatological talker when he heard one.

An hour later, by bureaucratic standards faster than Burlane could say beam-me-up-Scotty, he found himself in the cozy office of Winston Monzon, Vice President Estrada's executive secretary. Monzon, strikingly handsome but so slender as to be nearly emaciated, flipped through Burlane's articles, and said, "How can we be of help, Mr. Lattimore?"

Burlane repeated his story of meeting two blonds in Davao. They were going to ride an interisland boat to Zamboanga, where he was to meet them, but they didn't show up. Zamboanguenos said a Muslim named al-Jabar claimed to have scored the girls by hijacking the ship, but they thought he probably bought them from the ship's captain. Sergeant Canizares of the Zamboanga police said that if al-Jabar did have the girls, there wasn't much that could be done about it.

"Mmmmmm," Monzon said.

Burlane didn't know whether Monzon's "mmmmmmmm" was good or bad. He said, "For what it's worth, I do more than sports. My contacts in the *New York Times Magazine* and *Esquire* are still good. *Atlantic Monthly*, too."

Monzon, still looking at the articles, thought about that. Finally he said, "The vice president is a very busy man, as you might imagine, Mr. Lattimore. I'll have to check his schedule to see if we have any time in the next few days. If you'll leave me your number, I'll have my assistant call you back this afternoon with a yes or no, either way. Is that fair enough?"

"Fair enough," Burlane said. "Thank you."

He had lunch and went back to his pension for an air-conditioned nap while he waited for his call. Twenty minutes later, the phone rang. Quick action. He snatched the receiver from its cradle.

It was the purring Filipina from the night before, her voice still oozing sugar and sex. "You haven't changed your mind, have you?"

Wearily, Burlane said no, he hadn't changed his mind.

The Filipina said, "If you do, just ask for Melanie at the desk. They say I look real hot in the afternoon light. Also, if you're really in the mood, and if the price is right, I have a girlfriend we can persuade to come along."

Burlane sighed. "No, thanks, Melanie."

At four o'clock, Winston Monzon called, saying Vice President Joseph Estrada would be pleased to grant Darryl Lattimore a few minutes of his time, at ten o'clock the next morning.

SEVEN

The next morning, after a forty-minute wait in the reception room, James Burlane was ushered into Joseph Estrada's splendidly appointed office, where Estrada waited with Winston Monzon. The crime buster was a mustached Filipino gone to gut and jowl, but with no-bullshit, penetrating eyes that Burlane supposed had much to do with his movie persona. Estrada as Erap was, as Burlane understood it, sort of a Tagalog Robin Hood, a Heroic Defender of the Little Guy.

With Monzon taking notes, Burlane told Estrada/Erap his story, saying that in addition to finding the girls, he wanted to do a magazine article on the Japanese sex trade for a magazine with some clout. "It'd be fun to shake them up with the truth," he said.

Monzon glanced at Estrada.

Estrada bobbed his eyebrows, a quick up-and-down.

Burlane had noted that Filipinos used their eyebrows to greet one another, to ask questions, to agree with one another, and to register shock or surprise. Where a longnose would wink, Filipinos used their eyebrows. In this case, Estrada had used his eyebrows to give Monzon permission to continue on his present course.

Monzon said, "As it happens, we have a special investigator looking into the *japayuki* traffic. Maybe he can help you find the young woman." He arched one eyebrow and let his voice trail off suggestively.

"I receive, and I give in return," Burlane said quickly. "I'm a veteran. I know how to scratch backs. I know how to write a story so editors won't mess with it. Besides, it can't hurt to have a vice president on my side, can it? Don't most vice presidents yearn to be president?"

Monzon, amused, glanced at the vice president. The glance said, What do you think, boss?

Estrada grinned. He bobbed his eyebrows twice. The meaning of this was also clear: He agreed to the deal. Joseph Estrada would help Darryl Lattimore; and Latimore would make sure the crime-busting vice president didn't get edited out of his *japayuki* story.

Estrada said, "I guarantee we would like nothing better than to put the scumbag *yakuza* recruiters out of business, but there's so much money being made by everybody, except the girls, that progress isn't easy."

Monzon said, "Our investigator is named Rene Alburo, Dr. Alburo, actually. He's a professor of Japanese history at the University of San Francisco. He is a *japino*. Have you heard that term, Mr. Lattimore?"

"I don't believe I have."

"Half Japanese, half Filipino. Dr. Alburo's mother was one of what the Japanese called 'comfort women' during World War II. These were women from occupied countries who were forced to provide 'comfort' to Japanese troops. Korean, Chinese, Thai, Malay, Indonesian, and Dutch women, and Filipinas, all had their turn as the imperial army captured territory. It was, we think, the first use of the term *japayuki*. After reading about the death of a young woman named Maricris Sision a couple of years ago, Dr. Alburo called Vice President Estrada and volunteered his services."

Estrada nodded his agreement at the explanation.

"Dr. Alburo is now checking out leads on Cebu. If you like, I can call him and arrange a meeting for you."

"I'd like that very much."

"You'll have to go to Cebu."

Burlane imagined that most of the *japayuki* action was centered in Manila. Why was Alburo in Cebu? He said, "No problem."

Monzon grinned. "Done then. I'll call you at your pension when I have a time and place."

A bobbing of eyebrows couldn't be quoted or taped. The vice president had said almost nothing the entire meeting. As he rose to leave, Burlane thought that if Richard Nixon and his connivers had communicated by eyebrow, Nixon might have saved his presidency.

On his way out, he wondered whether he had the discipline to withstand a third call from the determined Melanie. As his curiosity grew, he knew, so would his cock, while his will to resist simultaneously wilted. Melanie knew that, too.

Before she could charm him a third time, Winston Monzon called to say that Lattimore could meet Rene Alburo in the Cebu Chess Club the next two or three mornings. "After that, he doesn't know where he'll be," Monzon said. "Look for a man who looks like a Filipino Richard Boone, only shorter and more stout. If the PAL people tell you their flights are booked, call me."

EIGHT

The desk clerk said the Cebu Chess Club was about a block and a half up Palaez Street from James Burlane's hotel, The Century. "Up" meant toward the mountains in the center of the island. The Century was the cheapest of the medium-range accommodations listed in Burlane's hippie guidebook, and it turned out to have its own disco and massage parlor, so that inebriated longnoses didn't have to risk the streets late at night.

A half-block toward the sea was the teeming corner of Colon and Palaez, the heart of downtown Cebu City. Three of the corners were dominated by movie theaters in the old-fashioned grand style, featuring kiss-kiss, *rat-a-tat-tat* movies in Tagalog; the sidewalks were a confusion of vendors hawking *kalamansi*, guavas, mangoes, *lanzones*, bananas, peanuts, newspapers, and magazines.

Although the clerk had been certain he knew where the chess club was located, Burlane was stumped at first. The stretch of Palaez Street in question contained a *carenderia*, a hole-in-the-wall tailor shop, and a massage parlor. There was not a hint of anything having to do with chess.

Finally Burlane asked a woman in the *carenderia* for help, and learned that the club was located in an interior courtyard with an unmarked entrance. Following her directions, he stepped off the sidewalk into a large square or courtyard that took up most of the inside of the block. This area was loaded with gossiping women, naked children, cavorting puppies, a speckled pig in a bamboo cage, and several tethered fighting cocks. A touring brown rat paused to inspect the invading longnose; after demonstrating its indifference, the imperious rat, lethargic, not to be hurried, blinked its rodent eyes and continued on its way.

The open-air quarters of the chess club, separated from the courtyard by a bamboo lattice, were to Burlane's left. He could see ten or twelve figures inside, including Rene Alburo, who was watching two players bent over a board in intense concentration. After each move, their hands shot like adders' tongues to punch a button on their half of the clock, which had a face for each player.

Behind him, two fighting chickens clucked at one another across the courtyard. James Burlane stepped inside the chess club. He could tell by Alburo's eyes that the Crime Commission investigator recognized him immediately.

Alburo abandoned the chess game and strode toward him, hand outstretched. "Welcome, Mr. Lattimore. Rene."

"Darryl. Winston Monzon said I should look for the man who looked like Richard Boone. But how did you know me?"

Alburo laughed. "You were in Zamboanga. The police down there have to keep an eye on foreigners in town."

"I see. I suppose I should add that I saw you following a woman and a Japanese man down to a yacht in the harbor, the *Sagawa Maru.*"

Alburo looked surprised and a little concerned. "You did?"

"I was in a *carenderia* watching the parade."

"Was I that obvious?"

"You didn't look like Inspector Clouseau, but I figured it out."

Alburo frowned. He glanced at the chess players and lowered his voice. "What do you say we go have a beer and talk? There's a good place just a couple of doors down. Joe Estrada pays. They've got American and German food there that foreigners say is just like home. Estrada's good for pepper steak or Wiener schnitzel in addition to the San Miguel.''

''Sounds like a deal to me,'' Burlane said.

They walked down the sidewalk to Our Place and scored a table beside a Spanish window overlooking the street. Below them, the corner of Palaez and Sanciangko was choked with horse-drawn carts, bicycles, motorcycles, jeepneys, cars, and trucks.

Our Place was something like an American cowboy bar with an international touch. The walls were covered with Bavarian travel posters, a black velvet painting of beer-drinking dogs, plaques commemorating memorable drunks by visiting seamen. John Wayne, looking to Burlane like a man suppressing gas pains, hung above the Coca-Cola refrigerator where the San Miguel was stored. B-movie overhead fans pushed languid air past grateful customers, especially suffering, sweating longnoses.

Alburo was a deep-voiced Filipino with a rugged face and stout belly. Here was a man who liked his rice and San Miguel. He was not fat, however. ''Stout'' was the word. They ordered San Miguels and peanuts, and Alburo told Burlane they were dealing with the *yakuza* and the *japayuki* trade. Did Lattimore know anything about *japayuki*?

Burlane shrugged. ''Only in general.''

''For years, the *yakuza* ran regular sex flights to Bangkok and Manila. However, the Japanese prime minister stopped the practice on the eve of his visit to Southeast Asian capitals in 1981. How, for example, was he to explain the Casio watch company's party in Manila for two hundred male employees? Each employee was given a number; at the appointed hour, two hundred Filipinas with matching numbers spilled into a ballroom . . .''

''What?'' Burlane, suppressing a grin, leaned back in his chair, eyes wide.

''The eager watch men plunged into the crowd to find their screw for the night. Great sport.''

''Oof!'' Burlane laughed. ''I suppose that says something about the Japanese, but I'm not sure what. Something impolite, I suspect.''

"After the sex flights were stopped, the *yakuza* concentrated on importing *gaijin* females to Japan. In the Philippines something called the Philippine Overseas Employment Agency was supposed to watch Filipinas dance three dances and listen to them sing three songs before they were issued cards certifying them as 'entertainers.' " Alburo rolled his eyes. He beckoned to a waitress. "Popcorn, please, *inday*."

The waitress gave him a heavy-lidded look and headed for the kitchen.

"By 1991, when a girl named Maricris Sision was killed by sexual torture in Nakajima, about seventy-five thousand Filipinas worked as club and cocktail hostesses in what the *yakuza* call the 'water trade.' Only about five percent work as legitimate entertainers; the rest are forced into prostitution of one form or another. The stories of use and abuse of *japayuki* are nearly incredible. They're used in porn films. There is even a Japanese magazine that offers them for sale."

At the bar, a bespectacled longnose with white hair gestured toward a tape deck with his hand. He waggled his fingers and an earringed gay man in tight jeans twitched his way to the machine.

"But the Philippine government can't stop it, I take it."

"No, it can't, I'm embarrassed to admit. I regret that we are so pathetically poor that our women are forced to do this, and we lack either the political will or the physical means stop them. We must have help from the outside. That's why I volunteered to write a report for Joseph Estrada, and that's why he sent you down here."

On the jukebox a husky-voiced man with a southern accent sang:

Poor old Bobcat Bill
Poor old Bobcat Bill
Oh, oh, Friday-Night Fayyy
Friday-Night Fayyy
Friday-Night Fay-ayyy
On down to Waco wayyyy.

Burlane looked mildly back at the bar. The white-haired man tapped his hand to the rhythm of the music. Behind him, the gay man wiggled with his eyes closed, but the look on his face suggested that listening to cowboy songs wasn't his druthers. Burlane said, "The white-haired guy looks like the boss."

"His Filipina wife actually owns the place. Foreigners can't own the controlling interest in property here."

"I see. What happened after Ms. Sision was murdered?"

"The government passed a law that an 'entertainer' had to be at least twenty-three years old to be a *japayuki*, but that was a joke. This is Asia. You can order counterfeit birth certificates by the gross. An 'entertainer' in Japan is supposed to get about fifteen hundred U.S. dollars a month, but after the Filipino and Japanese 'recruiters' get their nick, a girl might earn three fifty a month if she's lucky, and that paid in pesos at the airport. Some Filipinas have come back with stories of having to do twenty-five after-hour 'dates' a month, with the clubs collecting from the customers. If a girl misses a date, she gets docked a hundred bucks. My God, they charge twenty bucks for a glass of beer in some of those places. Can you imagine the tab for a tumble with a Filipina?"

The waitress arrived with the popcorn heaped up in a bowl, and Alburo set about giving it a hit of salt.

Burlane snagged some popcorn. He said, "I suppose the price for securing the assistance of Filipino cops is a bargain to the *yakuza*."

"Pocket money. By the way, the yacht you saw in Zamboanga belongs to Shoji Kobayashi, the *oyabun* of Takeshita-*kai*, which is the main *yakuza* dealer in *japayuki*."

Burlane, munching on popcorn, said, "*Oyabun*. Meaning 'godfather,' if I'm not mistaken."

"Correct. We think Kobayashi himself is aboard. The Philippine National Police have been helping me track the *Sagawa Maru* through the islands. That's why I was in Zamboanga behaving like Inspector Clouseau."

Burlane laughed.

On the tape machine, the cowboy sang:

They feed in the coolie
They water in the draw
Their tails are all matted
Their backs are all raw.

At the bar, the man with the white hair looked pleased. The gay man, having ceased his wiggling, looked bored.

Eyeing the room, then Burlane, Alburo grabbed a handful of popcorn and said, "We're dealing with a Japanese *yakuza* organization called Takeshita, which is named after the gang's founder. Takeshita-*kai* literally means Takeshita's gang; internationally, it's an industry leader in porn films. It publishes the magazine I told you about. In view of Kobayashi's presence aboard the *Sagawa Maru*, I told Estrada I wanted to document her voyage all the way to Japan. The Japanese would get touchy as all get-out if they found a Filipino investigator running around on their soil, but he said to go ahead. If anybody asks him, he'll claim I'm an overenthusiastic professor." He grabbed more popcorn.

"A pragmatic Mr. Estrada. Not for nothing was he elected vice president."

"He knows we don't stand a chance if we're too fastidious about the rules. You know, I wouldn't bet my last peso on it, but there's a chance that Beth Anne Holden and her friend are on board the *Sagawa Maru*."

Really?" Burlane took a swig of San Miguel.

Alburo said, "The *yakuza* love North American women, especially blonds. American and Canadian readers would be interested in that, wouldn't they? Estrada said, why not take you with me to Japan?"

"Me?" Burlane signaled with two fingers that he wanted another round of San Miguel, pointing to both his and Alburo's nearly empty bottles.

Alburo said, "Why not you? We can give your editors evidence of the *japayuki* trade they just can't ignore. If you score a solidly documented piece in the *New York Times Magazine*, say, what would the Japanese do then, call you a liar? They can ignore stories in the Filipino media, but they just loathe having barbarians from the West call them uncivilized."

"Estrada called? Really?"

Alburo grinned. "Well, okay, Winston Monzon called."

"*And* did the talking," Burlane added.

Alburo bobbed his eyebrows: yes, Winston Monzon did the calling and the talking.

The cowboy now sang:

Oh, Dan, can't you see
The waters running free
Just waitin' there for you and me-ee
Oh, wa-ter
Cool . . . clear . . . wa-ter

The white man, even more pleased, wanted the music louder. He liked his cowboy songs. He motioned to the machine again.

The gay man, making a face, turned up the volume.

Burlane said, "What kind of music does the gay man like?"

"He's a *bayut*. We call them *bayuts* in Cebuano. He likes Barry Manilow love songs."

"Ahh. Which brings us to the question of why you're in Cebu?"

"I'm waiting for the *Sagawa Maru* to show up, and my wife's family lives here."

"You seem confident about the *Sagawa Maru*. Do you know where it is, exactly, and why?"

"Yes to both questions. I'll take you for a drive tomorrow morning and show you."

"Bring an extra pad for my notes?"

"I'd think so. This will very likely be the *Sagawa Maru*'s last stop in the Philippines." Alburo raised his hand to order two more San Miguels. *"Day! Day!"*

NINE

Pickpockets cruised the packed sidewalks of Cebu's teeming, smelly downtown, and drying clothes hung unembarrassed above sidewalks cluttered with hawkers of everything from imitation Swiss army knives to green mangoes. This was was the stuff of old movies, and James Burlane loved it; he wanted to plunge into the throng to see what there was to see, but first there was Shive to take care of, and he needed to study Rene Alburo's summary report on the *yakuza* connection.

He bought himself a cold San Miguel *grande* and some Cebu peanuts and took them back to his room. The Filipinos had discovered that peanuts would grow between rows of sugarcane, and the peanuts, cooked in oil spiked with garlic cloves, were wonderful. They had their skins on and were salty, so good that eating a handful of them probably reduced his life expectancy by five minutes, but he didn't care.

Having to call Shive was in the nonwonderful category. He took a deep breath and dialed the personal number Shive had given him.

"Yes, sir?" said the operator.

"Collect call. From Sid Khartoum."

He listened to the ringing. Then Shive answered. Just like

that. The president and vice president had always been distant, almost mythical figures. Godlike.

"Khartoum? I'll take the call."

Burlane told Shive where he was. "I've got a line on your daughter. A lead only. I haven't seen her myself. I think, but I say again I'm not certain, that she's headed for Yokohama. She may be in the hands of *yakuza*."

"What?"

"I said may be, not is. And, remember, as far as anybody knows, she's Beth Anne Holden."

"Shit!"

"The Yokohama Bay Stars will most likely be playing the Seibu Lions in the Japan series. The Stars are a Yokohama team, so the hotels are likely all booked. In the event I need to go there, do you suppose you could use your political weight to score a place for me and a Filipino to crash in Yokohama?"

"I should be able to get elbow space for you somewhere. I'm going to Japan myself on this trade thing, did you know that?"

"So I see by the papers."

"When will you know one way or the other?"

"Maybe tomorrow. Maybe not. It's hard to say."

"Call me immediately, either way. Whatever I'm doing, I'll find the time to talk to you. If somebody answers and says I'm busy you tell them to unbusy me pronto. You've got my number. It's good no matter where I am."

"Will do, Mr. Vice President."

To: Vice President Joseph Estrada
From: Dr. Rene Alburo
Subject: Trade in Filipina *japayuki*
Re: *Yakuza*

The history of the *yakuza* may be traced to gangs of *kabuki-mono*, the crazy ones, or, as they were also called, *hatamoto-yakko*, servants of the shogun. Stories of these swaggering, sword-bearing rebels are repeated endlessly on Japanese television. When the first great shogun, Ieyasu Tokugawa, unified Japan in 1604, a half-million samurai were put out of work. Thus were born the *ronin,* or masterless samurai, who found themselves in a rigid world with few opportunities beyond crime.

Today's *yakuza* gangs see themselves as champions of the weak, and identify with the *machi-yakko,* the servants of the town, young men from all occupations who united to take on the murderous *ronin* in the 18th century. In the thousands of stories and kabuki plays heralding their good deeds and wonderful exploits, *machi-yakko* are called *otokodate,* chivalrous commoners.

The spiritual godfather of the *yakuza* is Banzuiin Chobei, who rose to become the head of the *machi-yakko* in Tokyo after he moved there in 1640. This doer of good deeds declined all offers of thanks for the help he gave, saying, "We have made it our principle to live with a chivalrous spirit. When put to the sword, we'll lose our lives. That's our fate. I just ask you to pray for the repose of my soul when my turn comes."

In the end, Chobei was murdered by his treacherous archenemy, Mizuno, who had invited him to drink sake in a ceremony of reconciliation. Chobei knew Mizuno planned to kill him, but he went anyway and died an honorable death.

Modern *yakuza oyabuns* popularly trace the lineage of their gangs to bands of gamblers and peddlers, the *bakuto* and the *tekiya,* who appeared about a hundred years after Chobei's death. The *yakuza* are organized into families, as in the Mafia, but with a Japanese touch—the *oyabun-kobun* relationship. The *oyabun* is the father; the *kobun* is the child. The *oyabun* helps and protects; the *kobun* owes the *oyabun* his absolute loyalty. Apprentice *kobun* are expected to be *teppodama,* literally "bullets," to protect the *oyabun.* That is, they are expected to stand in the front line and accept the consequences, as necessary, of blade or gun.

The *oyabun-kobun* bond is formed by the ceremonial drinking of *sake.* The *oyabun*'s cup is nearly full, the *kobun*'s nearly empty. If two *kobuns* drink, the amount is equal. An older brother gets six-tenths to a younger brother's four-tenths.

The *bakuto* introduced *yubitsume,* in which an errant *kobun,* by way of apology, offers the *oyabun* the end of his little finger for amputation. *Yubitsume* spread to other *yakuza* gangs, although the gamblers are most known for it. In 1971, government researchers found that 42 percent of *bakuto* had severed finger joints; another 10 percent had lost the tips of two fingers.

In medieval Japan, authorities tattooed black bands around the arms of convicted criminals. The *bakuto* responded by tattooing themselves as a badge of honor and to demonstrate their toughness and courage. The practice spread to other *yakuza* gangs and grew to elaborate full-body tattoos depicting flowers, animals, gods, and folk heroes. These tattoos end at midcalf, upper arm, and the neck, so a *kobun* can wear long trousers and a short-sleeved shirt without revealing the tattoos.

The *yakuza* follow Bushido, the code of the samurai. To prove their manliness, *yakuza kobun* are willing to endure hunger, pain, or imprisonment; violent death, such as that suffered by the noble Chobei, is poetic, tragic, and honorable.

At the heart of Bushido are the concepts of *giri* and *ninjo*. *Giri*, a difficult concept for *gaijin* to understand, is a complicated feeling of duty and obligation which is at the heart of Japanese notions of moral debt, loyalty, and gratitude. *Ninjo* is also hard to translate, but means roughly "emotion" or "human feeling," and is expressed in a generosity to the poor and disadvantaged. The tension between *giri* and *ninjo*, that is, obligation versus passion, lies at the heart of almost all popular Japanese culture.

Translated by the *yakuza*, *giri-ninjo* becomes "chivalry-patriotism."

There are roughly 2,500 *yakuza* gangs all over Japan who work with Japanese police agencies in a complicated system of payoffs, bribes, and various forms of "gifts" that maintain the *wa*, or harmony. These gangs have neatly divided turfs, both geographical and occupational. The largest number are *bakuto*, or gamblers, followed by the *tekiya*, the peddlers, and the *gurentai*, hoods. There are the *sokaiya*, who extort money from corporations, extortionists who use the threat of scandal-sheet exposure. Finally, there are seaport racketeers, involved in smuggling guns and methamphetamines, and those *yakuza* involved in the water trade, the world of hostess bars, sex shows, and prostitution.

* * *

To: Vice President Joseph Estrada
  From: Dr. Rene Alburo
  Subject: Trade in Filipina *japayuki*
  Re: Takeshita-*kai*, Yokohama

The largest gang involved in *japayuki* traffic is Takeshita-*kai*, headquartered in Yokohama. Takeshita-*kai* is believed to smuggle *shabu* from Taiwan, and both guns and *japayuki* from the Philippines.

Any Japanese club owner can buy or lease *japayuki* from Takeshita-*kai* by browsing through the gang's magazine that contains photographs of current offerings. If an owner wants to see more of a particular girl before he makes a commitment, he can request a videotape of her dancing and being screwed; Takeshita-*kai*, a leading international producer and distributor of S&M pornography, produces superior audition tapes.

The Japanese National Police Agency keeps dossiers of leading *yakuza* figures. The details are, on the surface, impressive, but on closer examination, the reader understands that there is nothing that could convict anybody of anything. These are dossiers of "maybe" and "might be" and "could be." There is nothing here to seriously disturb the *wa* that marks the cooperation and even open friendship between the Japanese police and the *yakuza*.

For example, it is clear that the power of both Yamagumiguchi in Kobe and Takeshita-*kai* in Yokohama can be traced to their intimidating presence on the waterfront. Takeshita-*kai* is widely believed to control the powerful Sagawa Rice and Sugar company. Sagawa's many acquisitions include the Yokohama Bay Stars baseball club, formerly the Taiyo Whales.

The *oyabun* of Takeshita-*kai*, a rabid Stars fan, is Shoji Kobayashi, who owns a town house in Yokohama which is said to have a special room with walls adorned with swords and photographs of *oyabuns* and baseball players.

Kobayashi's chief *kobun* are Tsutomu Kamina, who lives in a Takeshita-*kai* seaside compound near the gangster-dominated Atami hot springs south of Yokohama, and Nobito Kao, who heads the gang's Manila operation and lives in a Makati penthouse.

TEN

James Burlane, wearing a photographer's vest and lugging a large daypack jammed with gear, had no sooner stepped out in front of the Century Hotel in Cebu City than Rene Alburo pulled to the curb in a once-white 1964 Volkswagen bus with a leaking exhaust manifold that made a *puff-puff-puff* sound.

Burlane slid onto the front seat, almost immediately receiving the passenger's end of the cool sweep of an oscillating fan screwed to the dashboard. As Alburo lit a cigarette, Burlane noticed that the plastic top of the shift knob featured a miniature photo of a naked longnose woman with outstanding tits.

Alburo, eyeing the daypack, said, "You come prepared."

Burlane mopped sweat from his forehead. "They say the Boy Scouts teach that, but I dropped out after my third meeting. All that saluting and those merit badges and stuff." He rolled his eyes.

Alburo drove toward the mountains on Jones Boulevard, ticking off the landmarks. Camp Sergio Osmeña of the Philippine National Police on their right, followed by the Philippine Long Distance Telephone Company and the Silver Dollar Saloon and Restaurant, favorite of longnose aficionados of Filipina dancers.

As they slowed for Osmeña Circle, the white-domed capitol of Cebu province appeared straight ahead, with a denuded, jagged ridge of mountain behind it. Alburo said the long, narrow island of Cebu was dominated by mountains, and the population lived along the edges. Traditionally Cebuanos ate ground corn, grits, that they could grow on the slopes of the mountains, rather than rice, which was the staple of the rest of the islands, flat land of the kind needed for rice paddies.

Alburo told Burlane they were headed for Danao City, about thirty kilometers north of Cebu City.

Everybody in Burlane's business knew about Danao City. In the world of casual creeps, it was as famous for its product as Edam was for its cheese or Frankfurt for its sausages. For the moment, Burlane felt rather like a tourist. He had long been curious about what the place actually looked like; now, here it was, laid before him like a splendid lunch. "Danao? I know Davao, ate that awful fruit there. Should I know about Danao?"

Alburo, suppressing amusement, took a drag on his cigarette. "Maybe. I want you to see the town, then make a guess. More fun that way."

"I'm game," Burlane said.

They passed down narrow, crowded streets that could have been in any number of tropical Third World countries—a sprawling jumble and hodgepodge of huts and shanties nailed, wired, and cobbled out of a miscellany of scavenged boards, bamboo, cement blocks, and corrugated tin. The walls around these fortresses of poverty inevitably had broken beer bottles cemented on top as a deterrent to casual thieves. Walls facing alleys or the street ordinarily had a hip-high, off-color base of brownish yellow crud; this was the malodorous pee line, established by generations of unembarrassed Filipinos past. When a man's gotta pee, he's gotta pee.

With all the Spanish surnames above the *carenderias* and *sari sari* stores, Burlane thought he might as well have been in Central or South America.

They passed out of Cebu City, immediately entering the congested, formless urban confusion that was Mandaue City. Patiently and expertly, cigarette rarely leaving his lips, Alburo wheeled the microbus in and out of the traffic-dodging bicycles, tricycles, and homemade trucks with aplomb. Twenty minutes later, most wonderfully, they were past the ugly cityscape and into the country.

The narrow macadam road wound through low rises and shallow vales flanked by patches of water lilies, banana groves, and clusters of coconuts hanging high, like bunches of green testicles. They passed the Stephen King Carenderia, which had a sign saying it had piglets for sale. Burlane looked back, wondering if the piglets might not be closet man-eaters, Satan's little sweeties. They passed brown goats. They slowed for a boy pulling a carabao by the ring in its nose. Soon the lovely aura of the tropical sea made its appearance on their right.

At Liloan, they passed a white church, built in *año de* 1847.

They passed some fish ponds and came upon a series of beach resorts. They passed Cebu Mitsumi, a factory that made cassette parts. They passed Feel Ann's Little Store. They came upon some low, bald ridges that had once been forested. Then, suddenly, they were at Danao City, no question.

"Wow!" Burlane was wide-eyed.

Alburo, smiling, shifted the microbus into second and slowed. "You like it?"

"It's lovely," Burlane said. Indeed it was. Danao was a tidy town nestled around a sweet bay perhaps a half-mile wide at the entrance. The bay was extraordinary because someone had prevented the water's edge from being overrun by vendors as was the custom in the other seaside towns Burlane had seen. Instead of the usual clutter of *carenderias* and hawker stands, the picturesque bay was flanked by palm trees and a strip of grass—a promenade of sorts—so that a pedestrian, well oiled with insect repellent, might go for an early-evening stroll and enjoy the beauty of the sleek and colorful pumpboats in the water. The bay, a splendid sight, had been preserved. On this day, the pumpboats were accompanied by the yacht that had been in Zamboanga.

Alburo said, "I got a call before we left that the *Sagawa Maru* had dropped anchor this morning. They won't be going anywhere this afternoon. Would you like me to take you for a tour of Danao?"

"It's beautiful, Rene. Is tourism responsible? Passed some beaches back there."

"No, not tourism." Alburo grinned. "Did the duo you saw in Davao and Zamboanga look like tourists? Tourists go to Moalboal to spend money and dive and smoke pot. They go to Cebu City to get laid or find a wife. Cebuanas have a reputation as making the best wives in Philippines, did you know that?"

"No, I didn't."

"The usual recommendation is to get one from the provinces. If they grow up in the city, they're spoiled. The women from Luzon are more frugal, but Cebuanas are sweeter and more faithful. Not to mention better looking. My wife's a good-looking Cebuana from the provinces, as it happens."

"And?"

Alburo took a draw on his cigarette. "It's possible it's all just a rumor." Then he grinned; he liked his wife.

They crossed two white concrete bridges over small streams that entered the bay, then turned to the left, inland, up a street that was remarkably free of trash. Dead ahead lay a green ridge with a sawtooth top. Not the Alps, but not a bad backdrop for Danao.

Alburo took a left and drove a few blocks, and then hung a right. He dragged the gut in front of the public market—about a hundred and fifty yards of motorcycles and their colorful sidecars. He retreated back to the bay and took a left, past the impressive, domed Fort Danao, made of cream-colored blocks of coral.

Suddenly they were on a white concrete highway, a Filipino version of a German autobahn or American freeway.

Burlane was amazed. "What's this?"

"Give me a minute, and you'll understand everything," Alburo said. Shortly, they came upon a huge sugar mill on their right, Durano III & Sons, Inc. Two hundred yards later, a sprawl of industrial buildings, the Durano cement company, lay to their left. The sugar mill looked inactive. There was some activity in the cement company, but not much.

Alburo slowed the microbus for a U-turn. "Danao City has been the private fiefdom of the Duranos for years. The mayor is a Durano or Durano relative. Most of the town councilmen are Duranos. Their congressman is a Durano. Their sugar mill and cement factory are on hard times now, as you can see. But the Duranos have always seen to the needs of the town, encouraging the development of several productive cottage industries to keep people working."

They were on their way back to town.

"What do they make?" Burlane asked.

"They make pottery. They make snakeskin handbags. They make a soft white cheese you longnoses compare to feta. That's just about the only native cheese you're going to find on Cebu, incidentally. They use carabao milk."

"Good for them! And . . ."

"And they make guns."

"What?" Burlane pretended to be amazed.

"When I asked you yesterday if you'd heard of Danao City, you might have if you'd been a gun buff or a reader of *Soldier of Fortune* magazine. The Duranos first got gun making going in the 1970s, with the connivance of Marcos. They started with simple shotguns, then worked their way up. Now they can even reproduce fake Uzis. They engrave 'Uzi-Dan' on the barrel instead of 'Uzi-IMI,' which you'll find on the Israeli original. At home I have a nine-millimeter revolver with a barrel that's been cut from an M-sixteen and rebored. The *oyabun* on the *Sagawa Maru* is likely here to pick up a load of Smith and Wasliks." Alburo, amused, glanced at Burlane.

"Okay, you want to tell me what a Smith and Waslik is? A revolver, I take it."

"An imitation thirty-eight-caliber Smith and Wesson. They're a favorite of the *yakuza* because they're cheap enough to chuck after they're used. *Waslik* is Tagalog meaning to throw away with disdain. If your Danao special misfires, you *waslik*, that is, you whip your victim in the face with the barrel as you throw it away."

Burlane laughed. "The Philippine government knows about this?"

"Oh, sure. They can't shut the trade down because the Duranos would object. Who would feed the families of the gunsmiths? The PNP allegedly prevents them from peddling weapons to the Moros or the NPA, but that's a joke. One thing is certain, the government doesn't care how many Smith and Wasliks they sell to the *yakuza*. Let the Japanese shoot one another, is how they look at it."

"Very sensible, I suppose."

"They'll load up after dark, at a private dock north of here. The official line is that Danao City owes its prosperity to pots, handbags, and cheese."

"And the beneficence of the Durano family."

"That too. It goes without saying."

"And what do you propose to do?"

"I propose to rent a pumpboat and watch the whole operation. You can come along if you want."

"Right out of the movies. Erap's man in action!"

"That's it," Alburo said. "Here we are." He slowed and took a left turn to the wharf on the northern end of the bay.

The line of stalls and *carenderias* was on their left, Cholly's, Ruben's, Moning's, and the rest. The remainder of the wharf was wonderfully free of the usual swarm of peddlers and hawkers. Burlane waited in the microbus while Rene Alburo negotiated for a pumpboat.

ELEVEN

When the *Sagawa Maru* pulled anchor and began moving, James Burlane and Rene Alburo responded to the call as though they had been rehearsing for it all their lives. Burlane took the tiller while Alburo, on the bow, watched the *Sagawa Maru*, and explained the nighttime geography to Burlane.

They were about halfway up the east coast of Cebu, a long, narrow island in the central Visayas—almost square in the center of the Philippine archipelago. To the southeast, behind them, lay the island of Bohol. To the northeast, in front of them, was Leyte, and beyond that, Samar.

They stayed well back of the *Sagawa Maru*, and when it stopped and dropped anchor, Burlane killed the Briggs and Stratton to knock off the *pop-pop-pop*. In the night lenses of his binoculars, he could see on shore four diesel vans with Filipino-made sheet-metal bodies parked in a courtyard above a jumble of bamboo nipa huts poking out over the water.

In the water, a half-dozen pumpboats were being loaded with heavy cardboard boxes by barebacked Filipinos in short pants. They laughed and joked as they worked.

Burlane gave Alburo the glasses. "The merry gunsmiths and their relatives. See 'em."

"Yep. Say, these night binoculars are good, aren't they?"

"My camera shoots on ultraviolet, too. Unless I screw up, I should should get some decent pics for your Mr. Estrada." Burlane focused his Hasselblad and snapped a few shots of the loading of the pumpboats. *Cl-click. Cl-clack. Cl-click.*

As the first pumpboat reached the *Sagawa Maru*, Alburo, who was watching through the binoculars, said, "That's him. Kobayashi. Can you see him?"

Burlane, watching through a two-hundred millimeter Leopold and Vary night lens, said, "Oh, sure. The guy in the middle."

"That's Kamina on Kobayashi's right and Kao on his left."

Burlane said, "Got 'em. Three assholes in a row. Look forward now at the bow."

"A longnose girl."

"Leanne Tompkins."

"I can only see the other one when she leans forward."

"Beth Anne Holden, I think, but she straightened up before I could take her picture. There's a Filipina in there, too."

The first pumpboat had arrived at the side of the *Sagawa Maru*, and two barebacked Filipinos were struggling to get the first box of cargo up and over the rail.

Burlane *cl-click-cl-clack-cl-clicked* several pictures of Shoji Kobayashi and his *kobun* as they opened the box. Kobayshi, grinning, retrieved a Smith & Waslik and examined it, turning it in the dim light.

In twenty minutes the pumpboats had unloaded their cargo, and the *Sagawa Maru* pulled anchor. When Burlane could hear its engine rumble to life, he gave a yank on the starting rope of the Briggs and Stratton.

The *Sagawa Maru* returned in the direction of Danao City, and when its running lights were well off Burlane's bow, he piloted the pumpboat *pop-pop-pop-pop* in that direction as well.

On the bow, Alburo looked thoughtful as the boat slid through the darkness in the balmy salt air. They rode in silence for twenty minutes. Then he said, "You know, Darryl, the chess game they were playing in the chess club yesterday is called blitz. The players each have five minutes to complete the game. They have the same pieces. The pieces have equal powers. The only advantage, a slight one, accrues to white, who moves first. There are no dice or cards. In short, whoever is best at strategy and tactics and avoids crippling blunders wins.

"By Japanese standards, we Filipinos live in anarchy. We know they look down on us. They think we're all thieves and swindlers, but we're far better than they are at chess. We're not as good as the Russians or the Hungarians, say, but real good. We've got leagues of company chess teams in all our larger cities and towns. Their games are routinely reported in the papers, and readers know what a king's Indian defense is. Why do you suppose that is?"

Burlane shrugged. "Beats hell out of me."

"One theory is that the Japanese avoid games and competition where they can't buy the officials, or where they can't adjust the rules to favor themselves, or where they have to compete as individuals. But in fairness, there's more to it than that. Their game is go. You have to think about go."

"Go has rules."

"Yes, it does. But you'll note that it's a game of opposing groups. All go stones look exactly alike. They have equal value. They work as a group, with each stone backing the others up. It's acquisitive; the one who collects the most stones, that is, acquires the most territory, wins. A successful player sticks rigidly to tactics worked out by go masters hundreds of years ago.

"Chess pieces also work together, but they have different sizes and shapes as well as a variety of moves and powers. In go, homogeneous groups compete. Chess is heterogeneous; diverse players cooperate. Standard chess openings have evolved for the first dozen moves or so, but then each player is on his own; in order to coordinate the powers of his pieces, he is forced to be flexible and creative.

"The Japanese won't trade with *gaijin* as equals because they don't regard *gaijin* as equals. They compete among themselves, but when faced with *gaijin,* they work together, and they will always insist on playing with an extra rook or extending the range of their knights. They feel that is their prerogative as Japanese. They cannot imagine it otherwise."

TWELVE

On the way back to the city, they rode in silence. Rene Alburo was intent on shifting the gears of the microbus up and down as he dodged lunatic jeepneys, darting motorcycles, and dawdling carabaos; James Burlane was sunk in deep thought.

Finally Alburo said, "Going to Yokohama is no problem. Finding a place to stay will be something else again. Remember, the Stars will be playing in the Japan series."

"Taken care of. I made a call last night."

"You made a call?"

"Right. We'll have our rooms."

"I see," Alburo said. "I take it you're not going to tell me how."

Burlane said, "Do you know how to make *kinilaw*? I really like that stuff."

Alburo smiled. No, he was not supposed to ask how. He said, "Sure. Coconut milk, *datu puti*—"

"*Datu puti?*"

"A white cane vinegar. Also *kalamansi* juice—from the little green *lemoncitos* you've probably seen—sliced onions and ginger, some strips of green onion, a little salt, and some hot peppers. Maybe a few chunks of ripe tomato. You should crush the ginger and the peppers up to put a little zip to it. *Tanigigi* is the best fish, but *bangus* will do too. You just cut it up in chunks and let it marinate for a half hour or so."

Burlane said, "Can we get some made this time of night?"

"Sure. If we've got the pesos."

"When we get back to Cebu, I propose that we settle down in my hotel room with some *kinilaw* and cold San Miguel and consider what it is we propose to do in Yokohama." Burlane whistled *weet-a-weet. Weet-a-weet. Tweetle doo. Tweetle doo.* "There's something I've been meaning to tell you, Rene. A confession, so to speak."

Alburo said, "I was wondering."

"The real Darryl Lattimore will be in Yokohama covering the Japan series for *Sports Illustrated.*"

"The real Darryl Lattimore?"

"Right. Now old Darryl can lug parabolic microphones and fancy cameras across international borders all he wants. He's a journalist. He could take them into Japan, no problem. Probably did, for all I know." Burlane whistled *weepeet, weepeet.* He reached for his backpack and retrieved a large envelope from which he took a half-dozen book jackets.

Alburo, waiting for traffic at a stop sign, glanced at the jackets in the dim streetlight: *Schoolcraft's Night Birds of the World; Schoolcraft's City Birds of the World; Schoolcraft's Birds of Asia.* He said, "What?" He flipped the book over. There was his companion's face. The blurb said Larry Schoolcraft, an adjunct professor of ornithology at Stanford University, had called birds on the Larry King show and on David Letterman.

Burlane whistled *whip-or-willlllll, whip-or-willlllll.* He said, "I had the idea of the legend years ago, but it took forever before I could whistle well enough to make the bona fides work. It's the whistling that does it." *Wheeeooooeeeeppp! Wheeeooooeeeeeppp!*

"You work for the CIA?" Traffic was clear, and Alburo pulled out onto the street.

Burlane frowned. "Used to, years ago."

"But no more." Alburo slowed the microbus for a carabao pulling a cart of firewood.

"No more. They sacked me, actually. In this case, a man hired me to find and return his daughter and bring her back, and I intend on doing just that."

Alburo said, "Listen. You help me pin these bastards, I don't care who you're working for. I wrote Estrada a little summary of Yokohama. You might want to take a look at that before you go to bed tonight."

> To: Vice President Joseph Estrada
> From: Dr. Rene Alburo
> Subject: *Japayuki* traffic
> Re: Yokohama, headquarters of Takeshita-*kai*

After his initial visit to Japan in 1853, Commodore Perry returned in January 1854, flexing the muscle of seven steam-powered warships. Perry required the reluctant Japanese shoguns to open their country to trade with the Americans; the details of the capitulation, signed on March 3, 1854, were negotiated at a special convention center at the bottom of what is now the five-block-long Nihon Dori, on the site of the present red-brick headquarters of the Kanagawa prefectural government.

After a further treaty was signed in 1858, the Japanese opened a port in Yokohama, and the fishing village wound up being the gateway to Japan. Western-style roads were introduced here, also electricity, telegraph and telephones, trains, modern water and sewer systems, gaslights. Yokohama had the first Japanese newspapers and laundries, the first schools to accept females as students, the first horse racing, ice cream, even beer. You name it. For example, beef was first eaten here; the dish they now call sukiyaki was originally a Yokohama dish called *gyu nabe.* This was all cumulatively called the Yokohama Wave. Yokohama is famous for its fashion accessories and shoes, handbags and whatever. The term is *hama tora,* or Yokohama traditional.

The Tokugawa shoguns had sealed Japan off from the outside world for 286 years before Perry came. To prevent the hairy barbarians from contact with the citizenry, the government established a reservation for the *gaijin* in Yokohama called the *kannai*, which means "inside the barrier."

Yokohama was destroyed by an earthquake in 1923 and American bombers burned it down in 1945, but it's a natural port, and it has risen phoenixlike each time.

The area of the *kannai*, which contains Yokohama Stadium—home of the Yokohama Bay Stars—is now the center of the city. Owing to its history, Yokohama has always been a city with a large number of foreigners. It's also a city that's long been associated with crime syndicates. It's been a port of entry for drugs, guns, and pussy. In recent years Takeshita-*kai* has allegedly become the dominant gang in Yokohama owing to its *japayuki* recruiters in the Philippines.

To a Japanese, watching a sex show or beating on a Filipina is no more moral or immoral than buying a Big Mac, so the *yakuza* run the trade for expense-account businessmen and their politician friends. It's a cliché that everything costs more in Japan. In like fashion, *japayuki* have become a high-yen executive perk; when there are hot-looking Filipinas to be fucked, the spending gets serious. Proletarians go home to their wives.

The business and financial world is the engine of the Japanese economy. Whatever business wants, business ordinarily gets, and Japanese businessmen have unembarrassed libidos; they want young, imported stuff. Although bullying money from business is an honored *yakuza* tradition, there appears little chance that any systematic opposition to the exploitation of Filipinas will emerge from within Japan.

In Yokohama, as in most Japanese cities, establishments with *japayuki* hostesses are not furtive and shabby. Usually found tucked back on up-market side streets, they are high-yen and high-tech. The hotter the hostesses and the fancier the premises, the more outlandish the tab.

Thus, the system works. Most of the *japayuki* are ours, Mr. Vice President, Filipinas who have been outright purchased or leased. Yes, leased! Human females.

It has now been 140 years since Commodore Perry opened Japan up to trade with the outside world. After all that time, it appears that the most demanded and valuable *gaijin* import into Japan is apparently pussy, followed by what, Chivas Regal?

(Erap: Instead of sucking up to the Japanese, we should build our case and take it before the World Court and sue the reprehensible bastards. Don't ask me on what grounds, but there's just got to be something in this day and age.)

THIRTEEN

It was hot sitting cooped up in their cabin all day. At night, when they were taken on deck for a breath of fresh air, they had weights locked around their ankles or a wrist cuffed to something. There was nothing they could do, except wait for whatever was going to happen to them next.

Linda Shive knew her friend Leanne was not holding up well. After an initial bout of hysteria, Leanne had now sunken into gloom, refusing either to talk or to eat.

Kao had arrived from Manila the previous afternoon. Then he and Kamina had held big powwow in Kobayashi's cabin—their idea of powwow being much grunting and sweating. Had Kao somehow found out who she was?

Later that night the *oyabun* and his pals had taken boxes aboard. The content of the boxes was no mystery to Maria. They were Smith & Waslik pistols, she said. Imitation Smith & Wessons. Danao was a chief source of *yakuza* weapons, everybody knew that. At that news, Linda relaxed somewhat. The powwow had been about the pending gun delivery. Had to be.

Now, the day after the guns, the *oyabun* and his two *kobun*, purposeful and full of energy, had gone to shore in a launch, which returned with lunch for the *japayuki* prisoners and their captors.

"They're going to White Gold," Miki said.

Linda had no idea what White Gold was; a shopping center, it sounded like. Although Miki didn't mind an occasional question, Linda didn't inquire further. She had learned that trying to be Little Miss Goody Two-Shoes didn't do her any good, and trying to fight her captors was out of the question. The best tactic was to remain as invisible as possible.

After lunch, Kobayashi and his lieutenants returned with two of the latest-model Sony videocameras to replace the single, slightly outdated model they had on board.

The *Sagawa Maru* put to sea, but when they were well offshore the engines fell silent, and they drifted in the late afternoon sun.

Then Miki unlocked their cabin door. She was naked except for a black G-string and gold rings in her pierced nipples.

"Come along, Linda," she said.

Linda glanced at Leanne and Maria.

"Just you," Miki said. "And you might as well leave your clothes here. You're not going to be needing them."

Linda slowly began peeling.

"All of it," Miki said.

Linda got it over with.

As they walked to the fantail, Miki let her hand drift across Linda's hip and over her butt. "Now is when we get serious, so brace yourself."

Miki tied Linda's ankles to the rail support and her wrists behind her back. Then she disappeared, leaving Linda sitting on the deck. A few minutes later she was back with Kobayashi, Kamina, and Kao and their new cameras.

Kobayashi told Miki and his assistants what he wanted, and Linda watched as a crewman hauled up four buckets of seawater.

When Kobayashi had the cameras positioned to his satisfaction, he gave the word to Miki.

She tapped Linda lightly on the breasts, looking at Kobayashi to see if that's what he had in mind.

Kobayashi, munching on his apple, said, *"Hai! Hai!"* Yes! Yes! He whipped his hand through the air to demonstrate how he wanted it done.

FOURTEEN

The trio gathered at Tsutomu Kamina's country house on a bluff overlooking the Pacific near the Atami hot springs fifty miles southwest of Yokohama. After instructing his servants on the needs of the *oyabun* of Takeshita-*kai* and his guests, Kamina-*san* discreetly withdrew to the pleasures of his garden.

They began by watching some of the pornographic tapes that Takeshita-*kai* marketed overseas, ending with the tapes Kobayashi had made of Linda Shive on the deck of the *Sagawa Maru*. The examination of the skills of Takeshita-*kai*'s video crews made them horny, so they retired to separate rooms to have the tension relieved by *japayuki*. Masayuki Yoshida and Koji Watanabe had quickie dick sucks, while Kobayashi preferred a fuck.

Thus refreshed and relaxed, they retired to the bath, where they leaned back with their elbows against the wooden sides, and let their bodies float in the enveloping warmth. They talked through steam that rose from the hot water.

It was discourteous to get straight to the subject at hand, so they did not.

Kobayashi talked about the vicissitudes of the international market for pornographic tapes, a subject rarely addressed by the *Far Eastern Economic Review* or *The Economist*. He said, ''The Germans are our chief competitors, although the English have some wicked spanking tapes on the market. English culture, they call it. They like to tape 'headmasters' whacking the butts of 'errant' young women in school uniforms. The Americans know their Krafft-Ebing, but the Germans take that extra, kinky step."

"Why is that, do you think?" Watanabe asked. He leaned back, letting his body float in the water.

Kobayashi said, "It's perhaps an Aryan thing. Or European decadence. Or something. They come up with some tapes you wouldn't believe." He squeegeed the sweat from his face with the palm of his hand.

"Mmmm," Watanabe said. "They say the Christian writer C. S. Lewis was fond of women with extra large rumps. I don't know whether that means anything. God's will, perhaps." Watanabe made grabbing motions with his hands, as though he were squeezing a woman's rump.

Kobayashi said, "Japanese-language sound tracks are no problem; although we dub some of our fancier productions, our customers want tits and ass, not dialogue. We actually torture our *japayuki* while we tape them, and our customers know it. They're willing to pay extra for the realism."

Watanabe, still floating, kicked his feet up and down. "The hard sex is where the money lies, I take it."

"No question. We can do anything we want with a *japayuki*. Fuck them with cattle prods if we want. We've got a donkey trained to the work. We made a metal shield for its cock, so he won't split them completely open. Our competition can't match us. If they try, word gets out, and they have the police at their doorstep. I don't know if you know it, but we were a pioneer in snuff films."

"Oh?" Watanabe said. He returned to the sitting position and cupped his hands, using the palms to make a popping sound on the water.

"We wasted a dozen *japayuki* before we sensed a backlash developing in our longnose markets. Incidentally, we called the snuff girls *wasliks*—disposables—just like the Filipinos' home-made pistols." He too used his hands to make popping sounds on the water. *Pop, pop, pop.* "Snuff them just like that. If we smuggle a *japayuki* in without a visa, and we think she'd be a good performer for our production crews, she's still a *waslik* as far as we're concerned."

Watanabe looked uncertain. *"Wasliks." Pop, pop, pop.*

"Longnose men will pay top dollar to watch nonpretend Japanese culture, and Japanese men like white skin and big tits with pink nipples. There you have the makings of *wa* in international trade." Kobayashi dug at his testicles with gusto.

Watanabe sighed. "It would be nice if our present quarrel with the Americans was so simple and complementary."

Yoshida gently cleared his throat. "Which is why I believe you invited us this morning, Kobayashi-*san*. Am I right?"

"The Stars made it to the series this year because they take advantage of the breaks. They stay alert. When a Stars batter is thrown a mistake, he jumps on it." Kobayashi slapped the water with his hand. "We can buy fake passports and whatever else we need to deliver a Filipina to a bar or sex club in Japan, or to a customer who answered an ad in our magazine, but the disposables have to be picked up and smuggled into Japan. We've had to do it this way ever since the Sision incident. If the Sision girl had been an unidentified *waslik*, there would have been no fuss. But she was in Japan on a passport. The smuggling is added overhead, but it can't be helped."

Kobayashi mopped the sweat from his face with his forearm, and spread his arms on top of the water before he continued his story. "A couple of weeks ago, I flew to Cebu in the Philippines to take a cruise on my yacht, which was recruiting and buying *waslik japayuki*. You've been on the *Sagawa Maru*, haven't you, Yoshida-*san*?"

"I have indeed. It's lovely."

Kobayashi closed his eyes and ducked quickly under the water, running his hand over his face when he surfaced. "Kamina-*san* and I decided to go around Mindanao with our people and fly back to Japan in time for the series. Our guide was a half-Filipina who is our chief recruiter. Among her many contacts in the provinces is a Muslim sea pirate, Abdul Somebody, who calls himself a sultan. Remember the girl in the last tape, Yoshida-*san*? The blond we gave the saltwater treatment?"

"Turnips," he said. More bubbles.

They laughed again.

"What if something goes wrong?" Yoshida asked.

Kobayashi said, "Nothing can go wrong. What could go wrong? That is why this is so sweet. The nature of the proof prohibits its use."

Watanabe said, "To answer Yoshida-*san*'s question, if something went wrong, we would suffer national humiliation. Can you imagine?"

"Humiliation in addition to the same trade sanctions they've already proposed or worse," Yoshida said.

"To do nothing is to commit national *seppuku*," Kobayashi said.

They lapsed into contemplative silence.

Finally Watanabe said, "The Shive girl has nice tits, I'll give her that. I'd love to lead her around by the nipples."

"We all would," Yoshida said.

Watanabe said, "But I suggest our answer should be no to this proposal of yours, Kobayashi-*san*. It really is only a form of delay, isn't it? And even if it works, it won't be in our best interest. Times change, and I suggest history tells us that if we are to thrive, we must change also. I urge you to let the Shive girl go while we're all ahead. Keep the tapes for your private library."

Kobayashi released a burst of bubbles. "Yoshida-*san*?"

Yoshida licked his lips. "I know that time is running short, but I have to think about it."

FIFTEEN

Buying the daughter of the vice president of the United States traveling on a fake passport was a steal. At two thousand U.S., a giggle even. It was also like handing Shoji Kobayashi an exotic, loaded pistol. The *oyabun* of Takeshita-*kai* had now weighed the weapon in his hand. He had felt the cool metal.

He had aimed it at a deserving target.

Now, the urge to pull the trigger was nothing short of irresistible.

To discuss his chat with the negative Watanabe and the indecisive Yoshida, Kobayashi invited Tsutomu Kamina for breakfast in his apartment in Sumiyoshi-Cho, two blocks from center field.

Kobayashi and Kamina sat on a straw tatami with their legs crossed. Kamina was junior. Although he was curious, it was not his place to address the issue of their proposal directly. So he waited patiently, going along with Kobayashi's small talk. When Kobayashi was ready, he would tell Kamina what was on his mind, not before.

A servant poured them both green tea and quietly disappeared. Kobayashi said, "I met with Yoshida-*san* and Watanabe.

I showed them our tapes so they know we did good work. They liked them a lot."

"I bet."

Kobayashi smiled. "After a refreshing fuck, we sat in a bath, and I gave them our proposal."

"Mmmmm," Kamina said.

"Watanabe-*san* doesn't like the idea, I'm afraid. I expected as much. They made him CEO of Sapporo Motors. Incredible." Kobayashi smacked his lips. "Can you imagine holding stock in Sapporo Motors? That'd be like buying into vacuum tubes." He bunched his face. "I'm having *soba* with a raw egg and an apple. You?" *Soba* was a form of vermicelli made from buckwheat flour.

"The same," Kamina said, although he had never learned to eat noodles Edo-style, as Kobayashi did. This behavior was called *itsukimi*, watching the fox.

Kobayashi, the fox of Takeshita-*kai*, eyed Kamina and took a sip of green tea. "A foreign minister's duty is to avoid such unpleasant confrontations. Yoshida didn't do that. He failed in his job, but won't admit it. There comes a time in a man's life when he has to face up to the deterioration of his energy and nerve. In this case, both Watanabe and Yoshida have become old women. Watanabe sucks up to the Americans, and Yoshida refuses to relinquish his post to a more capable man. I don't know which is worse."

Kobayashi clapped his hands, and when the girl appeared shortly, he ordered their breakfast.

Kamina, hesitating, said, "But there is a chance with Yoshida? He can be convinced, I take it."

"Possibly. But Watanabe is hopeless. He's not even Japanese as far as I'm concerned."

The girl arrived with their breakfast on a tray.

Kobayashi, using his chopsticks to dip a noodle in a bowl of cold soup, said, "He's spent too much time with books, and traveling in America and Europe. He's forgotten what it means to be Japanese. You should have heard him parrot the appeasement line. This is a time for heroes and leaders, but what do we get? Pretend bignoses."

"It's a sign of the times, Kobayashi-*san*."

Holding one end of the noodle with his chopsticks, Kobayashi opened his mouth and dropped it down his throat, not swallowing. He grinned at Kamina. "*Hai*." Yes.

Kamina said, "I don't know how you do that, letting them slide down your throat."

"Yoshida is oh so careful. He talks to this minister. He talks to that businessman. One says this. The other says that. What if this . . . ? he says. What if that . . . ? He weighs everything. You'd think he was peddling *shabu* instead of protecting the future of Japan. He's convinced by the last person he talked to, and in this case I'm afraid that will likely be Watanabe."

"He'll buy Watanabe's *gaijin* line, you think?"

Kobayashi let another noodle slide down his throat. "They did this three hundred years before Perry arrived. The *soba* were made the same way. A noodle felt the same sliding down their throats as it does mine. No difference."

Kamina took a turn at letting a *soba* noodle slide down his throat.

"Well?" Kobayashi asked.

Kamina grinned. "Takes practice, I suppose."

"Once you get the hang of it." Kobayashi looked amused. "Watanabe imitates the Western way of thinking, so they're all convinced he knows how to deal with the Americans. They're using the end of the Cold War as an excuse. If only we learned to think like Westerners, they say. If only we ceased being Japanese and agreed with people like Watanabe, that's what they really want."

Kamina said, "The cold soup is good. And the *soba*."

"Never did like *sukiyaki*. Give me fish any day. Or pork. Even better, whale. If you want real meat, eat whale."

"And Yoshida?"

Kobayashi said nothing.

Kamina said, "If Yukio Mishima were still alive, he'd be with us, no question."

Kobayashi said, "Yes, he would have. We could have gone to him, and he would have responded, no question. He understood what had once made his country great, which is what made him such a good writer. He was a Japanese man, not a pretend bignose. We copy Western clothes and buildings and food. You name it. Copy. Copy. Copy." Kobayashi looked disgusted.

Kamina made a face that said he agreed.

Kobayashi said, "In the process of becoming successful copiers, we have forgotten who we are. Now, to please rice growers in California, we're supposed to do away with backyard rice paddies. What kind of country is it that has to import its rice? We'd be at the mercy of *gaijin*."

Kamina tried another noodle.

Kobayashi said, "Traditional foods have a specific, simple taste. The beauty lies in its simplicity. We have allowed things to get far too complicated, I'm afraid."

Kamina said, "Perhaps one day we'll all be driving Fords and Chevrolets. They're already trying to tell us the Saturn is as good as or better than anything we've got on the market."

Kobayashi, finished with his noodles, admired his apple, then bit into it with enthusiasm. *Crrrunnchhh!* Munching, he said, "We need to remind Minister Yoshida that while he might be a toothless old woman, we are not. We know who we are, and we honor our past." He bit into his apple with a ripping pop. "Tell me, Kamina-*san*, how long will it take the *Sagawa Maru* to get to Yokohama?"

"I suppose seven or eight days if we pushed it. Five to Kagoshima, where we can put them on a train if we want. Shoot them right on up to Yokohama."

Kobayashi was down to the core, which he examined, looking for uneaten goodies. He grimaced.

Kamina said, "We could get them here faster, if Fukamori combined a *japayuki* flight with a *shabu* run."

"Oh?"

"Fukamori's got a run coming up, hasn't he? He could take

two trips for the *shabu* if he has to. It won't hurt him to show us a little *giri*."

Kobayashi said, "This is far more important than another load of ice. We need to get our priorities straight."

Kamina rubbed his chin. "We could meet Fukamori in international waters and top off his tanks for the flight back. What are the Filipinos going to do? They only have, what is it, five working planes in their air force? And their navy is a joke."

Fate had pulled Kobayashi from the dugout of Team Japan and thrust him into the center of the action. He remembered Jocho Yamamoto's admonition:

When one is frustrated, it is extremely difficult to make a decision. But if one approaches the problem with a razor-sharp mind—that is, calmly, with simple determination, and without worrying about minor issues—one will always reach a decision within the space of seven breaths.

Kobayashi said, "We'll do it. I'll call Kao. He can get things squared away in Manila."

Kamina said, "Miki can fly up Friday morning."

Shoji Kobayashi looked pleased. "We can start shooting Friday night."

SIXTEEN

The dancer waggled her pussy in front of the transfixed Winston Monzon. He had no idea where Takeshita-*kai* found them, but Teddy's somehow managed to feature the wildest women in Manila. *Oy!*

When the waitress arrived with the beer, Nobito Kao said, "Ellie, sweet one, I want you to see to it that Mr. Monzon has a good room in the Claridge for the night. Mona will take care of it."

Ellie scribbled the message on a pad. "Mona for a room for Mr. Monzon. Got it, Mr. Kao."

"One high up on the northwest corner so he'll have both city lights and Manila Bay. You been in the Claridge, Winston?"

Monzon, pleased at Kao's generosity, shook his head, no, he hadn't been in the Manila Claridge.

"I want the liquor cabinet stocked with some decent booze. You like Scotch, Winston?"

"Love it," Monzon said.

"Make sure Mr. Monzon has some Johnnie Walker and some Chivas Regal. I want the refrigerator stocked with some cheeses, white wine, and champagne. Fresh fruit and whatever. Tell Mona to do it right. I want to treat Winston to a night of good, old-fashioned decadence. How about it, Winston? You game for a little decadence? Perk up your humdrum life."

"Sure!" Monzon liked having Kao mister him.

"Did I tell you about Miki, Winston?"

"Miki?"

"I see I haven't. When someone does something truly special for us, we let Miki demonstrate our appreciation. She's not just another bar fine, believe me. She'll give you the time of your life."

"Really?"

"Miki is real, real special, Winston. She's something, the best the *yakuza* have to offer. Are you sure you're up to it?"

Monzon grinned. "Oh, sure, I'm game. I'll do my best to keep up." He bobbed his eyebrows and they both laughed. "As it were," he said.

Monzon took an air-conditioned taxi to the Manila Claridge, a modern—that is, sterile—five-star high-rise hotel on Roxas Boulevard. The American ambassador currently lodged his guests there. Many an official of the International Monetary Fund and the World Bank had had his dick sucked in the Manila Claridge as part of Malacañang Palace's stroking of the longnose money machine.

Winston Monzon explored his room. It was a spacious, air-conditioned sanctuary, and he thought it was wonderful, a place so very quiet, far, far from the hullabaloo of honking jeepneys and cabs and the incessant, annoying *ra-a-a-a-a-a-a* hammer of motorscooters and motorcycles.

Here a traveler was far, far from the milling glut of sweating bodies that filled every inch of available space in Manila, and the omnipresent stench of accumulated, proletarian piss, puke, sweat, and shit. If you went far enough into the mountains you could find quiet in the Philippines, but here, motorcycles with rotten or insufficient mufflers were ubiquitous, and their annoying racket seemed to carry for miles.

There was nothing in the room made of rattan, bamboo, or anything suggesting a guest was in Asia. The bed was big and solid and made of real wood; it had a real mattress over inner springs, not a stupid pad thrown over slats. On top of the bed was a silken, quilted comforter. The pillows were large and fluffy, not filled with hunks and lumps and chunks like poor man's pillows. The chairs and table were proper Western furniture; never mind that the grainy oak was actually veneer.

The room was decorated in calm, complementary beiges, reflecting what Monzon assumed were expensive longnose tastes. One did not have to wear plastic thongs, which the Filipinos called slippers, to keep one's feet clean. No, no, no. One could walk barefoot and wiggle one's toes in the lush beige carpet. Above the dresser, Monzon's pleased image was clear and sharp in the mirror that was clean and not cracked or warped.

There was a small, neatly wrapped bar of soap in the bathroom sink. The same soap, with *Claridge Hotel* on the wrapper, was found in the combination shower and bathtub, plus miniature plastic bottles of shampoo and hair conditioner. Big piles of fluffy white towels.

In the Claridge there would be no crowing of fighting chickens at four in the morning. There would be no cockroaches cruising by like crocodiles, much less mosquitoes. Everything was First World new and nice and clean. This was Monzon's idea of class, real living.

He turned on the water in the sink, and held his hand under it. Hot water! He had grown up scooping cold water out of a plastic bucket; he didn't fully understand the longnose craving for showers with hot water.

The bedroom had a color TV with cable and a remote. Flowers and a bowl of fruit stood on the table. As in the bathroom, everything was clean and new. And just as promised, the liquor cabinet was full.

Monzon cracked a bottle of Chivas Regal and poured himself a hit over ice. He liked it that the Japanese could be imaginative in their generosity. Take Kao, for instance. He could have laid a laundry bag of thousand-peso notes on Monzon, no problem. But Kao understood that life was to be enjoyed.

The reward of Miki was a cultural thing, an extra treat by

way of showing extra thanks. The *yakuza* rewarded loyalty, Monzon had to give them that. And they stuck by those who helped them out. Kao had told him that many times. Now Monzon would be entertained by Miki, the best the *yakuza* had to offer.

He had to pinch himself so he would know being Joseph Estrada's executive secretary wasn't all a dream. It was perfect. Just perfect.

Someone tapped softly on the door. Now for the rewards of staying alert.

Monzon opened the door to a lithe, short-haired Asian beauty in high-heeled black pumps and an outfit that was positively cock-hardening. Her black lace trousers, showing pale skin through diminutive flowers, ended just above her pubic bone. Her translucent black blouse, held together by a single pearl, ended just below her breasts, leaving bare her tiny waist and provocative swell of hips. She wore dangly gold earrings and gold chains around her waist and her left ankle; the gold chain around her neck rested on the swell of breasts that pushed against the blouse, showing dark brown nipples.

"My name is Miki," she said, looking at him with languid eyes.

This very nearly took Monzon's breath away. "You're beautiful," he said. "Won't you come in?"

She stepped inside.

"You're a *mestiza*," he said.

"My father was Japanese," she said, looking around wide-eyed at the magnificently sterile room.

"Ah, so that's it. You have beautiful skin."

"Thank you." Miki peered into the bathroom. "Do you mind if I take a shower before we have fun? They have hot water here, and I just love hot showers."

Winston was anxious to see what Miki looked like naked, but he wanted to be a proper host. He was no grasping Filipino male. He was the executive secretary of Joseph Estrada, vice president of the Philippines.

"Oh, well, sure," he said. "Go ahead."

While Miki took her shower, Monzon undressed and carefully folded his shirt and trousers and arranged them neatly in the top drawer of the handsome bureau. He put his shoes under the bed, lining them up neatly. That done, he sat down in one of the room's two easy chairs and lit up a Marlboro. As he smoked, his circumcised cigarillo got hard.

A few minutes later, the naked Miki stepped in the room, a bath towel in one hand. She was lean and trim and wildly sexy.

Monzon said, "All right, Kao!"

Miki, wide-eyed, did a double take at the sight of his cock. "My God, you're built like a horse."

"Naw, I'm just average," Monzon said, glancing at his hard-on.

"You must rip a woman in half with that thing."

"Aww, it's not that big."

"Would you stand up and turn to the side?"

"Aww."

"I mean it. You're huge. Stand up for me. Let me see that honker."

Monzon, grinning, lit another Marlboro. He was cool. He was in no hurry. He stood up, smoking, and turned so she could study his skinny form and erect dork in studly profile. His cock bobbed once, stiffening from the glow of attention. He said, "I love it when you lie like that. Don't stop."

She said, "I'm not lying, believe me. I'll do my best to show you a good time, but with an organ that large, I don't know."

"Whatever comes to mind I'm sure will be fine by me."

Miki said, "Okay, I want you to lie down on the bed and close your eyes and put your hands above your head. I'm gonna give you a real treat."

Monzon smiled. He was pleased to be a *yakuza* insider.

He snubbed his cigarette out. He turned the cover of the bed back and settled back on cool, clean-smelling sheets. He closed his eyes. He flipped his cock back and forth with his hand, then put both hands above his head as she had asked. "Like this? Is this how you want me?" He was unable to suppress a patronizing grin.

Miki removed a short pick from the towel.

"What a cock!"

"I hope you like it." Enjoying the darkness behind his eyelids, Monzon knew how to be a playful kind of guy.

Miki stabbed the pick into Monzon's left eye and pushed it to the hilt. She ripped the handle to and from with both hands, slicing his brains into a hash of fatty cells, then released the pick, stepped quickly back, and punched on the television set. She turned up the volume.

Monzon's mouth opened, but his circuits had been cut and his scream was silent.

On the television, an earnest Filipino in a business suit, his hair combed into an outsized pompadour, extolled the virtues of Emperador brandy. He was in a room filled with books and maps and a polished cherry desk. He held the glass high and admired the brown fluid. "Drink Emperador brandy." He put a strong accent on the second syllable and rolled the r, Spanish-style.

Monzon's eyes opened wide. The destroyed left eye leaked blood.

"Welcome back to World Volleyball League action in Nagoya, Japan. This is Bernie Cooper with Wes Mills bringing you all the action. Wes, when you've got those big American blockers up front doing their job, when they're in their rhythm, why, it's awfully hard to come from behind against them, isn't it? They've always got those long arms of theirs in front of you."

Monzon's mouth closed.

Mills said, "The determined Japanese know what they have to do now, Bernie. They make up for their lack of size by their quickness and desire and their ability to function as a disciplined unit."

Monzon's thin body arched.

Cooper said, "They're real scrappers, as we've seen time and again here in this exciting World Volleyball League action."

Monzon's mouth opened again.

On the television, Cooper described the action, beginning

with a serve by former UCLA All-American Brent Sumner, to Japan's veteran Nakata Hondo.

Monzon shook and shuddered. He twisted and turned. He flipped. He flopped. He jerked.

He flailed.

His chest arched.

His legs thrashed.

He sprinted for the end.

He stiffened.

His hard-on wilted.

Miki shook her head in disgust. "Oy!" She withdrew the bloody pick, went into the bathroom, and washed it in the sink, then slipped it back into her handbag.

On the tube, Cooper said, "That was a nice spike by Akaka. Cleanly delivered. Japanese side out."

Mills said, "Note the misdirection, Bernie. The Americans had no idea which direction that shot was coming from."

"Now, we'll see if Nippon can put some points on the board. The hard-hitting Enega steps to the line with that booming jump serve of his."

Miki slipped into her lace trousers and translucent blouse; she turned the set off, then stepped into the hallway and was gone.

SEVENTEEN

They had gone east, Linda Shive thought, around an island, Leyte, if her memory was correct.

Then east again.

By late afternoon they were well offshore, likely above the Philippine Trench, when the captain of the *Sagawa Maru* killed his engines. The sea was rolling, with only a flutter of whitecaps from the gusting wind.

Linda could hear activity on deck through her open porthole.

And in a few minutes, off their port, a pale blue seaplane splashed down. A few seconds later, there came a tapping at their door.

Miki.

"Linda and Leanne, come on along," she said. She motioned with her hand for them to follow her.

The consequences of disobedience discouraged independence. Linda gave Maria Reyes a quick hug and did as she was told. So did Leanne. Leanne had not eaten anything or spoken to anyone in three days.

The aluminum ladder was unfolded down the side of the *Sagawa Maru*. Leaving Maria behind, Linda and Leanne and Miki boarded a fiberglass powerboat for the trip to the waiting seaplane. They kept their heads down to avoid salt spray as the sailor piloting the boat plunged recklessly *thud, thud, thud,* through the waves.

Linda, eyes closed, held on as tightly as possible. It was now sixteen days since she had last called her parents from Davao City.

Thud, thud, thud. Bump, bump, bump.

Surely her worried father would have done something by now. Surely he would have sent someone after her. He was the vice president. He had the CIA at his disposal for something like this. No question.

Thud, thud, thud.

All he had to do was pick up the phone.

Then they were at the fat-bodied seaplane, which had outsized twin engines on wide, stubby wings. The sailor hooked a nylon rope about an aluminum hook on the float, and, one at a time, they ascended a folding ladder into the belly of the plane. It was an eight-seater, with a pilot, a copilot, and six passenger seats cramped into a tiny cabin. Linda, Leanne, and Miki were the only passengers.

They buckled themselves in as the powerboat returned to the *Sagawa Maru.*

Then they were off. The pilot had no brakes to lock while he revved his engines. It was just the brute force of the engines and the ruggedness of the floats against drag and the water. And this was no puny *thud, thud, thud.* This was WHAP, WHAP, WHAP as the seaplane shuddered against the waves.

Linda could see into the cockpit. The pilot, whose name was Fukamori, had his head cocked to one side and his teeth clenched as he took on the waves. The copilot, holding on to a duplicate stick, kept his eyes on the instrument panel.

WHAP, WHAP, WHAP! BAM, BAM, BAM!

Suddenly they were aloft.

Fukamori, grinning, peered back at his passengers and said something to Miki.

Miki translated. "He says he bet he had you wondering, didn't he?"

No trace. They had grabbed her, and they had her passport.

What if the Mafia stocked Palermo whorehouses with young women from Sri Lanka? Or what if crime syndicates filled Canadian brothels with peasant girls from Guatemala? There were just plain too many piggies for available teats, that's what it came down to. If you already had a teat, you held on for all you were worth; nothing was to be gained by opening your mouth for a teatless comrade.

If Holocaust and prison literature were accurate, Linda supposed she would eventually experience a deadening of the senses and withdrawal into herself like what was obviously happening to Leanne.

She knew she had to keep her head. She had to be aware of what was happening to her. To understand it. But most of all, she could not become despondent as Leanne had. She had to stay alert.

Maria had told them the Philippine rumor that when *japayukis* were kidnapped or taken to Japan without going through customs they were called *wasliks.* Disposables. They were used in hard-sex porn films and then snuffed.

Not a trace.

Wasliks.

As near as Linda could tell from the setting sun, they were going due north, if not slightly northwest. Then darkness.

At seven o'clock, three hours after they left the *Sagawa Maru,* with Linda and Leanne wearing blue jeans and T-shirts, the pilot murmured to Miki, and she proceeded to unpack circular ten-kilogram lead weights which she locked around their ankles.

A few minutes later, they landed on a calm sea. They could see dim lights in the distance. There was a white moon above the silhouette of hills rising into the blue-black sky.

Linda tested the weights by lifting her feet one at a time. She watched as a launch emerged from the darkness, and four large duffel bags, a Budweiser beer cooler, and a thermos touting Pokka brand "Parisienne" coffee were loaded aboard. The plane's fuel tanks were topped off.

After a brief palaver between Fukamori and his colleagues

on the barge, they were off again, with another thundering burst of revs but far less teeth-grinding and lip-biting than during the first takeoff.

After they were aloft, Miki removed the weights from their ankles.

Linda said, "Where was that, as a matter of curiosity?"

"An island between Okinawa and Taiwan."

"I see. We're headed northeast now, I take it."

"Yes, to the northeast. To Japan. Yokohama. You hungry?" Without waiting for an answer, she opened the cooler and removed small wooden boxes that contained steamed fish, sushi, and pickled vegetables packed tightly into neat little compartments. She served the captain and copilot first, then took care of the *japayuki.*

She said, "These are *ekiben.* You can buy them at train stations or wherever. Fast food." She opened the Pokka thermos and poured them paper cups of green tea.

Leanne accepted her *ekiben,* then set it down.

Miki said, "Be stubborn. When we get to Yokohama we'll find ways of making you eat. If it pleases us, you'll eat until you puke and beg for more."

Linda said, "Eat something, Leanne. You have to eat."

Leanne shook her head.

"Frankly, we don't care whether you eat or not, but our customers don't want skin and bones. They like a full set of tits and a good full ass. You have to eat."

Leanne said nothing.

Miki said, "You'll see. You have to learn consequences. When you don't do as you're told, you pay the price. I've been patient with you. Once more, I've asked you politely to eat, and you've refused. I want you to remember that when you learn your lesson." Miki glared at Linda. "You two eat. Now."

Linda ate.

"You, eat."

Leanne did not.

"Eat."

Leanne refused.

"We'll see," Miki said.

After a three-and-a-half-hour ride in which Linda tried to sleep but couldn't, the plane began to descend through clouds, and Miki returned the weights to their ankles.

The plane landed in the darkness.

They waited. After twenty minutes, a forty-five-foot-long white powerboat with a split-level cabin appeared, engine gurgling lazily in the darkness.

Awkward with their heavy, weighted ankles, Linda and Leanne were helped aboard. The powerboat idled clear of the plane and the engine fell silent. There were no lights in the cabin.

They drifted in the darkness as the plane took off.

Linda could see lights on a distant shore, only this time farther away.

They floated, alone with their thoughts.

The more *yakuza* stories Maria had told her, the more worried she had become. But beyond the pain and humiliation and rage, she felt genuinely bewildered.

How had it happened that a country like Japan was allowed to get away with importing, even kidnapping foreign women for its commercial sex? This was a country that seemed paranoid about the prospect of foreigners overstaying their visas. Linda had been in Japan twice with her father and remembered the warnings and admonitions on the seriousness of the offense. A visiting tourist was grudgingly granted permission to stay two weeks in Japan, but Maria had said immigration officials routinely issued six-month "entertainer's" visas to accommodate Takeshita-*kai* and other *japayuki* dealers.

The Japanese police either pretended there was nothing wrong with the business or did nothing about it. The public didn't seem to care.

There were less than ten years remaining before the twenty-first century. How had the Japanese managed to dodge responsibility? she wondered. How had they done that?

Linda's father was a politician. The vice president of the United States. She knew the score.

Too damned much money! What was the figure for money dropped by Japanese lobbyists on American congressmen? Three hundred million? Or was it four hundred? Some obscene figure. Money like that carried real weight with moral degenerates and mental pipsqueaks who were elected to office, her father excluded.

What was Leanne thinking? she wondered. Leanne who had withdrawn and wouldn't eat. It was impossible to try to talk to her. She remained steadfastly, resolutely mute.

A half hour passed. Forty minutes.

After nearly an hour had passed, Miki said, "They're waiting to see if it's safe."

Linda said, "What if it's not?"

Miki said, "Then it's *waslik* time. You two go swimming."

Leanne Tompkins said, "Oh?" This was the first word she had spoken in three days.

She stood, stepped over the side of the boat, and disappeared.

EIGHTEEN

The light was blinding.

Naked, she waited patiently.

The taping crew came and hung her by her wrists from the ceiling. Her feet were several inches off the floor. Her ribs pushed out. She was breathing hard.

They had three cameras: one for her body, one for her face, and one for whatever part of her anatomy was being punished.

They left the whip and the strap on the bench in front of her so she could see them.

Kao ran his hand down her spine. "See there, she's afraid. She knows it's going to hurt. Good for her to have a turn once in a while."

Miki, looking up at her wrists, licked her lips.

"How old are you, Miki? Thirty-one? Thirty-two? Not a bad body." Kao took her by the nipple and spun her hard.

Kobayashi-*san*, sitting on a stool holding his crotch, said something to Kao.

Kao said to Linda, "*Oyabun-san* wants you to see what happens when he is displeased, Ms. Shive. Miki allowed your friend Leanne to kill herself, thus wasting a *waslik japayuki* before she was used. A valuable longnose blond. Beg me, Miki. Do it in English for the benefit of our new *waslik*."

"Please," Miki said.

"Please what?"

"Please whatever you want."

"If you were a man and had lost a valuable *japayuki* through negligence, you would have been obliged to surrender the tip of your finger to Kobayashi-*san*. We're having Ms. Shive watch your punishment, so she'll know what to do when it's her turn. If you don't make her suffer more than I make you, I'll have to repeat this."

Kobayashi murmured to Kao.

Kao said, "*Oyabun-san* says Jocho Yamamoto regarded reprimanding and correcting faults as an act of charity, but one must be very careful to do it the right way." He gave Miki a tap on the butt with the strap. He spoke to the taping crew and the lights popped on. "Not a word until I say when. Then I want you to show your blue-eyed student what discipline is all about."

He gave a Miki a stroke.

Miki opened her mouth, eyes wide.

"What was that? Did I hear something?"

Miki took a quick, deep breath.

He lashed her again.

Her body arched.

To Linda, he said, "See her twist like that, biting her lip to not make a sound. That was well done. Not a peep. *Gattsu*. She has *gattsu*."

NINETEEN

As the 300A Airbus began its descent to Narita Airport, with the Tokyo urban sprawl to their right, James Burlane read the rules of what could be brought into Japan duty-free. He thought this list contained rather more prohibitions than one would have thought for such a prosperous nation.

Burlane didn't believe that if he used Polo cologne he would resemble the handsome model in the duty-free magazine; this patrician-looking hunk, wearing riding britches and mud-splattered boots, was supposed to be a polo player. Burlane thought it was unsettling that people were capable of believing that smell made the man; as far as he knew, greed did not literally give off an odor.

On the intercom, the purser instructed the passengers that anyone experiencing recent signs of illness was instructed to report to the quarantine officer immediately upon disembarking.

Burlane was a seasoned traveler, and nowhere had he seen a disease fetish work quite the way it did in Japan. The Japanese greeted visitors with a kind of sick slip, a quarantine form upon which dutiful passengers were to tell the authorities his or her recent symptoms of illness and write his or her name and address and where they would be staying in Japan.

Burlane wondered what would happen if a traveler wrote 'restless cock' on the form.

He had been in Japan a half-dozen times, beginning with his days as a Company spook. Before the new terminal was opened at Narita in 1992, there had been a line of quarantine officers on duty, presumably watching for sweaty foreheads and telltale coughs. Burlane regarded them as human white corpuscles, alert to incoming viruses. He thought they looked splendid in their spiffy blue-gray outfits and hygienic white gloves, but he never saw any self-confessed sickies.

In the new addition, Terminal 2, the airport designers had tucked the quarantine officers discreetly to one side.

The British ran a tidy ship in Hong Kong, but Burlane couldn't remember filling out any quarantine form. And there was no such anxiety betrayed to arrivals in ultraclean Singapore, where one could be fined for chewing gum or spitting. There were countries that didn't want plants or animals or even soil brought in, but that was to protect their agriculture and livestock. The drill at Narita was openly aimed at contagious, two-legged vermin infecting Nippon with their presence. Why didn't the *gaijin* just stay home and consume Japanese products and leave Japan alone? But no, they were always showing up at the airport with those noses of theirs and their unfathomable independence.

Now, handed an anal-compulsive form, Burlane dutifully checked the yes/no blocks. No, he hadn't recently had diarrhea. No, he hadn't been suffering from a fever. Et cetera. When he got to the block that asked for his address while in Japan, he wrote *"Osaka."*

He got into the line where one turned in one's quarantine form. The clerk, a trim, self-assured young woman with a thin face, looked concerned about that answer.

"Where in Osaka?" she asked.

"I don't know."

"You will have to stay somewhere in Osaka."

"Of course, but I've never been to Osaka. Why would I want to stay in a hotel I've never seen?" Burlane looked bewildered.

She gave him a sour face, squinting her eyes and bunching her mouth.

"It makes no sense. I'll go there and look for a place I like."

She said, "There are many wards in Osaka."

"I'll bet there are."

She made a sucking sound with her pursed lips. This was a form of remonstration; Burlane had disturbed the *wa*. "What are you going to do in Osaka?"

"I don't know. Go for a walk, maybe. Have a look around. Enjoy a bowl of buckwheat noodles. Have some of those delicious pickled vegetables of yours. Look for some birds. I take pictures of birds."

Burlane went *weet-weet-weet, weedle-weedle, weet-weet-weet.*

"One moment, please." She showed the form to the next clerk, a man, who was examining Rene Alburo's quarantine card. The form clearly called for address, and the hairy barbarian had simply listed a city, Osaka. A city was not an address. This would not do. Why were the *gaijin* like this?

The two clerks conferred, confident that the English-speaking Filipino could not speak Japanese.

The man glanced surreptitiously at Burlane.

Seeing this, Burlane made a warbling sound.

The clerk blinked.

The woman returned to her post. She sighed. This was a form of admonition.

"You must comprete the form," she said. "It is the rule."

"I must list an address."

"Yes."

Burlane printed *"Waldorf Astoria"* in the block.

"Thank you," she said.

Burlane said, "Kind of spendy for me, to tell the truth. But there's a helluv'n Irish bar a couple of blocks away. Got those big honkin' roast beef sandwiches. I just love 'em."

On the way out of the terminal, Alburo, laughing, said, "Your clerk said that Americans were the worst bignoses to deal with. Completely undisciplined. My clerk said *gaijin* from Australia were just as bad if not worse."

"Fun to push their buttons," Burlane said.

"Part of the Schoolcraft persona?"

"He uses eccentricity to draw their attention from his cameras and parabolics. Man, he put on a show once at the airport in Madrid." Burlane smiled at the memory. "But of course he was younger then."

The bus to Yokohama was new, air-conditioned and spotless. The driver, in his white shirt and white gloves, looked quite professional. As Burlane and Alburo waited for the last passenger to board, a woman's taped voice admonished the passengers to buckle their seat belts. She did this first in Japanese, then in English.

They were told that the bus had a toilet, and that they could make national or international phone calls. However, they had to have a telephone card or the right amount of yen. The driver didn't make change.

Burlane wondered which was worse, stepping into the den of hustlers at Manila Airport or arriving in spiffy Narita where you were about as welcome as a sow on the putting green.

Land being so scarce, the Daisan Kehin Expressway was elevated, as were all freeways in Japanese urban areas. Freeways in the U.S. sliced through cities, restricting the view to concrete walls or the façades of the buildings on either side. In Japan, vehicles entered cities rather like low-flying birds, swooping over a plain of closely packed rooftops and through thickets of smokestacks; in the U.S., they entered like moles, burrowing their way toward the tall buildings in the center.

Burlane had once read that the Japanese estimated the value of Tokyo's real estate as matching that of all North America. Across the plains of tightly packed factories and warehouses—the producers of this awesome wealth—smokestacks belched grayish white crud into a malevolent pall. The morning sun, barely perceptible through the smoke and chemicals, looked like a squashed turd floating in chicken soup.

In the distance, elevated expressways swooped and looped through the haze in high, futuristic concrete curls, part George

Orwell, part *Blade Runner*. The expressway signs were the same style and color as those on American freeways; they looked identical, in fact, but Burlane dismissed the idea that the Japanese had for some reason copied them from the U.S. The Japanese couldn't have gone that far. Just couldn't.

They crossed the Tamagawa River. Below them, tiny houses with blue roofs were packed tightly together, separated by the narrowest of narrow streets. Then came a lot packed with yellow cranes. Spools of heavy cable, neatly stacked. A mound of discarded gears. Green and red barrels of chemicals. Above this hive of activity, the company logos familiar around the world. Panasonic. Toshiba. Toyota. Fuji. Mazda. Mitsubishi. Burlane had no sense of leaving Tokyo or entering Yokohama; the two cities were part of a single industrial sprawl, a productive growth that, year by year, edged outward from the capital city.

As the bus passed a sign indicating that they had entered Yokohama proper, Burlane said, "From the standpoint of the shoguns, the *kannai* was a form of condom, wasn't it, Rene?"

"What? A which?"

"A rubber to stop the spread of what the Japanese regarded as cultural AIDS." Burlane looked amused. "Commodore Perry brought the virus with him, and *gaijin* traders spread it through the orifice of Yokohama's port, which was seen as a dirty place, if you think about it. Trade with *gaijin* was a form of buggery."

"God!"

"Idle speculation," Burlane said quickly. "I was thinking about white gloves and quarantine officers."

TWENTY

The Japanese had not only responded to Jack Shive's request for a room in Yokohama for two friends but had surpassed themselves. No doubt thinking the vice president's friends were baseball fans, they had lodged Larry Schoolcraft and Rene Alburo in a two-bedroom corner suite of the Hotel Sansei with a view of Yokohama Stadium from one window and Yokohama harbor from another.

The refrigerator was stocked with Kirin and Beck beer, plus a bowl of marinated whale meat, a plate of sushi, a small Western ham, decorated with pineapple rings and maraschino cherries, and a roast chicken spiffed up with sprigs of parsley—a nice balancing of East and West. The coffee table bore a bottle of Chivas Regal, an English-language guide to the city, plus six everything-on-the-Hotel-Sansei passes: two for the Mutekiro, which according to the guide book was a French restaurant with entrees beginning at ¥7,000 or about $57 at ¥123 to the dollar; two to the Ohtanawanoren, a Japanese restaurant with courses priced at ¥7,500 up; and two to The Tavern, a block from the Hotel Sansei, a reasonable ¥950, which was listed as being owned by foreigners.

Burlane could remember no other country that had a separate listing for "foreign-owned" bars and restaurants.

He noted that he and Alburo had not been given passes to any of the "live bars" that charged ¥2,500 to ¥5,500 for admission and the first drink. "Live bar" and "hostess bar" were code for "with *japayuki*" and were where they would most likely find Linda Shive and her companions.

But the real prize, treat of treats, was a pair of passes for the Yokohama Stars' home stand with the Seibu Lions in the middle of the following week.

Alburo, seeing the tickets, said, "All right! What do you think?"

"I say we go if we're still here and can make it. Sagawa Rice and Sugar Limited owns the Stars, doesn't it? And Sagawa Rice and Sugar is in fact a wholly owned subsidiary of Takeshita-*kai*."

"Kobayashi owns a block of tickets just behind third base."

Burlane popped the cap from a bottle of Kirin and sampled the whale meat with a pair of pull-apart Japanese chopsticks. Gesturing with them, he said, "These are a lot easier to use than Chinese chopsticks, did you ever notice that? They're made of bamboo so they grip better, and these that you break apart have edges that help out." He clicked them together. He had some more whale.

"Well?"

"Well, what?"

"How does whale taste?"

"It tastes more like beef than fish, which shouldn't be surprising, since whales are mammals. It seems decadent eating it, I have to admit. Maybe it's no match for cannibalism, but right up there. Perhaps that's the attraction. Not that I've ever eaten human flesh, mind you. Try a piece."

Alburo did, then thought a moment, chewing. "It's probably a developed taste," he said.

The Japanese obviously wanted to please Shive, no matter what the cost or whom they had to dislodge from the Hotel Sansei. Burlane and Alburo, drinking Kirin and eating sushi and whale meat, enjoyed the view of the city.

They couldn't see over the lip of the stadium onto the field, but they did have a superb view of the *kannai*. And the thoughtful managers of the hotel had included two beautiful wall mountings in the suite: an aerial photograph of the stadium and a large, annotated map of the *kannai* so that out-of-towners could understand and appreciate the view from the corner windows.

Burlane, gnawing on a piece of whale, studied the map. The *kannai* was bounded by the Ooka River to the northeast; a belt of freeway and rail lines to the northwest, the stadium end of Yokohama Park; the Nakamura River to the southwest; and the waterfront with Yamashita Park to the southeast. According to the map's scale, this area was some two miles long and two-thirds of a mile wide.

In the park at the bay end, kitty-corner from the Hotel Sansei, lay a small lake. Just below the lake a short avenue ran to the waterfront.

Looking out across the sprawling city through his binoculars, James Burlane thought that these buildings, while modern in every way, symbolized an enduring frustration to the Japanese.

The American architect Frank Lloyd Wright, one of the pioneers of what later became known as the International Style of architecture, had traveled to Japan as a young man and had been influenced by their spare, utilitarian houses—free of the architectural gingerbread and classical bric-a-brac that cluttered western buildings. Later, Japanese architects copied the American and German pioneers, and themselves became masters of the International Style.

But the one triumph and symbol of the International Style, the skyscraper, was forever denied them in their homeland. Alas, Japan sat astride the Pacific Rim of Fire, an accursed crack in the earth whose earthquakes had once destroyed both Tokyo and Yokohama, among other Japanese cities. Otherwise, Burlane knew, they'd have built skyscrapers halfway to Mars, hardons for Nippon.

He thought Japanese cities were beginning to have the look

and feel and even the smell of American suburban shopping malls, as though the consumerist sanctuary of the new and fashionable had overtaken an entire country. It was difficult for him to figure out precisely what it was that made First World markets so dispiriting, but something there was about a shopping mall.

Alburo, flipping through his notes, said, "It may be impossible for us to get into any club with longnose girls in it. You have to remember that the *japayuki* trade is a Japanese game, and we're *gaijin*."

On the TV screen, a female reporter was doing a voice-over on a live shot of Japanese foreign minister Yoshida greeting Vice President Jack Shive at Tokyo's Narita Airport.

Alburo said, "She's saying Shive is coming here to press Washington's trade complaints before the economic summit meets. The Japanese wanted President Olofson to come early as well, but he declined, citing a lingering illness. Yoshida says it remains Japan's goal to maintain amicable trade relations with the United States, and he's sure that, in the end, the Americans will understand Japan's positions as they have in the past."

TWENTY-ONE

Toji's was flanked by a fashion boutique and a fancy candy shop on a spiffy, upscale lane east of the baseball stadium and south of the *kannai* subway station. The posh foyer was all maroon and gilt and bric-a-brac. The carpet was maroon. The maroon walls were covered with large photographs of famous American striptease artists of yesteryear: Blaze Starr, Lili St. Cyr, and Gypsy Rose Lee. A group of businessmen browsed through the pictures before they went inside.

On the way through the foyer, Linda Shive took a quick peek in at the ramp Takeshita-*kai*'s performers shared with Yokohama fashion models. There were television monitors in the corners of the large room. The gentlemen guests, sitting in a crush of tiny tables and chairs, could watch close-ups of the action on the ramp or small stage—the cameras concentrating on a *japayuki*'s face or whatever part of her anatomy was desired.

Linda thought no way would a European or American woman attend a fashion show in a place that displayed photographs of Lili St. Cyr and Gypsy Rose Lee in the foyer. But then, perhaps the photographs were changed on fashion day.

Miki said, "*Oyabun-san* wants to put you on the ramp tomorrow."

Linda, wearing jeans, Nikes, and a Princeton Tigers T-shirt as instructed, followed the smartly dressed Miki through a side door and down a narrow hall into a tiny dressing room used by models and *japayuki.*

Leaving the door open, Miki stripped and put on a black G-string, lacy garter belt, and black net stockings. *Oyabun-san* liked the gold rings in her pierced nipples, so she didn't wear a bra. As she pulled on her second stocking, she said, "You know, the submissive really has the fun. The perp has to do all work."

"The perp?" Linda asked.

"The perpetrator. The dominant one."

Speaking of perps, *oyabun-san* appeared suddenly in the open doorway. He spoke quietly to Miki in Japanese, and waited politely as Miki translated.

"*Oyabun-san* says when a Star commits a critical error in a game he must complete a *gattsu* drill of fielding five hundred consecutive ground balls or collapse of exhaustion, whichever comes first. *Gattsu* means guts. A guts drill. Kobayashi says errors are the result of inadequate training and lapses in concentration. He does not allow his baseball players or his *japayuki* to display poor form. You were shown the proper way to behave last night. You know what to do. If you make a mistake, he will remind you with the memory wand."

"Memory wand?"

"*Oyabun-san* asks you to bend over and drop your underpants."

Linda did as she was told. She saw that Kobayashi was holding a rod with a plastic shield six inches above its bullet-shaped tip.

"It's something like a cattle prod," Miki said as she oiled the end of the rod.

In a large room behind the theater, a Takeshita-*kai* cameraman slowly panned the exterior of a circle of cubicles, each with its door open so the camera could see inside the booths. Each cubicle had a window, actually a one-way mirror, that faced a glass-enclosed, circular room in the center.

Miki said, "The room in the center turns. You see how it works. As we go round, each booth gets a close-up of the action. We're taping you tonight, so they're shooting an establishing sequence."

"A star."

"If we're featuring a Filipina *japayuki*, it costs five thousand yen to lower the screen over the window and a thousand yen a minute to keep it that way. A clock tells the viewer how much time he has left. A European or American blond costs seventy-five hundred to open the window and fifteen hundred a minute to keep it open."

Linda followed Miki through one of the cubicles that functioned as an entrance into the inner circle; a Takeshita-*kai* taping crew waited with their Sonys at the ready.

Miki said, "We get repeat customers, but once they see one pussy and a single pair of tits three or four times, they get bored. A red light over a window means there's a customer inside. If there's no light, it's empty, and we can relax a little. As we slowly complete the circle, the customers watch you from a constantly changing angle. I try to show them something new each pass."

She gave Linda a set of restraining anklets and bracelets. "I want you to begin by standing at the edge, near the booths, and undress and put these on. Give them a wholesome, American-college-student kind of look."

Linda took her place. Undress she would. To act like a wholesome American college student under these circumstances was ludicrous.

The cameramen took their places.

Miki said, "Okay, take it off. Show the gentlemen what you have to offer."

As Linda bent to untie her Nikes, the floor began to turn. She stripped her T-shirt off, aware of the red lights above the mirrors. When she was naked, Miki instructed her to kneel, facing the mirrors with her knees wide. Miki then fastened her wrists together behind her back and tied her ankles to rings on the floor. Miki had a basketful of clothespins and a leather strap.

Over an intercom, Kobayashi gave Miki some instructions. She said, "It is *oyabun-san*'s wish that you remain silent until he says otherwise. Otherwise, it's the wand. You remember the wand."

Linda Shive clenched her jaws. "I remember the wand," she said.

TWENTY-TWO

Koji Watanabe was gloomy as his limousine slid silently along the winding coastal road to Tsutomu Kamina's retreat at Atami, where he had first seen Takeshita-*kai*'s tapes of Vice President Shive's daughter.

Ordinarily it would have been madness for the CEO of a Japanese automobile company to rendezvous at a *yakuza* retreat a second time. Watanabe could make an excuse for one visit, but two was not good.

They were in a swirling, thinning fog, but when the highway overlooked the Pacific, Watanabe could see the slate-gray ocean below them.

He was well aware of what had happened to the so-called kingmaker Shin Kanemaru, when he got caught accepting the yen equivalent of a $6-million bribe from a trucking company owned by mobsters. It was pocket money for Kanemaru. That was what had made the fiasco so pathetic. Everybody took bribes; everybody knew that. Kanemaru had disgraced himself by getting caught, not by taking a bribe. The same with Yoshio Kodama in the Lockheed scandal twenty years earlier. It was not that Kodama had accepted bribes; it was that he had gotten *caught*.

It was right that Kodama and Kanemaru had been scuttled. The public had to be allowed its comforting fictions, for on the other side of the fictions lay the dragons of the truth. The brilliant Italian writer Niccolò Machiavelli had been quite perceptive on this.

The wet, temperate marine climate and the mountainous terrain of Japan, covered by mixed evergreen and deciduous trees, were similar to the west coasts of Oregon and Washington and British Columbia in Canada. In fact, the Cascade Mountains of Oregon and Washington, and the Coast Mountains in British Columbia, were part of the Pacific Rim of Fire, that unstable crack in the earth's crust. And here, as in places in Oregon and Washington, geologic folds, or ridges of mountains, plunged directly into the sea, making for winding roads and turnouts over vistas of beaches far below. The curving coastal road was commonly referred to as the "old road" to Atami; the new one, slightly inland, swept through everything in its path so as to hold more traffic, only occasionally offering motorists a glimpse of the sea.

The driver slowed for a tight curve toward the mountain, where the road bridged a small creek that flowed down a narrow ravine.

Ordinarily Watanabe would have stayed well clear of anything associated with Takeshita-*kai*. But Kobayashi had obviously not given up on his hare-brained scheme. There was a high wind of unrest in Nippon; under the circumstances, Watanabe felt his presence was required as a ballast to help steady poor Yoshida, whose future was listing to the lee.

The whole country risked being swamped if Kobayashi was allowed to follow through with his proposal. He could not. It was madness.

The driver negotiated a seaward curve, and Watanabe could see the outlines of several large, rock monoliths poking out of the water.

Watanabe was worried that his countrymen were in for a serious jolt. Their security had always lain in the conviction that trade wars were madness and the Westerners, understanding this, would always be the first to yield. But if he had read the combative American media correctly, this time the Japanese were in for a rude awakening. But that was the least of the Japanese problems.

For now, he knew, the government had to find a way to calm the *oyabun* of Takeshita-*kai.*

As he slowed for the curves, the driver kept his eye on the convex metal mirrors mounted above the highway to warn of coming traffic.

Watanabe thought he knew his history. He was aware of the rhetoric that had led Japan to its doomed war with the United States. The recession in the 1920s and 1930s had rekindled a Japanese fascination with myths in which good conquered evil and in which action, honor, and loyalty were understood and appreciated. Insubordinate officers of the Japanese overseas army, infatuated with romantic notions of the noble samurai, invaded Korea in 1929 and China in 1931. Ignoring world opinion and the instructions of the Foreign Office, the overseas commanders did what they pleased—invoking high-minded notions of chivalry and national honor to murder people if they wanted, or rape them, or steal whatever struck their fancy. Two enthusiastic Japanese lieutenants competed to see who could behead the most Chinese in one week; details of this sport were reported in Japanese newspapers.

In one episode, a spirited contestant told how he had split a Chinese in half by bringing a sword down on the top of his head. Whenever a Japanese official in Tokyo protested such fun, the right wing simply called him a Western sellout. Assassination was a favorite sport of the *yakuza* in the 1920s and 1930s.

The driver eyed another mirror and took the inside path of the road.

By 1945, what any sensible person could have predicted in fact had happened. Japan lay in rubble.

The way Watanabe saw it, if the Japanese had sensibly chosen to compete economically, instead of militarily, they could have made a fortune selling airplanes for American and British pilots to fly against the Germans. He felt like shoving a sixteenth-century sword up Kobayashi's ass, along with a couple of dozen Yukio Mishima novels and General Tojo's riding boots.

Watanabe supposed they existed, but he had never been in a country where the government was so concerned about the safety of its citizens that it mounted traffic mirrors on country roads. It helped that the Japanese had the money to afford such mirrors; still, it was quite an accomplishment.

Watanabe's countrymen were willing to pay four or five times as much for a kilo of rice as their Asian neighbors, as long as it was grown in Japan. Stand up to the farmers, Watanabe had urged the government. If the Japanese had to buy California rice to keep the U.S. car market open, they should do it. Three-fourths of the Japanese trade surplus with the Americans was due to cars. Rice was parking-meter money.

The French farmers had bullied their government for years before they surrendered to the efficiencies of American agriculture. Government subsidies couldn't save small French farms that grew soybeans. Watanabe didn't think stubbornness would save the backyard rice grower in Japan. More efficient Japanese robots had replaced American assembly-line workers. Now it was Japan's turn: mechanized agribusiness in California was sure to overtake the diminutive Japanese rice paddy.

The code of Bushido was a snare and a delusion. Weren't good cars and safe roads what people really wanted?

Understand the forces of history, Watanabe had told the government. The Liberal Democratic Party loved to talk about discipline, as though discipline was a kind of cultural Gator Ade, a highly advertised, slightly acidic yet sweet tonic to be consumed in quantity whenever a quick pick-me-up was called for or there was a goal-line stand to be made. This tonic even had a hit of salt in it to take care of lost sweat.

Well, then, if discipline was so wonderful, Watanabe said, then show some. Stand up to the rice lobby. Legions of greedy little peckers were calling their rice paddies the "soul of Japan," saying if they bought their rice from *gaijin*, they'd be at the mercy of outsiders, that to eat Japanese rice was a matter of national defense. Such nonsense! In fact, most of the rice growers were part-time farmers who depended on the American car market for the high-paying, full-time jobs that supported their families.

The American and European desire for consistent trade rules shouldn't be so odious. If Japanese were truly superior and not all talk, they shouldn't have anything to fear, right? In Watanabe's opinion, Japan could accept the American challenge and still prosper. Change the patent laws. Compete, he argued.

The car began to wobble. They were in an isolated stretch high above the water.

The Japanese had to learn how to consume. They were first-rate producers but parochial consumers; markets were what the new competition was all about. Even if Shive hadn't put it in so many words, that was at the heart of the American fuss.

The driver slowed the car.

But what had the government in Tokyo done in the current crisis? Appealed to the *yakuza* for help. The *yakuza!*

And what had the *yakuza* proposed?

Watanabe shuddered to think of Kobayashi's crazed scheme.

In the intercom, the uniformed driver in front of the glass partition said, "I'm afraid we have a flat tire, Watanabe-*san*."

Watanabe said, "I don't think you should try to fix it on these curves. It's not safe. Take your time and pull over at the next turnout."

The car wobbled along slowly for a hundred yards before the driver turned it into a graveled overlook for sightseers. The overlook had two freshly painted green benches and a domed garbage can, as well as the entrance to a hiking trail that zig-zagged its way down to the rocky shore far below.

As the driver got out to retrieve tools and the spare tire from the trunk, a dark blue Toyota sedan pulled alongside and parked. A man and a woman got out, asking the driver if he needed help.

Watanabe was pleased that common courtesies yet obtained on Japanese country roads.

Then the rear door opened.

Watanabe found himself staring at the muzzle of a revolver.

"Watanabe-*san?*"

"Yes," Watanabe said. He felt stupid saying it, knowing from the cycles of history that he was about to share the fate of those who had opposed the Kobayashi clones then commanding the Kwangtung army.

The man behind the pistol was polite and respectful, and spoke refined Japanese. He bowed his head and said, "This is Japan, Watanabe-*san.* Unfortunately, you have forgotten what it means to be Japanese. Where is your *giri?*"

"More like riflings in a gun barrel."

The man with the pistol looked puzzled. "Huh?"

"The cycles of history," Watanabe said.

TWENTY-THREE

Miki watched for cars coming around the bend while Kao quickly dragged the bodies of Koji Watanabe and his driver to the trunk of the limousine and locked them inside. The driver had been surprised at his pay for delivering Watanabe so neatly. Owing to the nearby hiking trail, the car would be left alone until Watanabe's worried wife called the cops or the bodies began to smell.

Their chore completed, Miki and Kao hopped into the stolen Toyota and took a leisurely drive down to a stretch of the ocean where rocky jetties stuck out at irregular intervals. The jetties, built to protect small fishing boats from the surf and to check erosion, were such favorite hangouts for fishermen that regular sidewalk vendors operated at the approaches from the parking lots.

There were whitecaps on the Pacific; a chilly wind gusted off the water as Kao and Miki got out of the Toyota, so they retrieved nylon windbreakers from the rented Nissan they would drive back to town.

They bought peanuts from a vendor and cold cans of Georgia-brand café au lait from one of the red, roofed machines that were ubiquitous in Japan. The wind puffed up their red

L. L. Bean windbreakers, overpriced Taiwanese imitations of the real McMaines.

They wore spotless white Nikes, Indonesian-made, Portland, Oregon, marketed; his were white with red swooshes, hers mint green with mellow yellow swooshes.

They hiked down the path on the top of the jetty, pausing to watch two old men fish, then pushed on to the end of the jetty, near where three teenage boys in Stars baseball caps fished with spinning rods.

Kao turned his back on the wind and lit a Marlboro with his French cigarette lighter. He and Miki sat down on a rock and watched the boys fish.

Suddenly one of the boys had a fish on.

While he and his friends hopped from stone to stone, occupied with the difficulties of maneuvering the fish around the rocks and snags, Kao took the murder weapon from the pocket of his windbreaker. He took a satisfying drag on his Marlboro and gave the pistol a heave far out into the green water.

"Good throw," Miki said.

"Such a dangerous piece of shit," he said, letting the smoke drift through his nose. "Every time I pull the trigger on one of these things I wonder if it's going to blow my hand off."

"They're *wasliks*, made in somebody's backyard," Miki said. "What do you expect?"

"The question is, which cylinder won't hold up?"

"Or which one will?"

Kao smiled. "Shooting one's a form of Filipino roulette."

They watched the boy successfully net the fish, a wiggling perch.

Kao called, "Nice fish! What're you using?"

"Pieces of squid," the boy said.

Miki said, "It's a beauty. A big one. Your mama will be pleased."

"Thank you. It's all right, I guess. You should have been here last week. For a while it was really something. Hooked a fish with every cast."

The boy concentrated on removing the hook from the perch's

mouth. Then he held the still jumping fish up by the gills so Kao and Miki could see it better. Miki applauded.

Kao said, "Hard job to get it past all those rocks, I bet."

The fish still struggled.

The boy said, "Just when you think you've got it made, the fish throws the hook. Or else something snags your line. Or the stupid thing wraps itself around a rock. Always something."

That said, the fish jerked off the boy's finger, but he quickly pinned it with his foot.

He knelt and strung it on a line with two other fish before anything else could happen. "See. It looks simple, but it's amazing what can go wrong. One thing is sure—this is when they hit, at dusk. When the sun is setting, they get hungry."

TWENTY-FOUR

Miki had been right. The Japanese were avid fans of bignose *japayuki*. Toji's was packed.

As on the previous night, a Takeshita-*kai* camera crew taped everything.

Linda and a Filipina named Fely, whom Linda had met only minutes earlier, were oiled down and made to "wrestle" while wearing Seibu Lions and Yokohama Bay Stars baseball caps.

Then Linda was hung by her wrists and strapped by Miki, after which the lights were turned up and she was made to lie naked at the edge of the stage, displaying her welts. The customers, laughing and having a good time, brandished beer mugs and cocktail glasses as they gathered around for a close-up look.

Miki occasionally whacked Linda with a quirt, a signal for her to change positions and give the gentlemen a new look.

TWENTY-FIVE

They wore black suits and white shirts with odd, gangsterish black ties. One of them was a small, almost effete-looking man with a neat part in his shiny black hair.

The other was larger, with a broad face and a small scar on his chin. They wore dark glasses. Were they trying to imitate the Blues Brothers, was that it? Jazz musicians in a Fellini movie?

Vice President Jack Shive glanced down the hall outside his room. What the hell? Where were the security people? He didn't like the idea of people drifting in from the streets and banging his door unannounced.

The broad-faced man, reading his concern, answered his question. "The guard downstairs is a friend, and this is Asia. Friends help friends. Your Secret Service people have no idea we're here. They think everything is . . . how do you Americans put it? A-OK."

Shive looked alarmed.

The broad-faced man said, "Truly, there's no need to worry, Mr. Shive. You're perfectly safe. We mean you no harm. You're our guest in Japan, and it would be embarrassing in the extreme if anything happened to you. Rest assured that this is a civilized visit. You are Mr. Shive, the American vice president, are you not?" He spoke good English, but with an accent that, strangely, had a hint of Spanish about it.

"Yes, I am," Shive said.

"My name is Nobito Kao. This gentleman is Shoji Kobayashi."

The solemn penguins both bowed. In turn they shook Shive's hand. It was clear to him that Kobayashi was superior to Kao in whatever hierarchy they inhabited. The Japanese did not like to do things alone. They wore identifying outfits so people would know where they fit, so strangers would know how they were to be treated.

Kao said, "We would like to talk to you. May we come in, please? The hallway is no place to do business. We shouldn't be long."

"Excuse me. Business? This is about what, if I might ask?"

Kao said something in Japanese to Kobayashi. Kobayashi, pressing his lips, nodded his understanding and apparent approval.

Kao said, "About your recent conversation with Foreign Minister Yoshida in Washington."

Shive said, "Are you connected with the Foreign Office or the government?"

"No."

"Is this official or unofficial?"

"You might say, 'unofficially official.' We're here in the interest of Japanese national honor."

Shive thought that perhaps Olofson and he were right after all; if the Japanese were pushed to the brink, they would yield, but only then. They had pushed their interests remorselessly for more than 130 years since Commodore Perry's unwelcome arrival, but for all their constant talk of international this, international that, they remained the most isolated and parochial of all industrial countries.

Was this the way it was to be, then? The embarrassing details of capitulation agreed upon in private so as to save face in public? Shive didn't care how the Japanese went about their unpleasant chore, as long as they finally did something, anything, except stall. If saving face was so important to them, it wouldn't hurt him to go along with whatever odd drill was required.

Shive said, "It's true, I've spoken with Yoshida-*san* on a number of occasions. But anything I may have said to him was in strict confidence, intended for him and the Japanese government."

"We understand that."

"He would correctly be disappointed if I broke our understanding without his permission."

Shive thought the whole notion of confidential diplomacy was a joke; when more than one person knew about something, it was no longer a secret.

Kao said, "You told Yoshida-*san* about your disappointment in American failures to penetrate our domestic market and our alleged dumping, and you complained about our patent and copyright laws, which you feel are unfair. You told him that if we don't alter our way of doing business, you will retaliate with import duties and legal action. Is that a fair summary?"

Shive said, "I told him that you Japanese are superior producers, but you need to learn how to consume as well. I told him the Cold War is over, and if Japan is to sell on the international market and earn income from the rest of us, it should also learn how to buy from us."

Kao translated this for Kobayashi. He listened respectfully to Kobayashi, then said, "We feel that our way of life is at stake, Mr. Shive. As you might imagine, it's difficult to decide what our best action might be."

"Does Yoshida-*san* know of your visit tonight?"

Kao bowed.

"Ahh. Well, then, won't you come in and take a seat, please." Shive opened the door wider and stood aside. He gestured toward several easy chairs arranged around a coffee table. This was an encounter he should remember for his memoirs. When they were gone, he would write himself a note with the details. The white shirts. The black ties. The dark glasses. The small scar on Kao's chin. Publishers wanted details, he knew. Remember the details. The more details, the bigger the contract.

The penguins sat.

Shive saw that Kobayashi was missing the end of the little finger of his left hand. Shive's stomach twisted. Were his visitors representatives from the *yakuza?* What could the *yakuza* conceivably want with him? His stomach sugared. Something was wrong.

Suddenly he was thinking of what had happened to Koji Watanabe last week. Two days after Shive had talked to him, Watanabe had been murdered and stuffed in the trunk of his car along with his driver. Investigators determined that he had been shot in the face with a .38-caliber pistol, likely what English-language translations rendered as a Smith & Waslik from the Philippines, the *yakuza* weapon of choice.

Somehow Shive didn't feel threatened by the penguins. He wouldn't have hired them as baby-sitters, but surely they'd be more circumspect if they planned to harm him physically. He calmed slightly. A witness might be nice.

He said, "Would you like some tea? I can have some sent up. It will only take a minute."

Kao said, "You're very gracious, Mr. Shive, but that won't be necessary. We won't take up your time. We'll conduct our business and be on our way." He placed six videotapes on the coffee table.

Shive picked up one of the tapes and examined it. "And these are?"

"Little movies. Your daughter Linda is a star of the action."

Shive quickly put the tape back on the table. "My daughter?"

"To answer your recent query to the Filipinos, Mr. Shive, your daughter and her friend Ms. Tompkins foolishly booked passage on an interisland boat on southern Mindanao. The boat was hijacked by Muslims, who sold them."

"Sold them?"

"For the entertainment business. We Japanese are great admirers of your Western women, especially blonds and redheads. We like their white skin and those nipples of theirs. Pale pink! Filipinas are desperate to help their families and so volunteer themselves. Longnoses are more difficult to come by."

Shive leaned forward. "Where is my daughter? I want my daughter."

"Commodore Perry was able to sail into town and tell us what to do, but you are not. If we prefer to eat Japanese rice and drive Japanese cars, we will do so. President Olofson will propose that our governments establish a bilateral commission to study the long-standing trade issues between the countries. After tempers have cooled, the commission will suggest some reasonable compromises. If Olofson fails to make the proposal, Takeshita-kai will kill your daughter. If the administration sends an anti-Japanese trade bill to Congress, we will make copies of the tapes available for the amusement of the public."

Kao, looking grave, said something to Kobayashi. Kobayashi, suppressing a grin, held a make-believe camera to his face, and pretended to tape Jack Shive's daughter in action.

Nobito Kao said, "We market our tapes all over the world. To the Dutch, Germans, and Scandinavians. To the French. To the Americans and Canadians. No need to translate screaming; it's an international language. The look on a girl's face says everything."

Jack Shive popped to his feet and strode from the room. Behind him, Kao called, "Do enjoy the tapes, Mr. Shive. Do what you're told and your daughter will be fine. We'll be in touch."

TWENTY-SIX

The Japanese had chosen to house Vice President Jack Shive in one of their highest of high-tech offerings, which they no doubt found impressive but which James Burlane found slightly bewildering if not a little crazy.

Burlane supposed that over the centuries, the Japanese imagination had been largely formed by a lack of space. The Japanese were able to buy oil, which they also lacked, but they were forced to create space by making everything smaller, from bonsai gardens to cars, Walkmans, and left-field walls.

When their fascination with smallness was combined with their compulsive determination to remove yucky human beings from the transactions of daily living, they wound up with Shive's suite, where everything was miniature and all services were performed automatically, by machine. In this hotel, it appeared, only the guest, the desk clerk, and possibly a chef in the kitchen making fresh sushi were not robots. Each room had a computer monitor with which one called up menus of services: everything from rubbers to whiskey and taped tours of restaurants and night clubs. Whether it was news, sports, or movies, each room except the toilet had a high-definition television monitor on which the guest and his friends, forever spectators, could watch whatever they wanted.

Burlane was not sure of the necessity, even sanity, of some of the offerings, such as the sink in the toilet, wherein a guest— responding to a diagram and explanations in English, French, German, Spanish, and Chinese—waved his or her hand in front of a vertical sensing device to start the water. One moved one's hand up or down for more or less pressure, and over colored chips to make the water hotter or colder; red left for hot, blue right for cold. Burlane assumed that this transformation of the human hand into a wand was intended to spare the guest the offensive chore of turning a utilitarian knob, which required touching something that might have been handled by others. Dirty, dirty!

Burlane and Rene Alburo watched the *yakuza* pornographic tapes of Shive's daughter in the master bedroom, while Shive waited in the living room or salon, or, more accurately, what might have been a control room of Moon Base Alpha. Shive, still shaken, waited and sipped a Scotch on the rocks, looking out at the sprawl of Tokyo at dusk.

When Burlane and Alburo emerged, solemn-faced, Shive studied them for clues. That they hadn't immediately volunteered good news was in itself bad news. He ground his teeth together. "Well?"

Burlane cleared his throat. "Good that you had us watch the tapes first."

"And?"

Burlane flipped on the monitor offering the menu of services and began scrolling through the listings. He eyed Alburo. "I bet we could order ourselves up some hot little Filipinas if we wanted. We could all get drunk and get our rocks off."

"Mr. Burlane?" Shive ground his jaws together.

"Ahh, here we go. International restaurants. I wonder if they have any Hindu restaurants."

"The tapes, Mr. Burlane."

"I'm afraid all kinds of bad shit, Mr. Vice President. Truly."

"Featuring Linda."

Burlane cleared his throat. "They do have some Malaysian restaurants. And Thai, see there. Do you know what they do in Thailand, same as in Hawaii? They fly there in Japan Airlines; they ride buses owned by Japanese companies; they eat in Japanese-owned restaurants; they get laid in Japanese whorehouses; they buy gems at their own jewelry stores; and they play on their own golf courses. If it isn't Japanese-owned, it isn't for them. The Hindus don't eat meat, so they've learned how to use spices and yogurt to make food taste good. I love it."

"You said they subjected Linda to bad shit. Like what bad shit?"

"Well, you know." Burlane missed Ara Schott. If his friend had been there, Burlane would have conned him into this terrible chore of telling Jack Shive what had happened to his daughter. Schott was steady and had an almost fatherly way about him. But no, Burlane was on his own; he had to do it himself.

"No, I don't know," Shive said. "That's why I asked you to watch the tapes. Somebody had to watch them, as we all know."

"I truly think it would be better if you just used your imagination, Mr. Vice President. I'm not sure there's any point in going into detail. 'Pornographic tapes' ought to cover the territory."

Shive sighed. "We both know there's pornography and there's pornography. I have to have some idea on something like this."

Burlane shook his head in resignation. "Okay then. Hard sex."

"What do you mean 'hard sex'?"

Burlane continued scrolling through the menu until he arrived at the offering of condoms. These included multicolored rubbers, ribbed rubbers, and specimens that featured painful-looking spikes and evil-looking knobs. "Have you ever heard of a book by a woman named Ruth Benedict called *The Sword and the Chrysanthemum?*"

"Tell me, Mr. Burlane."

"This is a culture that deliberately isolated itself from the world for several hundred years, and now qualifies as one of the most repressive on the planet, with the possible exception of the Islamic world, and we see what happened there. This is a hotel frequented largely by Japanese businessmen. As you can see for yourself, they're unembarrassed by this shit." Burlane tapped the button and scrolled the listing of available condoms.

"Tell me about Linda."

"They've subjected your daughter to various forms of sadomasochism, Mr. Vice President. Straps. Whatever. You name it. There's no pretending that this is anything but the worst."

Shive swallowed.

"I just hate like hell to have to lay something like this on you." Burlane bit his lip. He glanced at Reno Alburo. Alburo swallowed too. He stared at the backs of his hands.

Burlane scrolled the listing again. "But look here. You can go see *kabuki* if you want. Or No theater. It's not that the Japanese are completely uncivilized. It's just . . . what do I say? They're just turned in on themselves to a degree most Westerners just cannot conceive."

Shive said, "Okay, let's get down to it. Getting hysterical is no solution. They've got her. They've set an impossible deadline. We proceed from the facts. Will you tell me again, Rene, how this *japayuki* business works?"

Alburo said, "The girls are imported from all over Asia, Mr. Vice President, from the Philippines and Thailand mainly, but occasionally from the West. The gentlemen who visited you are leaders of a *yakuza* gang called Takeshita-*kai; kai* translates something like the English 'syndicate.' Sometimes they're called *gumi*, which means, roughly, 'gang.' Shoji Kobayashi is the godfather of Takeshita-*kai*, which is the dominant gang in Yokohama; its power comes from its successful *japayuki* operation in the Philippines, headed by a man named Nobito Kao."

"And the Japanese and Philippine governments tolerate this?"

"The Filipinos have their laws, but they're either not enforced or Kao buys off the cops and judges. The Japanese police like *japayuki*, too. It's one of those businesses, like drugs, where there is just too much money involved. Money is a form of social asbestos, a carcinogen that absorbs all objections. There are periodic complaints by Japanese women's groups, but those go nowhere and probably never will. The *yakuza* permeate Japan, and this is a culture that caters to the desires of men."

Burlane said, "You should know that Rene is a *japino*, Mr. Vice President. His mother was a 'comfort woman' who served Japanese troops in World War II. Their offspring are called *japinos*." Playing with the monitor, he scrolled the night club listings.

"Comfort women?"

"Sex slaves," Burlane said.

Shive said, "Is that putting it too coarsely, Rene?"

Alburo shook his head. "In 1991, I read the story of a young Filipina *japayuki* who had been tortured to death, and I decided I had to do something about the horseshit. For my mother, if nothing else. I speak fluent Japanese, so I got in touch with Joseph Estrada. I may not be as motivated as you, Mr. Vice President, but I'm right up there."

"Which brings us to the bottom line: What do we do now?"

"Now we retrieve your daughter." Burlane called up the movie listings.

"How?"

If the price was right, they could watch *Jurassic Park, The Raiders of the Lost Ark,* whatever they wanted. "It depends on what set of rules you want to follow. Are you willing to give me a generous strike zone, or do I have to stick with a conventional one? Should we watch Indiana Jones? I take it the Japanese are springing for your tab?"

Shive said, "We do whatever works without the entire world getting its kicks watching my daughter on their VCRs."

Burlane scrolled through the movie listings. "*Lawrence of Arabia.* All right! Oh, and look here. They've got *Zulu* with Stanley Baker and Michael Caine. There's a real movie. They know how to chose their movies, you have to give them that."

Shive, understanding that this business was nearly as tough on Burlane as it was on him, pushed on. "And Linda is where, do you think?"

Burlane said, "Most likely somewhere in Yokohama, which is Takeshita-*kai*'s turf. But as Rene and I are finding out, it's virtually impossible for us as *gaijin* to find her. This is a closed world, and we stand out like the clichéd sore thumb. Even if we could find her, she'll likely be well guarded." He hesitated. "The Japanese public knows all about *japayuki*. They just don't talk about them. That would be a serious breach of *wa*."

Shive closed his eyes. "*Yakuza* money smothers everything."

"Correct. So it's to Kobayashi's advantage to keep Linda alive until he gets what he wants. If you try to go through government channels or Japanese police agencies, the *yakuza* will know immediately, and they'll snuff her in a second. Make no mistake. They'll put her under."

"He's right," Alburo said.

Shive sighed.

"If the *yakuza* want to call the game, fine. I say we show 'em how it's played in the bigs." Burlane punched up the drinks list and keyed in a request.

"Specifically what is it that you propose, Mr. Burlane?"

Burlane cleared his throat. "Remember the scene in *Raiders of the Lost Ark* where this muscular, malevolent-looking asshole steps forth brandishing a scimitar with which he intends to decapitate Indiana Jones?"

Shive half smiled. "I remember."

"Right! Jones takes out his revolver and casually blows a hole through his chest. Well, I don't like to fuck around with bush-league stuff either. Mr. Vice President, I bet if you really wanted to you could get the State Department guys to smuggle some special gear into Japan for me, couldn't you? You're the vice president."

"What kind of special gear?"

"Spook stuff. Professional couriers know it's none of their business what they're escorting. It could be an envelope, a trunk, or a truck. They don't have any need to know." From a slot Burlane retrieved three miniatures of Suntory whiskey and a can of soda.

"I can do that."

Burlane held a plastic cocktail glass under the suite's ice machine and tapped a button. The machine spit ice cubes into the glass. "Ask for Eddie Tanaka. If he's still with the Company, I want him. If he's retired on Maui or somewhere, unretire him and get him on a plane. He's not too old for a job like this."

"Eddie Tanaka, if I can get him."

Burlane poured their drinks. "If you can't get Tanaka, I want a Japanese-American with some experience. The Firm has them, I know. I want one who really knows his Japanese and has a Tokyo accent. No longnoses. I'll want the goods delivered to Rene in a new Toyota minivan. It seems unlikely that Shoji Kobayashi and Nobito Kao would know the details of your conversation with Foreign Minister Yoshida unless Yoshida wanted them to. Do you agree?"

Shive accepted a drink. "I think Yoshida either told Kobayashi what I said or he wrote a report of the conversation which Kobayashi got his hands on."

"So it's possible Yoshida knows about this extortion horseshit too, isn't it?" Burlane took a sip of imitation Scotch.

"Yes. Likely, even, although he may not agree with it."

"Will the president cooperate with us?"

"You don't have to ask." The vice president finished his drink quickly and took a turn at calling up another round.

Burlane said, "We get old weird Harold to show 'em a knuckler in Washington. Then I come in from the bullpen. I brush 'em back with a couple of inside fastballs, one after the other, then give 'em a roundhouse curve. After that we'll see if they've still got the fighting spirit. They're always talking about the fighting spirit, aren't they?" Burlane accepted a Suntory and soda from the vice president and held up his plastic glass for a toast for the job ahead.

TWENTY-SEVEN

President Harold Olofson was a tall, sandy-haired man who cinched his paunch in with a corset before entering situations in which there were cameras present. If Ronald Reagan could dye his hair black, there was no reason Olofson had to look like he'd spent most of his life on a barstool. Olofson had been the dean of faculty at the University of Idaho before he ran for the Senate. When he was dean, he had worn a Vandyke beard that, together with his spectacles, made him look vaguely Lenin-like. He'd distanced himself from that likeness by shaving the beard. But the paunch that had come upon him in his late forties refused to go away, despite his determined efforts to conquer it.

The other thing that refused to go away was a form of amoebic dysentery that lingered in his guts. He had apparently acquired it by eating a salad on a visit to Egypt. He had assumed that the Egyptian president would see to it that the salad greens were properly washed before they were served at a state dinner, but no. Now he had bugs in his insides, and they wouldn't go away. It didn't seem fair or proper that such low forms of life could infect the president of the United States.

Olofson remembered the passage in *The Brothers Karamazov* in which a dead priest began to smell almost immediately upon his death, a reminder to everyone of what happens to the flesh, no matter what the soul's claims on immortality.

Still, he felt in fighting trim despite his drooping belly and the bugs inside it. He was from Idaho, a state with silver, Nazis, a beautiful lake in the north, and potatoes and Mormons and good ski runs in the south. In addition to the ambitious Olofson, Idaho had also sent the isolationist William Borah and the internationalist Frank Church to the Senate.

He studied his notes from his conversation with James Burlane.

A mellow *bong* sounded. He picked up the receiver of the safe phone. "Do I have Minister Yoshida?"

The White House operator said, "Yes, you do, Mr. President."

"Put him through, then . . . Good evening, Yoshida-*san*."

"A pleasant good morning, Mr. President."

Olofson slapped his belly with his right hand, as he had seen old-timers do in Nampa bars when he was a kid. "Jack Shive sent me some videotapes of his daughter Linda. He said he sent you some copies too. Did you receive those videotapes, Mr. Yoshida?"

"Yes, I did, unfortunately."

"The daughter of the vice president of the United States being whipped and having her breasts covered with clothespins. If I showed those pictures to Congress, they'd insist that I declare war."

"Please, Mr. President . . ."

"The country would back me, too." Olofson felt a disconcerting twinge in his lower bowels.

"I assure you, Mr. President, the Japanese government has nothing to do with this. I know nothing of it."

Olofson said, "The idea is that I'm supposed to propose a bilateral commission to 'study' the trade issues: Is that your understanding of this tidy bit of extortion?" The twinge in his insides had become more insistent.

"I have no idea."

"Kobayashi knew the details of your conversation with Jack

Shive last month. Jack and I are both wondering about that. How did that happen, do you suppose?" Suddenly the urge was upon the President. The misery inside Olofson pressed for release.

"Kobayashi?"

"Shoji Kobayashi," Olofson said.

"I know of a Yokohama businessman named Kobayashi who is a generous contributor to my party, but I can hardly be held responsible for what he does."

Olfson clenched his jaws, together with his buttocks. He would see it through. Had to. "The Japanese National Police Agency says this Kobayashi is the godfather of a *yakuza* gang— Takeshita-*kai*, is it?—that saved your family's bacon during a strike ten years ago. Is that true?"

"I . . . I was as shocked as you when I received those tapes, I assure you, Mr. President."

"I am the president of the United States. The daughter of the vice president is being held captive by sadists trying to dictate American trade policy. We don't have any way of knowing whether you know about this outrage or not. Do you see our problem?" Boy, oh boy, did Olofson have a problem.

"Yes, I do."

Olofson bit his lower lip. "Under the circumstances, the American voters would demand that I ask these questions, and by God I will. I say again, Yoshida-*san*, do you know Kobayashi?"

"I'm a public servant and a politician, Mr. President. In Japan, a political supporter has the right to give without being investigated, and we never accept a gift if there are strings attached. This is our inheritance from your own General MacArthur."

The pain was now blinding. Olofson said, "We're told that if we seek the help of the Japanese police Kobayashi will murder Jack's daughter. In short, there's not a lot we can do on this short a deadline. You have two daughters, Yoshida-san. You can understand how Jack feels." Olofson mopped the sweat from his brow, hoping his alarm wasn't creeping into his voice.

Yoshida cleared his throat. "Yes, I can, Mr. President."

Olofson's mouth was dry. "What do you propose we do about this? If I have to, I have Shive's permission to show the tapes to leaders of Congress in closed session. We can just gather them together, from both parties, and lay it on this line: This is what Japanese gangsters are doing to Linda Shive. This is what we're faced with."

"I truly don't think that would be the wisest course of action."

For Olofson, the wisest course of action would be to tell Yoshida he would phone him back. But he didn't. He said, "Well, then what do we do? They say a picture tells a thousand words, but in this case, Yoshida-*san*, I don't think that even begins to tell the story. The truth is the only weapon Jack Shive has against the barbarians who are holding his daughter."

Yoshida said, "This is the *yakuza* we're dealing with, Mr. President. I'm not sure we could stop these people even if we wanted."

"You can't stop them? No? What are you saying? That they're the agents of the devil?" Suddenly, mercifully, the pain ceased. For whatever reason, Olofson's bowels were giving him a temporary break.

Yoshida said, "I know that you're aware by now that Koji Watanabe was murdered. Considering what the Mafia likely did to John Kennedy, do not be surprised at what the *yakuza* are capable of doing, Mr. President. We can huff and we can puff as we please, but the *yakuza* remain the *yakuza*."

"When Linda Shive is safely back in our hands, we'll talk again. Otherwise, make no mistake—we'll take you sons of bitches on for money, marbles, or chalk, you name it. And I guarantee you it will cost Japan big, big time."

"Please, Mr. President . . ."

Another twinge. An alarming contraction this time. Olofson narrowed his eyes. "If you're in contact with the assholes who did this, you can tell them Harold Olofson says they can take their proposal and their ultimatum and shove it. If you're not in touch with them as you claim, then please do get in touch with them. The last time you pulled shit like this we had to pop nukes to straighten you out. If you don't release Linda Shive and her friends now, immediately, I can assure you there again will be unwelcome consequences. Sayonara, Yoshida-*san*."

Olofson slammed down the receiver and ran for the toilet to forestall other, more immediate, consequences.

III
SHOBU

ONE

James Burlane and Rene Alburo crossed the street to the park below the stadium. They cut at an angle to the left of the small lake and emerged at the head of the broad, tree-lined Nihon Dori that headed toward the harbor. At the bottom of the Nihon Dori, on the left, was the headquarters of the Kanagawa prefectural government.

Here Burlane lagged back and fished his binoculars out of his daypack.

Alburo angled to the right, along a curve of Kaigan Dori, the main harbor thoroughfare. He walked down Kaigan Dori as it straightened out, with Yamashita Park and the port on his left. Straight ahead on his right lay the Hotel New Grand, which General Douglas MacArthur turned into his occupation headquarters following the Japanese surrender. Beyond the New Grand loomed Yokohama's Marine Tower, looking like a miniature of the Seattle space needle.

As he approached the New Grand, Alburo crossed Kaigan Dori and entered Yamashita Park. He passed through the middle of the narrow park to the promenade along the water.

In a minute a Japanese man in a blue business suit approached him at an angle. He was flipping an orange. This would be Eddie Tanaka.

"Is that orange from Valencia? A Spanish orange?" Alburo asked.

"Belize, more likely," the Japanese man said.

"Stann Creek?"

"Between there and Belmopan."

They fell in together.

"I hope I did okay," Alburo said.

"You knew your lines."

"I'm an amateur, you know."

Tanaka smiled. "Nice that they've kept this park along the harbor, don't you think? The Americans covered it with temporary buildings during the occupation. I've got your goodies parked in a garage a couple of blocks over."

Alburo said, "I have a further request."

"Oh?"

"We would like you to buy a sex doll."

"A what?"

Alburo looked foolish. "A sex doll. You know, one of those full-size rubber things that you blow up. With the fake pussy and everything."

Tanaka grinned. "You're joking."

Alburo shook his head. "Plus a half-dozen S and M porn tapes, whatever brand that's produced and marketed by Take-shita-*kai*."

Tanaka said, "This is not your idea, I take it."

"I have an imaginative partner. He called it refining his pitch. He says you'll know where to get the doll, and you can buy it without drawing attention to yourself, which we can't. He says you should wrap it and leave it in the lobby of the Sansei Hotel for Mr. Alburo. That's me."

They walked on. Suddenly Tanaka said, "Say, you're not working with a guy who carries a wok around with him? Hangs out in public markets and likes to cook?"

"A wok?" Alburo's partner did have a wok.

Tanaka smiled.

"You know him?"

"You might try calling him Sid and see how he responds."

"Who?"

"Sid Khartoum. Major M. Sidarius Khartoum, spelled like the city in Sudan."

"Is that his real name?"

"That's the way he's listed with Interpol."

Alburo said, "That doesn't mean it's an authentic name."

"To be honest with you, I'm not sure I know his real name. What difference does it make what his original name was? If he's a professional, he's a chameleon. If he's the guy I'm thinking of, he's been doing Sid Khartoum so long he's almost become Khartoum."

"I see."

"Besides, we are who we are now, not who we were ten years ago, isn't that right? That's the way I look at it."

"I suppose."

"I take it he's lurking around here keeping an eye on us."

"He's around somewhere," Alburo said.

He followed Eddie Tanaka to the parking lot, where Tanaka gave him the keys to a dark blue Toyota minivan.

Alburo said, "I almost forgot. Our friend, Sid Khartoum or whatever his name is, says you should get one with big, outsize tits."

"On the sex doll?"

"A longnose sex doll if you can get one. One with blue eyes and light-complexioned plastic skin."

Tanaka grinned. "You tell Sid I'll do my best. And tell him to stir you up a mess of his gingered fish sometime. *Mmmmmmmm.*"

TWO

James Burlane checked out the figure at the far end of Yamashita Park: Eddie Tanaka. He panned the narrow, rectangular park with his glasses. Here was where the Americans had built their administrative offices during the occupation. Burlane could see the hotel that MacArthur had made his headquarters. When the Americans left, the Japanese tore down the temporary buildings along the harbor and turned the area into a park which they named for the vanquished General Yamashita.

Seeing nothing that concerned him, Burlane lowered the glasses, leaned against the top rail of the fence along the harborside promenade, and reread the dossiers on Kobayashi and his lieutenants. The dossiers had been given to Rene Alburo by the National Police Agency.

Reading the stilted and oddly phrased English, Burlane remembered that J. Edgar Hoover had for years denied the existence of the Mafia because he thought it was too much for the FBI to handle. See no evil. Hear no evil. Responsible for no evil.

The JNP was less disingenuous than Hoover in addressing the obvious. On the surface, and judging by their thickness, the dossiers on the Takeshita-*kai* leaders were impressive, but within the bun of gaseous lingo there wasn't much legal meat.

The details offered were either disconnected or worthless, and there was no explanation at all as to why the police had not pursued the matter further. It was as though yes, people claimed the *yakuza* tiger was mean and had big teeth and terrible claws, but no, the police didn't want to go inside its cage to check it out. That would disturb the *wa*, if not the *oyabun*. The report on Takeshita-*kai* had the clarity of a snapshot taken from the window of a speeding vehicle.

Alburo said it was public knowledge that Takeshita-*kai* owned Sagawa Rice and Sugar, but Kobayashi's dossier only suggested a connection. Alburo said it was clear that Sagawa had elbowed control of the Stars from the Taiyo Fishing Company; the JNP report only hinted at it. The gang's role in the *japayuki* traffic was cited in passing, but downplayed as speculation. The same with Takeshita-*kai*'s smuggling of Smith & Wasliks: rumor.

It was possible to discern that the *oyabun* of Takeshita-*kai* had friends in any number of high places, including the Japanese Diet and Foreign Minister Yoshida. It was widely understood that the latter friendship dated to 1983, when there was an attempt to organize the Yoshida family's chain of American-style "quick food" outlets. Yoshida was said to have hired Takeshita-*kai* goons to bust the upstarts.

One of Kobayashi's obsessions, detailed at some length, was his passion for samurai literature in general and the *Hagakure* in particular. (Burlane assumed this was included because it was socially approved.) Kobayashi was said to be an "acknowledged expert" on the *Hagakure*, the original of which contained the teachings of the samurai-turned-priest Jocho Yamamoto (1659–1719) as written down and edited by his student Tsuramoto Tashiro.

In the militaristic fervor of the 1930s, *Hagakure* was believed to reflect *yamoto-damashii*, "the unique spirit of Japan." On the home front during World War II, *Hagakure* was socially obligatory reading. It was then, as a boy, that Japanese author Yukio Mishima discovered it. It became his personal bible, and after he killed himself by ritual suicide in 1970, it again became a best-seller in Japan. The JNP said Kobayashi was fond of requiring Takeshita-*kai kobun* to memorize long passages.

Tsutomu Kamina, who ran the daily affairs of the gang's Yokohama operation, lived in Takeshita-*kai*'s seaside compound near the Atami hot springs fifty miles southwest of Yokohama. Kamina had a garden that overlooked the sea. In this garden, lesser *oyabuns*, feudal vassals in the *yakuza* hierarchy, were said to pledge their fealty to Kobayashi. Kamina was reported to meditate in this garden each morning.

Possibility one: the garden.

When Nobito Kao was up from Manila, he was a regular at a harborfront Scandinavian restaurant, the Scandia. The dogged Japanese sleuths, serving the taxpayers in near-fan-magazine style, breathlessly informed the reader that, on his visits to Yokohama, Nobito Kao liked Scandia's salmon and pickled herring. These meals were dubbed "late-night eating binges."

Possibility two: Scandia.

Burlane was only a couple of blocks from the Scandia, but he had to keep his distance; for all of Yokohama's history of contact with the outside, to be a longnose in the *kannai* was to have the anonymity of a naked woman at high tea.

As he looked inland from the harbor toward Yokohama Stadium, six blocks from the water, Scandia was slightly to the left of the base of Nihon Dori, the five-block-long boulevard that ran from the bottom of Yokohama Park to the waterfront. Four restaurants were housed there in two narrow buildings that faced the harbor; Pomodoro and Suginioki were sandwiched between Mediterranean on the left and Scandia on the right.

Kaigan Dori, the broad, main arterial that followed the waterfront, ran directly behind the restaurants. Osanbashi—South Pier—lay thirty yards in front and slightly to the right of them at six-thirty, with the baseball stadium at high noon.

Beginning from the entrance to Osanbashi, the restaurants were circled, clockwise, by the waterfront police headquarters at seven o'clock; the regional maritime safety headquarters at eight; the city's silk museum at nine; the Yokohama archives at twelve; the Kanagawa prefectural headquarters at two; the customs house at three; and the immigration and quarantine office at five.

In the middle, geographically the center of the Western infection 140 years earlier, lay Scandia. In Scandia or outside Scandia, James Burlane proposed to show Nobito Kao what hairy barbarians could do if they put their minds to it.

THREE

Rene Alburo drove the Toyota minivan while James Burlane studied the map of the city. They cruised slowly by the row of restaurants kitty-corner from Osanbashi, where the insistent hairy barbarians had first unloaded their strange inventions.

The Yokohama city guide Burlane had consulted at the Sensei Hotel said steaks in the Mediterranean started at a yen equivalent of forty American bucks; the spendy Pomodoro offered Western food; a frugal *gaijin* or a Japanese unconcerned about losing face could buy a bottle of beer for five bucks in the Suginioki; but at Scandia, Koa's hangout, the smorgasbord was a sixty-buck minimum. Burlane supposed *yakuza kobun* had to do something with their *japayuki* profits.

Burlane said, "I'd like some height, if possible. Easier to shoot down on someone. You get a clean line of sight, and the victims don't have any idea where the shot is coming from. Sweet."

"God!"

"It's a hard world, Rene."

"The top of the police headquarters looks good. How about that?"

"It'd be perfect if I could figure out a way to get up there. It'd be a turkey shoot from the customs house or immigration office, but Japanese executives like to punish themselves with hard work and long hours. I don't want to be doing second-story work in a building with people in it."

"There's the island with transit sheds, but that'd be a longer shot. It looks like, what, maybe two hundred and fifty yards."

Burlane glanced across the water. "Let's go take a look."

They drove over the bridge to a harbor island and parked near the tip of a triangular tit next to Osanbashi pier.

Alburo said, "Well, Chief?"

Burlane focused his binoculars on his target across the harbor. "No height, but this is clearly my best shot. Easy in and out. There shouldn't be anybody out here late on a Friday night."

"Can you see well enough?"

Burlane grinned. "Night's the best time. When do these establishments close? Do we know that?"

"The Japanese-run establishments close early, between eight-thirty and nine-thirty, but these are both foreign-owned. The Scandia shuts down at midnight, and the Mediterranean at two A.M."

"Past my bedtime, but I can stay awake if I drink some coffee. There are only two car bridges to the island; safer for me to swim in and out."

"From where?"

"Good question." Burlane studied the map, then stabbed it with his finger, twice. "I think here. Or here, maybe. Shall we drag the gut and see what we're working with?"

They first drove to the seaside park in Noge, the ward just over the Oka River, the *kannai*'s northeast border. The park was part of Yokohama's ambitious Minato Mirai 21, aiming for the twenty-first century in the international style. The airy and open development by the water so far included the Yokohama City Museum, a maritime museum, the ultramodern Yokohama Grand International Hotel, and an exhibition hall.

Then they cruised slowly along the banks of the Oka river— also known as Tsukumo Magari, Ninety-nine Curves—looking for a place where Burlane might pop quickly out of the car in his underwater gear and hop into the water. From there he could float leisurely downstream to the harbor, then follow the shoreline to the right, that is, to the southwest, toward Osanbashi.

There were plenty of places to push off from. It was getting back that was the grinder.

FOUR

Outside, the setting sun.

With Rene Alburo at the wheel listening to the Stars and Lions in game five of the Japan series, the Toyota microbus shot *wwhhheeeeeeooooooo* southwest down the Pacific coast. New tires on perfectly laid concrete, not a wrinkle or a bump.

Ssssshhhhhhhh.

It was to ride like Aladdin on a high-tech carpet swooping above the city on an elevated expressway.

Wwhhheeeeeeeooooo!

The microbus was carefully engineered, and comforting in its precision. Alburo and Burlane rode in a womb of close tolerances. Tight, tight, tight was the feeling of their ghastly flight.

Wwhhheeeeeeeooooo!

In the country. On the ground.

Seibu scored four runs in the top of the first. Alburo said, "They're saying the Stars manager needs to get a solid six innings from his pitcher, and it doesn't look good."

Burlane said, "Most runs are scored in the early innings, aren't they? Tough to come from behind."

Wwhhheeeeeeooooooo!

Outside, gray clouds tumbled and rumbled, tumbled and rolled.

Wwhhheeeeeoooooooo!

The Lions scored two more runs in the top of the third to lead 6–0.

Outside, on a country road waiting for the minibus to pass: two Toyota sedans and a Komatsu dump truck.

Komatsu. Burlane felt lulled, almost sleepy, as his body hoarded energy. He remembered the round-faced Sakyo Komatsu he had met twenty years earlier in a Waikiki Hotel. This Komatsu, bespectacled, chain-smoking, was a popular Japanese author of science fiction. Burlane, perhaps loaded, had asked him to tell him one of his favorite stories.

Komatsu, savoring his Primo beer, took a drag on a Marlboro, and thought about the request for a moment. Then he told the story of a schoolboy who took a shortcut across a vacant lot one day and discovered a derelict, abandoned automobile obscured by a snarl and tangle of weeds and brush. Each day as the little boy passed the wreck on his way to and from school, he stopped to clean and polish it. As the weeks and months passed, he began fixing and refurbishing the old car as best he could with tools he smuggled from his father's workshop.

One day the automobile followed him home from school.

Wwhhheeeeeeoooooo!

Outside, a troop of teenagers, members of an outdoor or hiking club, judging from their matching outfits.

Wwhhheeeeeeoooooo!

Outside, the small farmhouses had upturned Chinese-style red roofs. The roofs were tucked in neat jigsaws of tiny, odd-shaped rice paddies. It was the owners of these diminutive paddies who objected so vehemently to rice harvested by combines in California. The tidy landscape—of a type favored by *National Geographic* photographers—was beautiful, Burlane had to admit. Or maybe cute, which suggested something small. But God, the inefficiencies of agriculture on that scale!

Wwhhheeeeeeeoooooo!

A farmer wearing a straw coolie hat looked up from the middle of a yard-sized paddie.

Wwhhheeeeeeeoooooo!

A garden and a restaurant. He'd play the hand that was dealt him. He had no choice.

Wwhhheeeeeeooooooo!

An old man in a baseball cap, cock in hand, pissing, scratched his testicles in disdain as the traffic hurtled past.

Wwhhheeeeeeoooooooo!

Burlane dug at his nuts too.

Wwhhheeeeeeooooooo!

This was how the Japanese had done it. This was how they had penetrated foreign markets and earned the trade surpluses that paid for the malling of Japan. Simple formula. They made vehicles that went:

Wwhhheeeeeeoooooooo!

As Rene Alburo and James Burlane scouted a back road for a turnout where the minivan might spend the night, the Seibu Lions added three insurance runs in the top of the ninth. The Yokohama Stars lost. Lost 9–0! Not only had the Stars' overworked pitching staff fizzled, but its hitting had gone south too.

Alburo translated the postgame wrap-up. "They're saying it had to happen. The Stars are down to two starters with sound arms, and they're both exhausted. They're saying the Stars don't have a reliever that deserves to be on a professional roster."

"Uh-oh."

Later that night, as they lay in the back of the minivan listening to classical music on Radio Australia, Alburo said, "You know, Larry, the basic problem here is that over the years the Japanese have become passionate believers in a free lunch. They'd deny it, of course, and they'd cite the long hours they work, but the truth is they just don't understand why they're so resented. There are many of them who feel that their brains have literally evolved differently than the brains of the rest of us."

"They don't want to be weaned. Who does?"

"They didn't see anything wrong with keeping 'comfort

women' to screw during the Second World War, and they have no Western moral or ethical reservations about importing *japayuki* for their bars now."

"Mmmmm. Well, we'll show 'em how to play ball tomorrow. We'll give 'em a doubleheader on their off day. Do they really think they can continue this shit into the twenty-first century? I mean, hey! Come on."

"They'd be furious if anybody suggested otherwise," Alburo said.

"The short of it is we're dealing with gangsters pretending to be seventeenth-century *ronin*."

"We're dealing with a gulf of misunderstanding that may be far deeper than you might imagine. Just as the Japanese have trouble with English *r*'s and *l*'s, they have difficulty understanding the longnose imagination. They're indifferent to Western indignation."

"What it comes down to is, the *yakuza* will do as they please as long as they're allowed to get away with it."

"Our best pitch is embarrassment."

Burlane said, "They're assholes. If the grinch stole their samurai movies, they'd come unglued."

FIVE

After two early morning passes along the scenic coastal highway to Atami, James Burlane and Rene Alburo figured out the entrance to the Takeshita-*kai* compound. Here the road-builders had confronted a cliff; to skirt it, they had bored a tunnel through a ridge.

Two hundred yards north of the tunnel, a steep, winding macadam lane led up the mountain. A guardhouse was tucked discreetly off the highway.

To get a view of the Takeshita-*kai* compound, Burlane and Alburo had to climb the adjoining ridge until they could look down on it. This required an ascent of nearly two hundred yards through thick underbrush. They started at daybreak, and by eight o'clock they had pulled slightly above the Takeshita-*kai* property on the adjoining ridge.

With the rising sun above the Pacific Ocean on his right, James Burlane used his binoculars to study Tsutomu Kamina's garden, about fifty yards down a zigzagging trail from the main compound, which included a kind of pine lodge with a shake roof that was perhaps an imitation of something found in northern Minnesota or Canada where hearty fishermen drank strong coffee and ate bacon and too many eggs before a day of swatting mosquitoes or suffering from the cold on the lake.

The garden was situated on a geologic bump that poked out from the ridge, which then plunged in a 150-yard vertical drop to a narrow, rocky beach; this was the cliff that had forced the digging of the tunnel.

A wave crunched onto the beach, sending plumes of spray skyward. A hard wind whipped the water against the base of the cliff. It was now low tide, but the water was rising.

The garden, perhaps half as large as a basketball court, was designed around a miniature sea of light-gray granite gravel. The gravel sea, hardly larger than a living room, was raked in neat whorls around and between an archipelago of nine dark-gray granite rocks. The rocks, the smallest being the size of an inverted teacup and the largest as big as a head of cauliflower, looked like splendid, ragged islands jutting up from a tranquil sea.

Having the power to do what he wanted, a *yakuza oyabun* was a form of corporeal god. But did Kobayashi and his lieutenants not decay, like everybody else? Did they not have human desires?

Burlane doubted that Kamina actually contemplated every day the symbolic meaning of nine rocks sticking out of raked gravel. Then what *did* a *yakuza* lieutenant think about, if anything? That he was hungry or thirsty? That his thigh itched? That his mouth tasted sour? That he was horny? That he had to let a fart? What pedestrian, ungodlike concern coursed through the synapses of his brain?

On the other hand, Burlane knew, there were those who swore about the pleasure of no-thinking-at-all; sometimes they sat and thought; sometimes they just sat.

Above the garden, Kamina's lodge was built on a natural flattening of the ridge; then, down a forty-five-degree slope, ran the trail to the garden. The immaculately groomed path that zig-zagged down from the compound to the garden was lined on either side by potted bonsai, diminutive junipers and firs.

Although Burlane felt the bonsai were old and beautiful in

their delicate, elegant way, he also knew how they got that way. Their roots were skillfully trimmed to limit their nourishment. They were literally starved—in a traditional manner—in order to stunt their growth. A bonsai was wildness shrunken and inhibited. Pretend wild. By-the-rules wild. A miniature of what might have been.

Burlane identified with big old wide-bodies with beards of moss hanging from their limbs like ghosts of Rip Van Winkle. And he liked his bark well scarred and scabbed—evidence of droughts, lightning hits, and passing pissers. *Under the spreading chestnut tree, the village assassin stands.*

On the path above the garden, a single sleepy-looking *yakuza* soldier leaned against a tree and lit a cigarette. A guard? The *yakuza* were as gods. What mortal challenged gods?

The posting of a guard meant action was surely at hand. Kamina?

Burlane gave Alburo the glasses.

Alburo said, "Are you sure you want to go through with this?"

"I don't see many people selling subscriptions to *Ms.* magazine over here. Who, if not me?"

"All I do is watch, then?"

"You'll have the glasses. Watch and give me the word if you see anybody coming down that path, so I can haul ass. Believe me, I'll have the volume turned up so I can hear you."

Alburo said, "You get to the path from the side, through all that brush."

"That's it. If he goes back, let me know so I won't waste a lot of energy for nothing."

"It's a beautiful garden, don't you think? I like that moss and stuff and the neat little gravel sea. And with a view of the ocean."

"Looks like they rake the gravel every morning."

Alburo started to give the glasses back, then stopped. "You're right. A guard. It's him." He gave the glasses to Burlane. "Kamina just took his seat on the flat rock."

Burlane refocused the glasses.

"So he has. He must have come back last night."

"Big game tomorrow. I bet he wanted plenty of time to contemplate the Stars' sorry pitching staff."

SIX

James Burlane, mopping the sweat from his forehead with the back of his hand, rested from the exertions of his steep climb through the underbrush. Ahead of him stood the guard on the trail above Tsutomu Kamina's contemplative garden.

The guard was smoking a Marlboro and reading a comic book.

Burlane crouched in the underbrush and took his time laying a single shot behind the guard's ear with his silenced .22 Ruger automatic pistol, a sweet little 1949 Mark I original. The guard, not hearing the muted snap of the pistol, dropped the comic book and pitched forward on the path, mouth open.

Burlane rested for a moment, licking his lips at the thought of what he had just done. Then he strolled down the path toward the garden. He stepped casually from the bonsai-lined path onto the placid, elegantly groomed gravel sea. He crunch-crunched across the neat whorls of granite pebbles in his maroon Saucony running shoes.

Tsutomu Kamina, startled, rose. He glanced up the path, then down at Burlane's intrusive *gaijin* feet.

Burlane bowed politely. Then, as in a dream, he heard himself give Kamina a polite good morning. *"Oh-ha yo gozaimasu."*

Kamania bowed. "*Oh-ha yo gozaimasu.*"

"Sorry about fucking up your gravel." Burlane pulled out his Ruger and shot Kamina three times in the heart.

The *oyabun* dropped to his knees.

Burlane hopped back to avoid the sinking corpse.

Into his transceiver he said, "Rene?"

"You're still clear."

Burlane put on his disposable rubber gloves. He quickly opened the corpse's mouth and began stuffing it full of videotape. He packed it as tightly as he could, until Kamina's cheeks bulged with videotape, and videotape poked from his mouth like plastic vomit.

On the transceiver, Alburo, watching from the adjoining ridge, said, "Hurry!"

Burlane dug his Nikon from his daypack. He dropped to his knees and snapped half a dozen shots of Kamina's head, framing each shot with his adjustable lens. He shot six more looking down on his subject, then a couple from his belly, looking up.

This done, he returned the camera to his backpack, dragged Kamina's corpse by the feet to the edge of the precipice, and gave it a sling.

He peered down at the narrow strip of rocky beach below. He couldn't see Kamina's body because of a slight bulge in the precipice, but the corpse was down there somewhere, waiting for high tide to wash it away.

An anxious Alburo, still watching from the next ridge, said, "For God's sake, get out of there, will you."

"Did it go all the way down? I can't see the beach from here."

"It went all the way. I followed it with the glasses. Splat!"

"Later, then."

Leaving the plastic cartridges of the Takeshita-*kai* tapes strewn on the garden where Kamina had sat, Burlane began the climb downhill to the highway where Alburo would pick him up in the minivan.

SEVEN

James Burlane loved pickled herring and so understood the attraction of Scandia's. To a seafood-loving Japanese, Scandinavian food had to be among the most attractive of *gaijin* cuisines. Nobito Kao had been in Manila for years, and Burlane knew that outside of a few jars imported by specialty houses to accommodate Scandinavian expats, in Manila proper pickled herring was impossible to come by.

Night game.

Eight o'clock start.

James Burlane could take Kao on his way in, belly empty, or on his way out, belly full of dilled salmon and pickled herring; it didn't matter.

While Alburo cruised, trying to find a private spot near the water where he could park the Toyota, Burlane packed the waterproof compartment in the rear of the Honda UV—underwater vehicle, or diver's tractor—that Eddie Tanaka had purchased to tow Burlane's middle-aged body around Yokohama harbor.

Alburo finally parked near the mouth of the Ooka River, near the base of a pier used by fishing boats. He backed the Toyota to within ten feet of the water. Working fast in the darkness, Burlane and he unloaded the Nippon Shark and quickly got it into the water.

Burlane punched the starting location into the Shark's computer memory, and started the electric engine.

"Good luck, Mr. Schoolcraft."

"Larry Schoolcraft's a birdman, Rene. He shoots birds with a camera. You're talking Sid Khartoum here."

"Ahh, Eddie Tanaka's guess. Don't run into anything down there."

"I'll try to be careful."

"Let me know when you get into place."

"I'll keep in touch," Burlane said. He punched the handles together, which started the engine. Then he twisted his left wrist. And he was on his way. It was totally black under the water.

The left handle controlled the speed of the Shark's electric engine and the pitch of its single screw. The right handle, in the form of a protruding knob, functioned as a universal stick, controlling the Shark's angle and direction. A wire cage protected the vehicle's rudder, elevator, and variable-pitch screw.

The instrument panel was flush with the curved snout of the torpedo-shaped Nippon Shark, providing time, depth, water speed, direction, distance traveled, and hours remaining on its rechargeable fuel cells.

If a diver programmed the chart of an ocean or river bottom into the vehicle's memory and an estimated speed of any currents or tides—as Burlane had done upon entered the Ooka River and Yokohama harbor—the Shark would trace the vehicle's progress underwater. The data was displayed on a four-inch-high-by-six-inch-wide screen upon which the Shark was represented by a blinking green light and the contour circles or other lines charted in a steady yellow.

The Shark had a light in front, but Burlane kept it doused. As he rode through the water, he kept his eye on the pulsing green dot that marked the Shark's progress down the steady-yellow river contour. He had the same eerie feeling that he had had in the morning, climbing the ridge in pursuit of Tsutomu Kamina: of being outside himself, of objectively observing himself.

This turn of events in his life was one of the mysteries the existentialists had talked about. The mystery of original being. The mystery of why a person finds himself in a particular time and place.

Why him, now, gripping the stubby control handles of the Nippon Shark as he cruised down the Ooka River?

Burlane felt suddenly sad. He was lonely. He missed his daughter. He wanted to be back at his cabin on the shore of Lake Wallowa in Oregon. There he could fish and hunt mushrooms and forage for wild food, and read and do his watercolors and drawings and go his way unnoticed and left alone.

More than Lake Wallowa, Burlane wanted to kick back in his easy chair with a good magazine in his lap, a cold bottle of Henry Weinhard beer on the floor beside him, and the Chicago White Sox on the tube. Let other people do the ugly, crappy stuff.

But there was no turning back. Unseen judges of Burlane's honor were legion; they watched over his shoulder, urging him on. These were the ghosts of his father and his father's father. He could not shake the voices. Filipinas yet to be recruited as "entertainers" counted on him. Alburo's mother counted on him. So did Maricris Sision.

So, of course, did Linda Shive, Leanne Tompkins, and their Filipina friend. Burlane wondered if there might not be a primal urge to defend the tribal turf and protect the tribal women. Having failed to dissuade the Japanese from the *japayuki* traffic by more civil means, it now fell upon the hairy barbarians to live up to their name . . .

When the pulsing green told Burlane he was at the mouth of the Ooka River, he surfaced to check his position, and was surprised to find the Shark's computer was off by only twenty yards. Considering the unknown speed of the current, and the fact that he had covered more than a quarter of a mile, Burlane thought the Nippon had performed admirably; in a harbor or ocean where the Shark would be used the most, its navigation system would be far more accurate. The crafty Japanese had done it again.

Burlane corrected the location of the green spot and submerged again. He proceeded southwest along the harbor front. He passed slowly under the supports of a railroad bridge that connected the *kannai* with Shinko pier. Past the pilings of the railroad bridge, he surfaced under the first bridge for cars and trucks. Running true.

Five minutes later, he surfaced under the second bridge, which connected Shinko pier with the area at the base of Osanbashi pier. He was now directly below Yokohama Stadium. He could see his objective, the tip of a triangular-shaped part of Shinko pier that stuck out of the water, pointing toward Osanbashi pier. The tip of this triangle was directly in front of the Scandia restaurant.

He submerged again, and a few minutes later he tethered the Nippon Shark to the underside of the mooring at his destination.

He retrieved the waterproof plastic bag from the storage compartment, together with a pocket transceiver, his disassembled 7.9-mm Mitchell M-76—a 10.9-pound, made-in-Yugoslavia sniper's rifle with a Kalashnikov AK-47 firing action and a 21.8-inch barrel with silencer and flash hider—and an aluminum bipod for shooting from his stomach.

He found a walkway that led topside, and followed it up; it was dark, and he was dressed in a solid black wetsuit. The competition among workaholics was indicated by a few scattered lights remaining on Shinko pier, but Burlane, a few feet from the water, was by himself.

He lay down, ready for the wait. "The catfish has landed," he said into the transceiver.

"Good man." Alburo said, "See it?"

"See it clearly."

He checked out the Scandia through the night scope. He studied the red bricks, the narrow blue awning, the white cross placed sideways on red. Whose flag was that? It looked like a Swiss army knife, but he didn't think it was Swiss. The Danes?

Being alert took all the concentration Burlane could muster.

He would have one chance, if that. He would have just a second—or fraction of a second—to get his shot off. He had to hit his target, but Nobito Kao didn't necessarily have to die for the pitch to be a strike.

EIGHT

In an attempt to imitate NASA, the Pentagon justified its research budget on the grounds that the results often had civilian uses. Burlane had always had difficulty understanding what civilian market there was for radar-evading technology, but never mind.

In the good bad-old-days of the Cold War, the challenge had been to keep nukes and delivery systems out of the hands of Stalinist Megashits. Now, possession of Stingers by barley-eating Afghanis had been enough to keep MIG-23s at a respectful distance. Day games were low-tech. The future was high-tech.

In the Gulf War, General Schwarzkopf's troops had stayed put in the daylight hours. At nighttime, party time, they donned their infrared shades and did their nocturnal thing—hip pilots and drivers, cool gunners and grunts who could see in the dark.

Burlane should have been prepared when microchips hit the popular market, but still, the quickness with which miniature-nearly-everything had appeared on the spook market caught him by surprise. It was as though the shadow world had popped from Harry Lime to James Bond on a Friday afternoon.

Now he had fitted an American-made Leupold night scope

on his Yugoslav sniper's rifle. He was a hip mercenary, a cool dude boogying with eyes of eerie red.

He waited. He watched.

At eleven P.M., Nobito Kao was suddenly there on the sidewalk with four companions. Kobayashi was not among them.

When Burlane first saw him, Kao, laughing, was standing in profile.

Then he turned, pausing to light a cigarette.

Burlane laid the crosshair into place.

He paused at the ebb of his breathing.

Kao squatted to adjust his shoelace.

Burlane waited.

Kao rose. A frontal.

Burlane triggered the first round . . .

Kao dropped to his knees, screaming.

And a second round . . .

Kao grabbed his crotch.

Burlane triggered a third, and a fourth, and yet a fifth round, coolly holding the crosshairs in place as he pulped Kao's cock and balls. Burlane was after a genital mush, nothing less.

Nobito Kao, rigid from pain, tumbled forward on his face.

NINE

Tsutomu Kamina had been scheduled to have supper with Shoji Kobayashi and spend the night in town so he, Kobayashi, and Nobito Kao could go to the game together the next day.

At eight o'clock, Kobayashi called to find out what was holding Kamina up.

Takama, the head of the compound's household staff, didn't know where Kamina was. He said Kamina-*san* had gone to his garden to meditate that morning, but hadn't returned. When someone was dispatched to find him, he was not to be found. There were a half-dozen empty cassettes of Takeshita-*kai* S&M tapes at the foot of the rock where Kamina ordinarily sat, but not a clue as to where he had gone. Perhaps he had decided to hike down to the beach.

Empty cassettes? A hike to the beach? That was unlike Kamina, who was a man of routine. He liked to sit in his garden. Also, Kamina liked to talk baseball, and tomorrow was game six of the series. Kobayashi told Takama to have the staff check the garden with flashlights. What if Kamina had had a heart attack?

At nine, Takama called to say the garden had been searched, but Kamina-*san* was nowhere to be found.

At ten, Takama again. Blood. He said they had found blood on the gravel near the rock where Kamina always sat.

Empty cassettes?

Blood?

Kobayashi felt a rush in his stomach.

Kao would come after pigging out at the Scandia. He loved the pickled herring, but Kobayashi couldn't handle it. But later, after Scandia, Kao would come by, and they would maybe fuck *japayuki*. For now, he had to get his mind off the missing Kamina and the blood found in the garden.

He clapped his hands softly, and the geisha Tomi appeared, bowing her lacquered hair. *"Hai,"* she said. Her voice was as a bell.

Gaijin females were far better for fucking than Japanese women because they were outside Japanese codes of behavior. They had no police protection, so you could do anything to them you wanted.

Tomi served Kobayashi the rice and the miso soup first, together with some *mukozuke*, in this case *buri*, a yellowtail, less than an hour old, spread out in delicious, thin raw blades for his pleasure. This was the traditional beginning. She would present each course just so, as *kaiseki* had been served in the seventeenth century.

Longnose *japayuki* had tender-looking, pale pink nipples that begged to be twisted. Their outsized butts were big bouncers under your hand, and their white skin reddened quickly under the strap, producing beautiful welts. And there was something about the brown-skinned Filipinas, with those perfect little bodies, that made them just about the sexiest women in the world.

A geisha's charms were aesthetic. Tomi was graceful and so delicate and tender. Her voice was so soothing and comforting. Such a flatterer, she was. Her entire reason for being was to charm and please men.

Thinking about longnose *japayuki* made Kobayashi's cock stiffen; when Kao got back from Scandia, perhaps Kobayashi would have Linda Shive brought in for a session of fun with those tits of hers and that ass.

Tomi's black silk kimono matched the autumn season. It had two large blossoms on each sleeve; the colors of these blossoms, off-white and yellowish-beige, were repeated on small, abstract leaves that tumbled toward the bottom of the kimono. The collar and cuffs were decorated with abstract patterns of muted apricot and almost-fuchsia, which were duplicated on the *obijime*, the narrow band wrapped and tied around the waist sash, the *obi*. The *obi* supported a muted-apricot and almost-fuchsia *obiage*, or bustle—in Tomi's case a large, translucent bow.

Maybe Kobayashi would have Miki use the strap on the Shive girl. Miki knew how to make her white ass hop. That would take his mind off Kamina and the tapes and the blood.

Kobayashi loved the way graceful, elegant Tomi shuffled in and out in her *zori*, her *obiage* moving this way and that with the movement of her tiny hips. Her little spine was as a willow. She kept her large black eyes demurely downcast. And she was so very tender. By holding her eyes down, she exposed the nape of her neck, putting herself at Kobayashi's mercy—a gesture every well-trained geisha knew was powerfully erotic.

Kobayashi loved to fuck the *gaijin* when their asses were still on fire and their eyes moist with tears. Then they writhed most sweetly. Yes, that was what Kobayashi would do, have Miki use the strap on Linda Shive. Tell her to really lay it on.

Tomi wore a single ivory *kanzashi*, an oval pin rather like a flattened Chinese chopstick, pushed sideways through her lacquered bun. Once, after Tomi visited Kobayashi wearing that same *kanzashi*, his lieutenants had reported the beating back of a rival gang's attempt to horn in on part of the gang's Nagoya *japayuki* territory. Kobayashi felt the *kanzashi* was lucky, so the thoughtful Tomi always wore it for him. To have a leisurely *kaiseki*, the food of the tea ceremony, was to enjoy a sensual pleasure exactly as it was enjoyed by the Tokugawa shoguns. It was impossible for the boorish *gaijin* to appreciate *kaiseki*.

After their fun with Linda Shive, he and Kao would drink Chivas Regal and eat macadamia nuts and talk baseball. Even

Kobayashi had to admit that after years of trying, Suntory hadn't quite mastered the knack of distilling Scotch whiskey. There was some elusive quality of the original that eluded them. Suntory tasted like imitation, Japanese-made Scotch whiskey, not the soul-calming original.

Kobayashi couldn't figure Suntory's failure. All that was required was to have a chemist analyze the stuff, then duplicate it. Surely they were up to that. That didn't seem too much to ask.

The lack of proper peat was widely thought to be the reason for Suntory's embarrassing failure. But the Scots just burned the peat, didn't they? They used it for fuel; it wasn't an actual ingredient. Also, heat was heat. What conceivable difference did it make if the mash was heated by burning peat or burning natural gas? Kobayashi found it hard to believe Suntory's management couldn't find a way to imitate peat, if that's what it took.

In order to protect Suntory's failure to clone British-made whiskey, the Japanese government had socked a luxury tax on foreign brands that was four times higher than anywhere in Europe. Annoyed distillers in Scotland claimed the tax was unique in the world. There were times when Kobayashi had a flickering of doubt about the wisdom of such levies.

That the boorish Americans would launch a season of frenzied bitching about Japanese trade practices at least once a year was as predictable as the rising sun. The season of the put-upon *gaijin*, ordinarily peaking after two or three weeks of name-calling, had become an annual ritual. The Japanese had learned to live with it.

Kobayashi paused in his thoughts while Tomi served him boiled *kabu*, a kind of turnip she knew he liked, and roast *tai*, a sea bream. He picked up a piece of nearly translucent *kabu* with his chopstick and sampled it. Delicious. The *tai* was good too. As fresh as the *buri* had been.

What Kobayashi found infuriating this year was that the Olofson administration had chosen to begin its mulelike braying on the eve of the Japan series. And the U.S. was a country that called itself civilized!

Tomorrow the Stars would tie the series. On Sunday, they

would win it. Kobayashi would just love to pit the Stars against the winner of the American "World" Series. Kobayashi would match Japanese discipline, proper form, and team unity against so-called American creativity any day of the year. "Creative" meant sloppy and lazy; "individuals" were losers. In such a confrontation, *doryoku* would carry the day.

To win from the beginning is to be the constant victor.

Kobayashi poured himself a tumbler of hot *sake* as Tomi brought the next course, a soup called *hashi ari,* and broiled *tako,* or octopus, the representative dish from the sea, and marinated mushrooms, *matsutake,* the chosen food from the mountains.

Kobayashi wondered where Kao was. Kao was late. He poured himself some more *sake.*

Tomi politely removed the tray, moving quietly so as not to disturb her master's thoughts. The Yokohama Bay Stars were in the Japan Series, and she assumed Kobayashi-*san* must have a lot on his mind.

But Kobayashi was not thinking about baseball. Kamina had disappeared, leaving empty cassettes and blood behind him. What did that all mean?

Kobayashi's manservant came to tell the *oyabun* that he had a call from Yokohama Chuo Hospital. Something terrible had happened to Kao-*san.* He had been shot from ambush.

First Kamina, now Kao. Kobayashi felt an unsamurai-like rush of anxiety course through the pit of his stomach. He rose to call the hospital.

TEN

There were no vast acres of parking lots surrounding Yokohama Stadium as was the fashion at suburban ballparks in the U.S. Instead, commuters from Yokohama's far-flung wards emerged from the *kannai* subway station two blocks from the stadium, just opposite the Hotel Sansei. Two blocks west of the stadium, fans from Tokyo arrived on the fast train via the JR Negishi Line.

The stadium, built in 1978, looked to James Burlane a lot like Oakland Coliseum. Did Oakland also have burnt-orange seats and a blue fence? He couldn't remember.

Burlane believed that as circumstance forged the individual, and as citizens reflected their many cities, the nature of the home park molded a baseball team. Yokohama Stadium, like many awful American ballparks built in the seventies and eighties, was perfectly symmetrical, which he felt somehow smothered colorful baseball. Actually, the round stadium was stylishly tilted like a beret; that is, the lip of the stadium behind home plate was higher than that behind center field. This rakish slant was meant to be high modern, Burlane supposed.

He knew that American stadium architects, beginning with a new park in Baltimore, had come to understand that baseball, like life, was most interesting when it was varied and asymmetrical.

The St. Louis Cardinals concentrated on the hit-and-run, base stealing, bunts, and defense because Busch Stadium was so huge few players were capable of knocking one out. The Boston Red Sox, with that short, high, right-field wall, over the years had given their fans sluggers from Ted Williams to Carl Yastrzemski. It was not for nothing that the legendary Yankees were called the Bronx Bombers; sluggers from Ruth to DiMaggio and Mantle had blasted them into the tenements—and the Mick did it from either side of the plate. The Giants of the Polo Grounds had filled that vast space in center field with Willie Mays. The Dodgers of Ebbetts Field were far more fun than they ever were in symmetrical, yawn, Anaheim.

Likewise, Burlane thought, the Japanese had an enclosed, island mind, while the Americans, formed on a vast frontier, had restless, on-the-edge imaginations.

As Burlane and Rene Alburo emerged from the stairs onto their section behind first base, they would hear a *hut, hut, hut* shouting on the field. This turned out to be Tanda Sugimoto, the Stars' center fielder and team captain, leading his mates in spirited pumping of knees. The Stars did not laze their way through this drill. They were energetic, high-pumping baseball players, packed with the spirit of competition. This was it, the sixth game, and they were down 3–2. Lose this one and they could cry in their Kirin.

After they had settled into their seats, plastic cups of beer in hand, Burlane focused his field glasses on the section behind third base as Alburo fell into a conversation with his neighbor, a passionate baseball fan and devotee of the Yokohama Bay Stars.

Burlane studied the spectators. Then he found him, flanked by *yakuza* soldiers where Kao and Kamina would have been.

He gave the glasses to Alburo. "Our man, right?"

Alburo refocused the glasses and studied the figure. "That's him. That's probably Ito, his third-in-command on his right where Kamina or Kao would ordinarily sit. I don't know the man on his left." Alburo gave the glasses back.

Burlane, amazed, watched the Stars do vigorous push-ups. Up, down. Up, down. Up, down. To him baseball meant batting practice and maybe a game of pepper to loosen up.

Alburo said, "My neighbor here says when Sagawa Sugar and Rice bought the team, the Stars were competitive, although maybe not as good as the Yomiuri Giants or the Lions. They brought on Taji Nakamura as manager to institute good, old-fashioned Bushido baseball."

Burlane shook his head. "So that's what this is."

"*Shi no renshu*, or death training, works on the assumption that hard work and practice will overcome everything. The pitchers are supposed to throw a minimum of three hundred pitches a day; the batters take one hundred shadow swings when they get up in the morning, and at practice it's fifty swings each against a right-hander and a left-hander, followed by a hundred against a batting machine."

"And then another fifty before bedtime, I bet." Burlane grinned.

Alburo said. "You guessed it. Before they go to bed it's another one hundred shadow swings."

Burlane burst out laughing. "I was just kidding. What on earth are you saying? Is your neighbor making this up?"

"I don't think so. He says the Stars have instituted *gattsu*, or guts, drills for players who commit errors. The infielders are given the one-thousand-*fungo* drill."

On the field, the Stars did squat-jumps in unison.

"The one thousand *fungo*?"

"A player fields ground balls until he drops, which is usually after three or four hundred. The outfielders have a one-hundred-fly-ball drill. One hit far to his right. The other hit to his left. The next over his head. The idea is to keep him running."

"Whoa! The poor fucking Stars."

"This is to instill *yamato damashi*."

Burlane adjusted his binoculars, watching the sweating faces of the Stars as they did their squat-jumps. "Which is?"

"Japanese fighting spirit. Also *doryoku*. Effort. Same thing."

"An athletic boot camp!"

"That's what it amounts to, apparently."

The Stars fans, bearing orange plastic noisemakers that were combination rattles and megaphones, began a whack, whack, whacking sound in unison. Then, upon the instructions of a man with a microphone, they began a chant.

As they did, the Stars leaped up and began running in place again, kicking their knees as high as they could.

Seeing this, the fans increased the volume of their whacking and chanting.

Burlane said, "What are they saying?"

Alburo pursed his lips. "Nothing very imaginative. Go Stars Go. Go Stars Go."

"It's like a high school football game. Jesus!"

On the field, the Stars' Billy Radford, whom Burlane knew had played first base for the Houston Astros in his prime, performed the warm-up calisthenics along with his mates, but perhaps less energetically.

Burlane said, "Billy Radford used to play first base for the Houston Astros. Does you friend know the dope on him here in Japan? How old is he?"

Alburo conferred with his neighbor and said, "He says Belting Billy is now thirty-eight years old. He hit forty-six home runs this year, which is one of the reasons why the Stars made the series. He says Radford's forty-six home runs are the reason he's allowed to chew bubble gum while he plays."

"I see. Does your neighbor know the story with the black dude for the Lions?"

In right field, the Seibu Lions, including an African-American *gaijin*, did energetic squat-jumps in tight unison.

Alburo said, "The black man is Terry Williams. He has speed and is quick off the ball. He's a switch hitter and has a good arm. He also batted three-twenty-two and stole forty bases this year. But he only hit eighteen home runs, not good for an import."

"No?"

"He says Japanese managers have lots of players who can hit for average and steal bases. That's not what they want from imports. They want big macho sluggers. Guys who can knock 'em over the fence."

"I see." Burlane zeroed in on a right-hander warming up in the bull pen. It looked to Burlane like he was throwing fastballs full throttle. "Who's the guy warming up?"

"That would be Tobi Inouye. The Stars are starting him for the third time in the series. When he gets tired, he starts getting wild, my neighbor says."

"It's crazy, throwing that hard before the game starts. Guy's gotta be a fucking masochist."

"He wants to show the fans that he's ready, and he's not afraid of a little hard work."

Burlane shook his head.

Alburo said, "Last season, Nakamura used his ace reliever, Jojo Mieno, almost every day, and when he complained that he needed a rest once in a while, the Stars traded him to Seibu. He didn't have fighting spirit. He was not a man. He lacked *giri* to the team. Trading him was in the interest of *wa*."

"Well, I should hope so. Nobody needs a player who's dogging it," Burlane said. "What happened then?"

"Seibu rested him once in a while, and this season he leads the league in saves. In fact, it was Mieno who supposedly got Seibu to the series. Now, if the game's on the line in the late inning, the Stars will have to face his fastball."

"Oops!"

"My neighbor says the Stars pitchers suffer the most. Not only do they throw long and hard at practice every day, but in a game they're expected to throw the ball as hard as they can with every pitch. Doctors have been telling management this isn't good for a pitcher's arm, but they won't listen. In an important game, in order to show that he has *yamato damashi*, Nakamura is expected to use every pitcher on the staff. He uses starters as relievers, and nobody gets a rest."

The Stars switched to an exercise in which they stood with legs wide, arms extended, and twisted left, right, left, right.

"My neighbor says the Stars management puts much importance on how many complete games a starter can pitch. To make that work, a club needs a rotation of four or even five quality starters. The Stars had four, but one by one, their arms started going lame. Nakamura responded by making them throw more pitches every day."

"Why, for God's sake?"

Alburo looked amused. "Why, to strengthen their arms. Practice makes perfect, my neighbor says. He says the Stars have got *yamato damashi*, so he's hopeful."

"Who replaced Jojo Mieno for the Stars?"

"Shin Ozawa, a hard-throwing right-hander who's been out with a sore arm for the last two months. The club gambled heavily on Ozawa, who says he's now ready to throw. My friend says we'll see."

The Stars suddenly gave up their calisthenics and began running in a thundering herd around the stadium.

Alburo said, "My friend here says if Tanda Sugimoto stays hot and Radford keeps slamming them, and Shin Ozawa can come on in the late innings, then the Stars should have a shot. Bushido baseball will triumph. If not, then the owners have a lot of explaining to do."

ELEVEN

The report on Nobito Kao was not good. He was still alive and would likely remain so, but the doctors said whoever had ambushed him had used hollow rounds that exploded on impact. There was no chance, none, that doctors could reconstruct his genitals.

Unfortunately, Kao had fallen to his knees after the first shot, and his friends said he remained there for a moment in shock, paralyzed by pain. The doctors estimated his assailant then laid four more rounds on Kao's crotch, one on top of the other, although they conceded that was just a ballpark number. From three to five additional rounds, somewhere in that range. The damage was so severe they couldn't do anything but guess. After much polite talk, they finally came right out and said it:

Two shreds of skin remained between Nobito Kao's legs; don't ask about medical miracles.

The police across the street at the base of Osanbashi pier had acted immediately and sealed off the harbor at the bottom of the *kannai*, but found nothing. Nobody had heard the shots fired. The assailant had obviously used a silencer, the police said. And with accuracy like that, laying one shot on another, they were dealing with a professional.

Kobayashi knew the police had concluded this was *yakuza* on *yakuza*, and were waiting to see whether they had a full-scale war on their hands, or whether cooler heads would prevail. But the marksman was not *yakuza*, Kobayashi knew. He was working for Jack Shive, and was most likely a longnose. Longnoses operated according to invisible limits that Kobayashi didn't understand but knew existed. He was stunned that one could be so coldhearted and brutal as to have done something like that to Kao. He had obviously held his sights on Kao's crotch and pumped determinedly away until there was nothing left. A disciplined *yakuza* soldier could have done that, maybe, but not a longnose. It wasn't their style; it was not how they played.

Kobayashi did not like it that his adversary was playing out of form. What kind of treacherous longnose would do this, who even in the CIA? The *oyabun* didn't like the unpredictable.

The fluttering returned to his stomach.

That morning, Kamina's staff searched the garden again, and found more blood. But Kamina was not to be found. He was likely dead, Kobayashi figured. The garden was at the edge of a cliff. If an assassin had thrown his body over the precipice, it would have been washed to the sea by the tide, food for the crabs.

The Stars had made the World Series by competing, not by begging or trying to change the rules. The American complaints about Japanese trade practices were longnose *gaijin* envy at a superior culture, nothing more. Envy was a pitiful emotion. Losers envied. Kobayashi did not envy.

Also, since when did losers dictate terms to winners?

The last time Kobayashi heard the story, it was General Douglas MacArthur who called the shots after the war, not Emperor Hirohito.

Try as he might, Shoji Kobayashi could not understand the unfathomable Americans. Each night on the news, he and the astonished Japanese public watched televised glimpses of life in the filthy, barbarous pit that was America. Riots. The homeless. The unemployed. The ignored. Night after night, it was a nonstop spectacle of the alleged superpower lurching drunkenly toward the next century.

The Americans were always yapping about their so-called creativity. Did the *gaijin* think they could force the Japanese to consume trash? Did they expect Japan to voluntarily reduce its standard of living because of some odd and vague Western notion of "fairness"—in fact, ill-disguised sour grapes?

Fairness was not to envy a country that actually worked; fairness was to live by the competitive ideal you self-righteously held up as the standard for everybody else to observe. The willfully stupid *gaijin* embarrassed themselves with their sniveling and whining.

The Japanese didn't tell the Americans how to run their lives. Did Jack Shive honestly think a *yakuza oyabun* would yield to cowardly ambush? Did he? If Shive wanted to play by *yakuza* rules in Takeshita-*kai*'s home park, Shoji Kobayashi would have to show him what playing by *yakuza* rules was all about.

Few men are grateful for advice.

TWELVE

The Stars' second baseman, Joichi Kama, led off the bottom of the third with the score tied 0–0. He threw with his right arm, but batted leftie.

James Burlane noted the wad of tobacco in Kama's mouth. He said Nellie Fox, the second baseman for the go-go Chicago White Sox when Burlane was a kid, had similarly played with a wad of goo in his cheeks. Like Kama, he threw rightie and batted leftie.

"You know about Nellie Fox?"

"Well, sure. A little."

"Kama's supposed to look like Nellie Fox. But I guess I should tell you the story. It's in all the papers." Alburo said Kama's father had been captured by the American army at Guadalcanal, and a G.I. prison guard, a high school teacher, taught him English, mostly by telling him stories about the Chicago White Sox and physically demonstrating the action to match such words as run, catch, and throw. After the war, Kama's father corresponded with the American, who kept him informed of the Sox's latest woes and occasional triumphs.

When young Kama grew up to become a baseball player, he

decided to honor his father's friendship with the American by
becoming a Japanese Nellie Fox. Fox batted leftie and hit second
in the order; Kama batted leftie, second in the order. Fox played
with a wad of tobacco in his cheek. So did Kama, although it was
less flamboyant than Fox's trademark puffed-out cheek. Fox
choked up on a short, thick-handled bat. Kama also used a bottle
bat. Fox was a never-quit fighter. So was Joichi Kama.

Kama squirted a tidy splat of goo on the ground to show his
disdain for the Lions rightie, Jiro Kawana. A murmur rippled
through the stands. Such a wretched habit. Filthy. Yuch! Kama
spit tobacco like the disgusting, filthy American players. Ooooh!
As it was supposed to, the crowd moaned at Joichi Kama imitat-
ing Nellie Fox.

Kama settled in Nellie Fox-deep in the box and took a couple
of preemptive Nellie Fox-swings. He cocked his bat and concentrated, Nellie Fox-style, an old-fashioned ball player doing his
job.

Kawana gave a terrific kick and came at him high, inside, and
very fast.

Kama leaned coolly back. He spit disdainfully. He was Nellie
Fox all the way. He wiped his mouth with the back of his hand
and took a couple more practice swings. After a brushback like
that, Kama/Fox was entitled.

Kawana tried to slip a breaking ball past Joichi Kama, but
Kama slapped it into center field for a sweet single, Nellie Fox-
style.

Standing on first base, grinning, the scrappy Kama spit
again.

Burlane appreciated the performance, and watched it with a
critical eye.

Kama had obviously watched a lot of old film of Nellie Fox.
He knew the way Fox choked up on his fat-handled bat and
glanced at his feet as he settled in at the plate. There was the
obligatory spit of tobacco to please the fans.

Fox was said to be an old-fashioned kind of baseball player.
You could always count on him to get a piece of the ball on a

hit-and-run. And he had a hell-it-ain't-nothing' look on his face after he'd looped one of his chickenshit singles over the first baseman's head.

As far as Burlane could tell, Joichi Kama had mastered every major Nellie Fox mannerism except the half-embarrassed yet triumphant aw-shit-folks look on Fox's face as he stood on first base. Kama either wasn't aware of the look or forgot it in the excitement of having led off with a crisp single. Also, when Kama let fly with the goo, they were such prissy, teensy-weensy, sanitary little squirts as to hardly qualify as spitting at all.

Burlane wondered if Kama was really spitting. Maybe he wasn't. Maybe those were pretend spits and that was a pretend wad of tobacco in Kama's pretend bad-boy cheeks.

But Burlane knew those complaints were picky-picky, something only an observant Nellie Fox fan would probably know. There was something more fundamentally wrong with the performance. Nellie Fox was Nellie Fox. An original. He wasn't trying to imitate Ty Cobb or Lou Boudreau. The fans wanted to watch him, Nellie Fox. Nellie Fox was not a sissy spitter. He was from Allentown, Pennsylvania, dammit, not Nakajima, Japan.

When Kama reached first base he was, for the briefest of moments, himself. Then he spit. The fans expected him to spit like Nellie Fox.

When the pitcher toed the rubber, Kama took his lead, just like the gritty little Nellie Fox.

Joichi Kama was on with Tanda Sugimoto and Billy Radford coming up. The Stars had a rally going.

Burlane said, "Now's the time to throw our pitch, I think. See what he does with it. You want to see that he gets to the package. Spend what you have to get the job done. Here, give 'em a Benjie. It's Jack Shive's money, not ours. Here." Burlane gave him a crisp new bill.

"It will be my pleasure," Alburo said.

"And could you bring us each a beer and a couple of doggies? They got hot dogs out there, I saw 'em. Shive'll spring. In view of what I gotta do tonight, the least he can do is see that I'm fed."

"Beer and hot dogs. Got it."

"Lots of mustard on mine, please, and chopped onions if they've got 'em. I see these people eating squid. This is a baseball game. Jesus!"

"No, no, no," Alburo said. "This is *besuboru*."

THIRTEEN

All right!

A Star on first and the heart of the Stars' batting order coming up. Shoji Kobayashi felt a rush of confidence. Sagawa Sugar and Rice paid top yen for the Stars to score runs, and he wanted runs scored. He wanted the pennant flying over Yokohama Stadium.

On first, Joichi Kama did his best to distract Kawana. Hands outstretched, Kama stretched his lead as wide as possible, planting the question in Kawana's mind: Was he getting ready to steal?

Kawana stepped off the rubber.

"Excuse me, Kobayashi-san?"

"Huh?"

Ito bowed his head. "This came for you. 'Extremely urgent,' the kid said. It was given to him by a man who gave him a U.S. one-hundred-dollar bill and disappeared." He handed Kobayashi a large envelope.

Kobayashi took the envelope, but made no attempt to open it. The sender had paid U.S. dollars for its delivery; after what had happened to Kao, Kobayashi knew it was not good. He'd watch Kama first, then deal with whatever was in the envelope.

He'd invested hundreds of millions of yen in *japayuki* and *shabu* earnings in the Stars; they were going to win the pennant, and no sorehead *gaijin* was going to prevent him from enjoying the triumph. He would not allow it to happen. No.

He thought *bunt*.

Ito said, "A bunt, do you think?"

Kobayashi fiddled with the envelope in his lap. He made a bunting motion with his hands.

He thumped the envelope with his forefinger and bent it slightly. Photographs. There were photographs in the envelope. He could feel them.

Photographs of Kamina? Likely. He was obviously dealing with one very mean *gaijin*. He wanted to open it, but didn't. Tanda the Panda was due up for the Stars.

FOURTEEN

Tanda Sugimoto stepped to the plate.

James Burlane said, "Well, Kobayashi must be pleased. Stars've got a leftie Sugimoto batting against rightie Kawana and a duck on. What does it say about this guy? He's the captain, isn't he? Probably carries his weight."

Alburo translated from the program. "It says Tanda Sugimoto had a three-twenty-one season, third best in the Central League. He's a pull hitter with modest power. He's a switch-hitter, but he's better batting southpaw than right-handed. He got hot in September when the Stars came from eight games behind to win the Central Division pennant. They call him Tanda the Panda or the Panda Man."

Using the glasses, Burlane saw Kobayashi make a bunting motion with his hands. His friend nodded his head vigorously in agreement.

Did they think the Panda Man was going to bunt? This was only the top of the third. A .321 switch-hitter with a rightie on the mound and a duckie-wuck on first? The stats said righties were Panda meat.

The Lions manager moved his infield in.

The men to Alburo's right jabbered excitedly.

Burlane said, "What're they saying, Rene?"

"They say he's going to bunt."

Kawana delivered.

Sugimoto fouled a bunt off the tip of his bat.

"What's going on here?"

"Don't ask me. We play basketball in the Philippines, and I've never gotten involved in baseball in the United States."

Burlane said, "With the infield in like that, Sugimoto should be able to drill one right past them. Move his man to third." He thought: *It's only the third inning. You've got your main man at the plate, sport. Swing the fucking bat. Take a chance.*

Sugimoto bunted Kawana's next pitch down the third baseline, but the Lions' third baseman took it on the run to throw him out.

Kobayashi and his companions nodded their heads. The play had gone as they expected; Kama was in scoring position on second.

Then Kawana tightened his stuff.

Blasting Billy Radford, swinging with a mighty ripple, popped out.

And finally, with Joichi Kama still waiting on second base, the Stars' right fielder, Fuji Matsumoto, struck out with his bat on his shoulder.

FIFTEEN

James Burlane still couldn't figure the Stars' strategy. Tanda Sugimoto was a leftie who pulled the ball. A single into right field would have pushed Kama to third base, and he'd have scored on the fly ball that followed, but no. A bunt. A leftie had a one-step head start on a bunt, yes, but a pull-hitting leftie could also push the runner to third with a single, no sweat.

The Stars' overworked pitchers were arm weary. They needed the runs. Burlane couldn't figure it.

Then he understood. Of course. The sacrifice! It was a team thing. This was a team way to play baseball. To move a runner around the bases Japanese-style required the successive skills of several players rather than one big basher. The leadoff hitter had to get on base. The batter after him had to successfully bunt. Then two more players had a shot at bringing him home.

The Japanese liked roles and duty. They played team baseball, the way coaches taught it in Little League, all rah-rah and do-our-damnedest and we're-in-this-together-guys. They hadn't wanted heroics out of Tanda Sugimoto. He might have been the hard-hitting and much-loved Tanda the Panda, but before anything else the Stars manager wanted discipline and obedience.

Sacrifice bunt. Sacrifice fly. The very terms had a Japanese ring to them.

Burlane thought baseball was a good television game because the viewer was treated to close-ups of pitchers and batters locked in one-on-one competition. In football the combatants' faces were covered by helmets; in basketball, they bounded up and down the court like hyperactive kangaroos.

The stolid and unemotional second baseman Ryne Sandberg, a smooth-fielding Cubs slugger, hauled down the big contracts but somehow didn't have the spark or sense of pizzazz that landed him in the strato-bucks sports ads. Sandberg was quiet and unemotional, a private kind of guy, but a real fighter. He did his best for the Cubs and the Cubs fans every day, then went home to his wife and family. Ryne Sandberg was a second baseman à la Nippon. When he thought his skills had eroded and he was no longer contributing, he abruptly retired without a hint of whining.

A thoroughly American player was Pittsburgh Pirate right-hander Bob Walk, an unkempt, hulking man with the face of a morose hound. Walk would probably never make anybody's all-star team. His face said "addicted to *Mad* comics" or "plays a real mean whorehouse piano." Burlane liked Walk's goofy slouch and earnest, furrowed brows as he concentrated on his catcher's signal. If ever a pitcher's face pleaded to the strikeout gods for deliverance from Salinas or Walla Walla—a fate almost as bad as no baseball at all—it was Bob Walk.

Billy Radford was on deck.

Burlane could feel the tension in the air.

Billy Radford was about to take on the former Stars fireballer, Jojo Mieno, who had replaced the tiring Jiro Kawana.

Alburo said, "*Shobu.* My neighbor says this is big, big *shobu.*"

"*Shobu* being?"

"What your Mr. Hemingway would call *mano-a-mano*, a man-to-man showdown. It's like a swordfight or a duel. It's the essence of sumo, for example. My neighbor says the greatest *shobu* in the history of baseball was in the emperor's first baseball game, a momentous encounter between pitcher Minoru Morayama of the Hanshin Tigers and Shigeo Nagashima of the Yomiuri Giants."

"I would have thought that was the encounter between Ralph Branca and Bobby Thompson in the Polo Grounds, but never mind. What happened in the great Japanese *shobu?*"

Alburo consulted his neighbor.

"He says the score was tied four-to-four in the eighth inning, with the emperor scheduled to depart shortly. No one wanted him to leave before the end of the game. The Tiger manager, filled with *doryoku,* brought on Morayama, a rookie with an incredible fastball. The day before, Morayama had struck out the Giant side in the ninth, Nagashima included."

"Strong-armed kid firing aspirins in the clutch. All right."

"The emperor hung around to watch Nagashima bat once more. On a two-two count, Morayama threw Nagashima an inside fastball that Nagashima knocked ten rows into the left-field stands."

"What happened then?"

His neighbor, who was listening too but not understanding Alburo's English explanation, was quick to supply the answer.

"Shigeo Nagashima went on to win six batting titles. He played third base—quicker than Brooks Robinson, my friend says. He says Nagashima was the most popular figure in the history of sports. More famous than Babe Ruth, he says; Joe Dimaggio and Joe Namath and Muhammad Ali were nothing compared to Nagashima. He says Pelé might compare, or Michael Jordan, but we should keep in mind Nagashima had no detractors. None. Everybody in Japan loved him. They called him 'Burning Man,' a tribute to his fighting spirit. The women said he was *otoko rashii,* manly."

"What became of poor Morayama?"

"He had a brilliant career, but that one home run was like a permanent asterisk beside his name. Morayama and Nagashima developed a bitter rivalry. Morayama vowed to get his fifteen hundredth and two thousandth strikeout against Nagashima, and kept his word both times. But until the day he retired, he remained the man who had served Shigeo Nagashima a sayonara home-run ball in front of the emperor."

Burlane thought Billy Radford had something special going for him too, as he stepped coolly to the plate. Radford had baggy eyes and was a bit jowly. He was slightly thick around the middle, but not yet Ruthian in girth. Caught up in the spirit of *shobu*, he sucked in his mighty gut, tugged coolly at his jock strap, and blew a pink bubble. He took a couple of practice swings and gave his butt a little wiggle. He was ready.

There were no ducks on, and no score. Batters on both sides had been having their problems. But now, with Billy Radford facing Jojo Mieno, the fans wanted action. Radford had popped out in his last at bat. He was due.

The fans, following instructions from a loudspeaker, began a chant, in such English as they could collectively manage, a tribute to the *gaijin* slugger come *shobu* time: "*Wwwaaaadfowd, Wwwaaaadfowd, Wwwaaaadfowd! Bwwwaaassst one Biwwy!*"

Burlane, grinning, was moved to join them in their spirited support of the hairy barbarian. He cupped his hands around his mouth and yelled, "Do it, Billy, do it, you big tub of lard. Splash that sucker in Yokohama Bay!"

His neighbors, Stars fans, were amused at the solo, American-style cheer. They had momentarily forgotten the Japanese-*gaijin* business. Billy Radford was a Star. He was theirs. He wanted to win the pennant as much as they did.

"*Wwwaaaadfowd, Wwwaaaadfowd, Wwwaaaadfowd! Bwwaasst one Biwwy!*"

Billy Radford blew another bubble and waved his timber menacingly.

Mieno kicked high and, with a Nolan Ryan grunt, delivered his first pitch, a searing fastball.

Radford, concentrating on the ball, swung from his heels and extended his arms.

The ball exploded off his bat with an echoing *ccrraacckkk* and sailed high, high, high over the left-field wall. The home fans leaped to their feet, wild with delight. This was one of those truly nutty homers they would watch again on television when they got home. They would get to tell their friends how they had been there the day Billy Radford, on the line come *shobu* time, flat muscled Jojo Mieno's best heat outta the place. Put it into orbit. That'd show Mieno a few things.

Flashing a big *gaijin* smile, Radford tugged at his jock as he watched the ball, seeming extrawhite in the arc lights, soar out of the stadium. Then he began a leisurely, triumphant trot around the bases. Let them sneer at his paunch if they would. For the moment it was no beer belly; now it was a noble gut.

Radford gave the fans a bubble and a thumb-up as he crossed the plate. The Japanese paid him to hit homers, and, by God, Bwwwaaasssting Biwwwy Wwwaaaadfowd had delivered. He had bwasted home the bwubber and put the Stars up, 1–0.

Just six more outs. If only the Stars' *soba*-armed pitchers had hair enough to ride out the last two innings. The Lions had been hitting the ball hard all day, but always straight at someone. They had the top of their order coming up, and if anybody was ever due, it was them, and everybody in the park knew it.

SIXTEEN

Tobi Inouye was uncertain at his good fortune of being up 1–0 in the top of the eighth. He was getting a trifle pooped, yes, but under the circumstances it would be suicidal to tell that to Nakamura.

If Inouye could fight through it, if he could hang tough, he could win it, go the full nine. Just two innings. Six outs. It was unlikely that Jojo Mieno would give up another run, so he'd have to blank 'em to do it.

On the public address system, the fans were told that Radford's home run was only the second four-bagger Jojo Mieno had given up all year.

It was obvious from the worried look in Nakamura's eye that Inouye was tiring fast. "Keep 'em down," he had told Inouye before the game. "Keep 'em down. When you start floating them, they start hitting them."

Well, keeping them low was something else after you had pitched twenty-six innings in six days on top of going the distance for two wins in the last five days of the Central Division pennant race.

When the announcement was made that Billy Radford's home run had cleared Yokohama Park and bounced on the street in front of the YMCA, the crowd, responding enthusiastically to a loudspeaker prompting, rose and chanted:

"Biwwy, Biwwy, Biwwy, Biwwy, Biwwy, Biwwy."

In the excitement of the moment, Tobi Inouye reared back and threw the first pitch . . .

Awwwwwwww! High.

From first base, Billy Radford, who used the same English in his on-the-field exhortations as he had used with the Astros, said, "Hon now, big guy. 'Hon now. This guy's ass is pork, babe. Your bacon."

Inouye delivered again.

Awwwwwwww! High.

"Couldn't find his dick with both hands, Tobi. Do it."

High.

Inouye's mouth was dry. If fighting spirit could be measured, he had it in abundance, but his arm had plain wilted. Even if he did bring his pitches down, what then? He didn't have any zip left.

He caught the ball from the catcher and glanced to the dugout. Nakamura, grimacing, nodded: Do it.

Such craziness.

Inouye delivered, hoping he hadn't served up a home-run ball.

He gave up two straight walks. One on four straight balls, the second on three straight balls and then a luck-out strike, followed by another ball.

The Seibu Lions now had the tying and winning runs on with no outs.

SEVENTEEN

As Taji Nakamura strolled to the mound to talk to his pitcher, he signaled to the bullpen for Shin Ozawa to begin warming up.

Behind third base, Shoji Kobayashi fiddled with the mystery envelope, which lay unopened in his lap. Kobayashi liked Tobi Inouye's complete game numbers. This was still baseball, a nine-inning game. It wasn't a five-inning game. Or a three-inning game. Or a one-inning game. There was something to be said for a pitcher with the grit to go a full nine.

Watching this, Kobayashi signaled for another beer.

On the mound, a concerned Taji Nakamura, his mouth dry, knew he should give Inouye the hook immediately, but Kobayashi was watching from behind third base, and Kobayashi liked to see a pitcher go all the way; he wanted his pitchers to be men.

If Nakamura was to lose the game, he knew it was wise to lose it Kobayashi's way. Kobayashi was the owner; Nakamura was only the manager. American managers had to win, yes, but, with the exception of Yankee skippers under George Steinbrenner, they ordinarily called the shots on the field; there were no Tommy Lasordas or Whitey Herzogs in Japanese baseball, wheeling and dealing their way to pennants. In Japan, a club had a game form, approved of by the owner, and it was followed to the letter.

For the Stars, that meant Bushido *besuboru.*

While Kobayashi waited for Nakamura to palaver with Tobi Inouye on the mound, he studied the columns of numbers in the program. He sucked the sweet, hoppy foam from the top of his plastic cup of Asahi and took a sip.

Kobayashi liked it that baseball invited statistics. A pitcher either threw a strike or he didn't; the ball either got hit or it didn't. The same for a batter. When he stepped up to the plate, he either did or he didn't.

When a Yokohama player came looking for a raise, the first thing Taji Nakamura did was to sit down with him and say, "Okay, kid, let's take a look at the stats and see what they have to say." Once, at Takeshita-*kai*'s place on the coast, Nakamura, drunk, did imitations of his heart-to-hearts with players with dreams of matching the salaries they'd been reading about in the newspapers.

Nakamura said if a ball player led with a good batting average, he dinged him for his lack of power. If the player thought he should be paid more for his power, Nakamura shook his head solemnly at his lamentable number of strikeouts. If the player thought he played good defense, Nakamura brought him down with his lack of range. Just how many chances did he handle compared to other players at his position? Some guys were quick enough to be worth a few errors. Guys with lead feet had thick necks from watching catchable ground balls bounce by for cheapie singles.

There were numbers for everything. Unfortunately, one thing numbers didn't cover was injuries. What was Nakamura supposed to do with a pitcher who said he had a sore arm? There was no way to objectively measure pain, a machine with a needle that registered degree of discomfort. Nakamura had to take an athlete's word for it.

Take Shin Ozawa. Ozawa knew if his arm remained sore he

would have to give up fondling rosin bags for a living. A pitcher's natural inclination, at the first twinge of pain, was to give his arm a rest. Ozawa had fretted over his arm for months now. He said it hurt to come over the top, and that's where his fastball was. He had tried to deliver three-quarter sidearm, but that didn't work. The heat wasn't there.

Ozawa was a stopper. He lived and died by his heat. If there were ducks on, a medium-speed fastball was downright dangerous.

The club surgeon once showed Kobayashi a plastic model of the human shoulder, and gave the *oyabun* an involved technical explanation about something called a rotor cuff, which was supposed to be what was wrong with Ozawa's arm. Buying Ozawa had been Kobayashi's idea, and everybody knew it. He didn't want to hear crap about rotor cuffs.

Baseball was zen. One concentrated. One practiced. One overcame pain.

On the mound, his time up, Nakamura gave the ball to Inouye and said, "One more, Tobi. One more and we'll see what happens. Do your best to keep 'em down. If you can keep 'em down maybe we can work our way out of this mess. Ozawa needs to warm up, in any event."

Inouye was aware of the pressure on Nakamura. The responsible, sensible thing was to be honest, but that would disturb the *wa*. He didn't want it said that he was a quitter. "I'll do my best, I really will," he said.

"That's all anybody asks, Tobi. Let's both hope you can do it." Nakamura sighed and strode back to the dugout.

In the bullpen, the lame-armed Shin Ozawa, his eye on the fading Inouye, worked earnestly.

In the dugout, Taji Nakamura leaned against the wall and popped a fresh stick of Juicy Fruit.

Tobi Inouye, summoning all the fighting spirit he could muster and concentrating on good form, hit the third batter in the small of his back with a curve ball that didn't curve. Inouye had done everything right; his form was perfect; but there was no snap left in his wrist.

In the dugout, Nakamura waved in Shin Ozawa from the bullpen.

EIGHTEEN

The way Shoji Kobayashi saw it, so Shin Ozawa's arm was a little sore. Getting to the series was a once-in-a-lifetime thing. A series was a new season. Seven games. Win four of the seven. That's all it took.

If Ozawa's arm was sore, it would have all winter to rest. Why not shoot it up with something? Surely there was something the doctors could do. Weren't they always telling themselves that Japanese medicine was the best in the world? But no. They said pain was the body's way of telling the brain that something was hurt and needed rest. If you took away the pain, you took away the warning.

The Americans had taken to recording the speed of a pitcher's fastball, and when his numbers were too low, the manager gave him the hook. Kobayashi suspected that a lot of American pitchers started checking out the bullpen action even before they finished the five innings required to book a win. The fewer pitches they had to throw to win a game, the longer their career lasted. No *giri* to the team. No fighting spirit. The Yokohama Bay Stars were men.

On the mound, Shin Ozawa fiddled with the rubber with his spikes. He signaled that he was ready. Time to earn his yen.

Terry Williams stepped to the plate with a pond full of ducks. He was no clutch artist. He had his pride.

Shobu!

Shin Ozawa paused, ball cradled at his waist, then delivered.

Pennant on the line.

Gattsu time.

If Shin Ozawa lost *shobu* to a black man in the Japan Series, Kobayashi would see to it that he never played another game of baseball in Japan, for the Stars or for anybody else.

High. Ball one.

Kobayashi felt a pitcher's first loyalty ought to be to his team and his fans, then to his precious arm.

Ozawa started to massage his right shoulder with his glove, then quickly dropped his hand. He delivered his second pitch.

Strike one. A gift from the umpire. Ozawa punched his mitt.

Kobayashi couldn't stand it anymore. Somehow emboldened by Ozawa's high strike, he ripped open the envelope and took a look at what was inside.

He stared, transfixed.

Kamina!

Kobayashi didn't see Terry Williams turn on Shin Ozawa's next pitch, what had once been his famous fastball. He only heard the sound of bat meeting ball that echoed across the *kannai* like the crack of a rifle.

NINETEEN

The Takeshita-*kai* camera crews filmed their studio productions in two locations: at the gang's seaside retreat where Tsutomu Kamina lived, and in the top floor of Kobayashi's Yokohama town house. The retreat had a full dungeon with various racks and whips and a drawer full of clamps and clothespins which the film crews used on Linda while they filmed her. The studio in the town house, while less ambitious and with a smaller selection of rods, quirts, and paddles in stock, nevertheless had everything it needed in the way of lights and reflectors to capture the charms of female suffering in all their many subtleties.

Linda Shive had her own room at the retreat. When she was imprisoned in Yokohama, she was kept in one of two adjoining apartments Takeshita-*kai* kept for Kao and Miki to use on their many trips up from Manila.

Now, locked in Kobayashi's apartment—which meant more bad shit coming up—she read one of several paperback Agatha Christie mysteries that Miki had brought from Manila on her latest trip. Linda's left ankle was enclosed in a metal anklet tethered to the top rail of the metal footboard by a light chain.

It struck Linda that Christie's charm lay in the fact that the puzzle was the thing that interested her, the mystery. The stories were set in the 1920s and 1930s, yet the reader rarely got a hint that any of her characters were disturbed about their upstairs/downstairs world. The maids made beds. The cooks cooked. The gardeners spread dung. Everybody was happy . . .

. . . until the untoward digging up of a young man's body by a curious hound. Then, as a favor to the local innkeeper, the Belgian with the waxed mustaches began asking questions. A question here. A question there.

Linda Shive wanted to get lost in a puzzle. Screw the real world. She had a remote if she wanted to watch television, but she'd watched CNN and CBS until she thought she would puke the next time she laid eyes on Joie Chen or Dan Rather. She had even seen her own father on CNN. He was coming to Japan to talk about trade.

Linda's father, an old pal of Congressman Richard Gephardt of Missouri, was a member of the take-no-crap-from-Nippon club, and she was a *waslik japayuki.* Wonderful. Her parents had surely become alarmed by now, but what had they done? What could they do even if they had somehow discovered her fate? Send in the Marines?

Down the hall, they were watching the Stars play the Seibu Lions on television. Miki said Kobayashi owned the Stars through a dummy company. In his enthusiasm, Kobayashi allowed himself to show some emotion about the Stars.

Once, Kobayashi had unaccountably taken her into a room filled with swords and photographs of Japanese godfathers and baseball players. Something was on his mind, and he wanted the longnose girl to know about it.

With Miki translating, Kobayashi-*san* told her Sachio Kinugasa played third base for the Hiroshima Carp from October 18, 1970, until October 22, 1987, during which he played 2,215 games, eclipsing Gehrig's record of 2,130 games. At 1,130 games, he suffered a broken shoulder blade from a pitched ball, but he kept playing.

The Baltimore Orioles shortstop Cal Ripken Jr. was aiming for Gehrig's record, but Ripken had an odd form; when he batted, he held his fists the wrong way, and he pointed the tip of his bat to the rear. Also, he sometimes backhanded the ball when it was hit straight at him. How could American fans admire a player with flawed form?

Kobayashi said Japanese players learned to play *besuboru* the correct way. Kinugasa had perfect form. He took a minimum of a hundred practice swings a day.

Linda, thinking that a flattered Kobayashi might be a less sadistic *oyabun*, but knowing better, asked him about Sadaharu Oh. Was it true that Oh was the greatest home-run hitter of all time, not Babe Ruth? He had broken all of Ruth's and Hank Aaron's records, hadn't he? The greatest home-run hitter of all time was Japanese, not American.

Kobayashi said Oh's father was Chinese. Sadaharu Oh carried a Taiwanese passport his entire life. Didn't Ms. Shive know that? Then he added that Kinugasa was, in fact, half black. Shigeo Nagashima, who hit a *sayonara* home run in the emperor's first baseball game, was really Korean. Masaichi Kaneda, the god of pitching, who won four hundred games in his career and struck out Mickey Mantle three straight times in 1955, was half Korean.

He said the greatest pure Japanese player of all time was Kazuhisa Inao. In the 1958 Japan Series against the Yomiuri Giants, Iron Man Inao won all four games for the Nihitetsu Lions. He started five of the seven games and pitched forty-seven innings, of which twenty-six were consecutively scoreless. He won twenty games each year of his eight-year career, and in 1961 won forty-two games. Inao played samurai baseball, Kobayashi said. He knew *doryoku*. If the Yokohama Bay Stars could find a pitcher like him, they would be unstoppable.

The country was turning soft, he said. Nowadays pitchers spent half their time worrying about their precious arms.

Then, his lecture on baseball completed, it was on with the show, and Kobayashi supervised the taping of Linda being buggered.

Now, Kobayashi was presumably at the game with Kamina and Kao. She wasn't interested in watching the game and didn't care who won. She preferred the company of Hercule Poirot and his little gray cells.

As Poirot and his friend Captain Hastings were having a charming lunch at the South Devonshire resort of Torquay—which Ms. Christie referred to as the English Riviera—the watchers down the hall burst into cheers. With her remote, Linda flipped on the tube to catch a beefy, redneck-looking long-nose trotting around the bases.

Through the excitement of the Japanese broadcasters, she gathered that this was Biwwy Wadfowd. The *gaijin* slugger, it seemed, had socked one over the wall for the Stars.

She punched off the set. Her eyes were tired; she lay back to rest. The more she slept the better. When she was asleep she didn't have to think about what was happening to her. Sleep was the greatest blessing.

TWENTY

Shoji Kobayashi left the stadium by an exit behind third base and emerged opposite Yokohama City Hall. He strode quickly, with a determined stride. He was uninterested in the company of his lieutenants, who trailed by a respectful distance; the *oyabun* was a man with a lot on his mind, and they knew it.

Kobayashi bore to the right, toward the harbor. He worked his way through the glut of people headed for the *kannai* subway station two blocks away, and turned left at the YMCA.

Behind him, in the crowd, James Burlane said, "Good. He's on his way back to his apartment. If he'd headed for the coast or somewhere, we risked losing him."

The door popped open.

Miki said, "Wake up."

"Huh?"

"Kobayashi called."

Linda looked puzzled.

"The Stars lost four to one. Kobayashi-*san* says we're going to have some fun."

Linda blinked. "If the Lions won, won't their fans be the ones throwing the parties?"

"I suspect this has more to do with what happened to Nobito Kao than baseball. Although I'm certain Kobayashi-*san* isn't happy about losing the series."

"What happened to Kao?"

"He was ambushed last night. Somebody laid five slugs on top of one another, right here." Miki tapped her crotch with her forefinger.

"What?"

"Quickly, quickly now."

"Kao?" Her father had sent someone for her.

"Never mind Kao. The streets are packed with people going home from the game, and we've got a lot of work to do . . ." Miki freed Linda's ankle from its tether. As she tucked the anklet and chain into her handbag, she said, "And Kamina is missing, you might be interested in knowing."

"Oh?"

"He missed the game today. The Stars in the Japan Series. It's a mystery."

"I see."

"I wouldn't get my hopes up if I were you. Nobody outplays Shoji Kobayashi. Nobody. He is fearless, and he will not yield or be intimidated."

"And he doesn't like what happened to Kao?"

Miki said, "He doesn't like that one bit. Guaranteed."

They followed Kobayashi to a town house a couple of blocks from the YMCA where Biwwy Wadfowd had bounced his biggie in the Stars' loss. This was in Tokiwa-Cho, which referred to a neighborhood rather than a street, as was the custom in the West. Tokiwa-Cho was a high-rent district in the *kannai*, almost directly behind centerfield.

A paragraph about the town house was one of the useless bits of information tucked into the JNP dossier on Kobayashi. The house was a copy of the New Orleans French Quarter residence of interior decorator Jacques LeFleur. Kobayashi had seen photographs of it in an architectural magazine and decided to have it copied.

Alburo, who was listening to the postgame wrap-up on his Walkman, said, "They're saying the Stars should have listened to the doctors instead of trying to play samurai *besuboru*. Taji Nakamura just plain pushed his pitchers too far, and their arms couldn't hold up. You can't fault Tobi Inouye or Shin Ozawa for lack of fighting spirit."

"You have to grow with the game, I suppose."

"They're saying exactly that. If Inouye's arm stays sore or Ozawa's rotor cuff keeps giving him trouble, next season could be a full-scale disaster. It's easier to maintain and improve a pitching staff than it is to build one from scratch. That can take years."

"Would you just look at the Stars fans? Poor sons of bitches. To come this far and fold like that. What a disappointment."

Alburo said, "They're saying the Stars are going to have to forget about Iron Man Inao. There was only one Iron Man."

"Who is Iron Man Inao?"

"I don't have any idea. A famous pitcher, sounds like."

TWENTY-ONE

Maria Reyes was in the shooting studio, naked on the floor with her hands cuffed behind her back and one ankle tethered to a ring screwed into the base of the wall.

A matching brace of padded restraining tables were surrounded by lights and reflectors. On the floor was a bamboo cage with six white doves and a basket of apples. This one would be supervised by Kobayashi-*san*.

Miki said, "You will do as you're told. You know the drill."

Linda Shive nodded.

Miki had leather anklets and bracelets, and a gag with a rubber ball that went into the victim's mouth. This ball was held in place by a studded leather strap with a buckle in the back.

"Open."

Linda opened.

Miki poked the ball into her mouth and fastened the buckle.

"Strip and drop 'em. Make 'em neat."

Linda, her mouth full of rubber ball, stripped and folded her clothes.

"Leave 'em on the floor. Turn around. Hands behind your back."

She turned, hands behind her back.

Miki popped on the cuffs. She sat the doves on the floor. "Up you go."

Linda hopped up on the table.

"On your back, wrists above your head."

Linda did as she was told.

Miki fastened her wrists together at the head of the table and her ankles at each corner. Having done this, she added bands around Linda's thighs, just above the knees. She snapped a slender chain to one knee restraint, ran it under the table, fastened it to the other knee restraint, then pulled tight.

Linda was on her back, arms above her head, and legs opened wide. She could see but not move or speak.

Miki put a New York Yankees baseball cap on Linda's head and adjusted the plastic tab in back, then tied Maria down the same way on the other table. Maria got a Seibu Lions hat.

Then Kobayashi stepped inside, followed by a Takeshita-*kai* film crew—two cameramen, a lighting man, and a man who did the sound, plus a man in a top hat and full tuxedo. The man in the tux went straight to the bird cage and started talking to the doves in a soothing voice.

Miki informed Linda and Maria that this gentleman was Count Ikeda.

Alburo looked the narrow town house up and down. It had abstract floral patterns of beige, green, and yellow bricks worked into the dark redbrick exterior. The windows were arched with a pale, cream-colored stone swirled with lavender and green; each window had a diminutive balcony with wrought-iron railings. The stoop, of a nearly translucent white Italian marble with light gray specks, had wrought-iron handrails. The front door was a rich red wood, possibly cherrywood, with a cut-glass doorknob.

"What is it you propose to do?" he said. "Just walk up and ring the doorbell?"

Burlane said, "That's exactly what I intend to do."

"Oh?"

"This is the Yokohama residence of the *oyabun* of Takeshita-*kai*. One looks upon this town house with awe and respect.

These are not Italians; once the turf is divided and accommodation made with the police, everybody's goal is to maintain the *wa.* Isn't that what you said?''

"Ahh, I think so." Alburo looked impressed at his partner's chutzpah.

"In Yokohama, Kobayashi is an unchallenged predator. He has no natural enemies. I've been in places like this, and I bet you have too. It's narrow and tall. Ordinarily the front door will open into a small vestibule. There'll be steep stairs to the left and the kitchen dead ahead. The living and dining rooms will be on the second floor, with bedrooms and Kobayashi's room full of swords and *yakuza* memorabilia on the third and fourth.''

"She'll be on the third or the fourth floor."

"That's my bet."

TWENTY-TWO

Shoji Kobayashi grabbed himself an apple as the technicians snapped on the lights above Maria's table and began testing the sound. He assigned two cameras to Maria and one on Linda to record her face as she watched what was obviously in store for her as well.

Miki laid a knife by the side of Maria's head.

Maria, wild-eyed, looked at Linda.

Count Ikeda, rolling up his sleeves, began talking to the cameras. He addressed the viewers, apparently explaining what he was about to do. Stepping to one side, holding his hands open for the camera to see, Ikeda splashed some baby oil on his hand. He inserted his fingers into Maria's vagina.

With no further ado, he plunged his fist forearm deep.

Maria's body arched. She screamed into the rubber ball.

Ikeda, speaking to the cameras in a matter-of-fact tone of voice, twisted his fist inside Maria.

The photographers closed in on his wrist.

He suddenly pulled his hand out, and released a white dove.

Kobayashi, munching on his apple, applauded vigorously. "Hai!"

Then, with the cameras taping the action from different angles, he did it again, more slowly, so the cameras could inspect his every action for cheating, and yet a third time. Kobayashi, pleased with the wonderful show, applauded the release of each bird. *"Hai!"*

Miki said, "You always were a *waslik,* Maria; you've known that all along." She picked up the knife and slashed Maria's throat.

Kobayashi applauded. *"Hai! Hai! Hai!"*

Burlane, with Alburo at his side, went up the stairs of the stone stoop of Kobayashi's imitation Jacques LeFleur town house. As he rang the doorbell, he removed his Ruger from his shoulder holster. "Don't be surprised at anything I do. We're not competing for Ms. Congeniality here."

"Got it," Alburo said.

"Tell whoever answers that we want to borrow a cup of sugar."

"Sugar?"

"Sure, sugar. Why not? If you like, we can tell 'em we're Jehovah's Witnesses or aluminum siding salesmen."

A middle-aged man in a *hapi* answered the door.

Burlane, seeing he was the only person in sight, shot him in the heart with his Ruger and grabbed him by the throat before he could make a peep. Still squeezing him by the throat, Burlane lowered him to the floor; as he did, he checked out the kitchen in front of him.

Kobayashi watched, eating an apple, as Miki laid the knife beside Linda Shive's head.

Count Ikeda addressed the cameras.

As in a dream, Linda listened to Miki translate.

Ikeda told President Olofson and her father that he was the world's best pussy magician. He had removed doves from the pussy of the girlfriend of the British movie actor Brent McConnall, and from the pussies of the harem of Sheikh Ibn Said al-Hussein of Oman.

Then Ikeda recited a poem.

When he had finished, Kobayashi said, *"Hai!"*
Miki translated:

The dove,
released,
flies swiftly home.
The soul,
freed,
settles on a distant limb.

That was supposed to be a Zen koan, Linda knew. Settles on
a distant limb. Such pea-brained, sophomoric horseshit!
    Ikeda showed his hands to the cameras. Empty.
    She felt his fingers, exploring.
    Then, the vicious thrust . . .
    His fist was inside her.
    She was nearly blind with pain.
    He twisted his fist inside her.
    Sweet Jesus!
    She heard Kobayashi saying, *"Hai! Hai!"*

TWENTY-THREE

Inside, James Burlane heard a man say, *"Hai! Hai! Hai!"*

He tried the door. Unlocked.

He stepped into the room.

Two tables.

Lights:

A naked girl tied to each table.

Cameras: Three of them. Two were trained on a man in a tuxedo removing his fist from Linda Shive's vagina.

Action: As the man released a dove, Burlane drilled him in the center of the torso.

The silenced Ruger went *ka-snap.*

The man pitched forward, still alive. The confused dove fluttered its clipped wings and hopped onto his foot and looked up at Burlane.

Burlane, seeing that none of the camera crew were armed, gave the tuxedo man a coup de grace in the head. *Ka-snap!*

"Rene, please tell everybody to stand free from the tables. I want their hands on the backs of their necks. If they remove them, I'll blow their fucking brains from here to Fukuoka. Then please release Ms. Shive so she can get dressed. Your father is in

Tokyo for trade talks, Linda. We'll get you to him as soon as we finish this business."

For the first time, Burlane got a good look at the girl on the second table. A Filipina. He saw her throat. She was the Filipina he had seen in the window of the *Sagawa Maru* in Danao.

"Who did that?" he asked Linda.

As Alburo freed her left hand, Linda pointed at Miki. "She did, a few minutes ago. I was one dove away from having my turn." She was not hysterical. She did not blubber. She did not weep. She was in control, but furious. Later there would be time for emotion. Now she wanted revenge.

"I see." Burlane said. "She's not any kind of prisoner, is she?"

"No." Linda glared at Miki.

Burlane shot Miki in the stomach. "No sense even listening to somebody like that. It'll take a few minutes, and it won't feel good, but she oughta reach Mega-Bitch Heaven, no problem."

Linda Shive, pulling on her underpants, said, "The chief fruitcake ate an apple while Miki cut Maria's throat."

"Kobayashi?"

Grabbing for her bra, she nodded. "Prick." She looked at Kobayashi with raw hatred.

"Rene, I want you to use this bondage gear to secure these gentlemen to something solid. I want 'em gagged too, please. I don't want to listen to any of their fighting spirit and how-noble-it-is-to-die bullshit. Enough is enough. Tell the *oyabun* to take a seat on the floor until I'm ready for him. Take a load off."

Linda said, "They've got more tie-down gear in the cabinets over there. Everything you'll need and then some."

"Rene, remind them again that I don't play pretend samurai."

Linda stepped into her jeans. "Jesus, thank you guys, whoever you are."

"I'm Sid Khartoum, engaged by your father, and this is Dr. Rene Alburo, of the University of San Francisco, here courtesy of the President's Anti-Crime Commission of the Philippines."

"Our pleasure, ma'am," Rene said. He dug two more pairs of handcuffs from a drawer and fastened the cameramen and their helpers wrist-to-wrist in a back-to-back circle which he attached to a ring at the base of the wall, part of the room's apparatus of suffering.

"How's that? That do it?" Alburo said.

"That'll do just fine."

Alburo said, "The *oyabun* respectfully declines to sit."

Burlane looked surprised. "He does? Tell him again, please."

Alburo did.

Kobayashi remained standing.

Burlane shot him in the foot.

Kobayashi dropped to the floor, holding his foot.

Burlane said, "Tell him playing *yakuza* rules ain't no fun."

Kobayashi grimaced at the pain.

Burlane looked concerned. "Foot smart, does it, partner?"

"That poor little Filipina," Alburo said wearily, looking at Maria Reyes.

Linda said, "She was Maria Reyes from Zamboanga. She was here to make money for her family, she said; she was the oldest of eight children. She said when Miki recruited her, she showed her pictures of Filipinas in sexy outfits serving drinks to businessmen in what sounded like an imitation Playboy club. This is what she got."

Burlane said, "What happened to Leanne Tompkins?"

"From the beginning, they did whatever they wanted to us, and Leanne fell to pieces after a few sessions of sport. We were on our way here, on a boat that was to take us to shore, when she deliberately stepped in the water and was gone, headed straight to the bottom. They had weights locked around our ankles. After my first taping in Yokohama, I envied her."

Burlane said, "Kobayashi requires discipline for his errant ways. He himself would say so. You can stay or go as you please."

"I'm not going anywhere."

"They sent tapes to your father in an effort to blackmail the government, but Rene and I watched them for him. No sense him having to watch that crap." Burlane snatched an apple from the basket and flipped it up and down in his left hand.

Eyeing him, Linda pulled on her Princeton University T-shirt. "Thank you. After we finish this, I'll make my old man take us all to a big pig-out of American food. I don't care how much it costs him. By the way, that's not any old apple you've got there, Sid. That's a Fuji, a Japanese apple. Kobayashi doesn't eat apples from Chile or Canada."

On the floor, the fatal third dove stepped from the sleeve of the corpse's tuxedo. It hopped cheerfully up the dead man's bare arm and stopped, cocking its head inquisitively.

Burlane said, "Tell the *oyabun* good afternoon, Rene. Use an ultrapolite, respectful form of address. I don't want it said that I'm a barbarian. Tell him that I am now his teacher. I'm going to teach him how to be a man. Tell him we will have a *gattsu* drill. In this exercise, he will learn the consequence of uncivilized behavior."

TWENTY-FOUR

James Burlane unfolded the rubber sex doll from his daypack and began blowing. It was a long, flaccid, slightly ridiculous-looking bag of rubber. Breath by breath, it began to take shape. Burlane, pausing, said, "You translate, Rene." He continued puffing.

"Got it," Alburo said.

Watching Kobayashi, Burlane put this thumb over the stumpy valve stem, which was like a mole or wart on the doll's left heel. "You want a hard body or should I leave it a little soft?"

Alburo translated the first question.

In spite of his foot, Kobayashi seemed surprisingly calm.

"I know you're not supposed to display any emotion in these circumstances. Part of your Bushido horseshit. I bet you're wondering what this is for, eh, *oyabun-san?*" He continued blowing on the doll, which was shaping up to have long legs, blond hair, and blue eyes.

"I was wondering too," Linda said.

Burlane said, "Give me a few minutes. Why don't you tell the *oyabun* who you are, Rene? About your mother and everything."

Alburo did. When he finished, he said to Burlane, "That was a good idea."

"You told him?"

"I told him. Thank you for letting me get that off my chest."

Burlane said to Linda, "Rene is a *japino*. His mother was a *japayuki*. She was forced to serve Japanese troops as a 'comfort girl' in the war." He gave the doll three more breaths of life. "Ask *oyabun-san* what he would do if he'd walked into a roomful of Americans fist-fucking a Japanese girl in a snuff film. Ask him, Rene."

Alburo asked the question.

Kobayashi looked impassive.

Burlane was finished with the doll; he screwed the cap on the air valve, and dug a marker pen out of his pocket. On the spacious left breast of the sex doll he wrote, *No more japayuki or we'll be back. Sisters of Sudden Justice.* "Okay, Rene. Same thing in Japanese over the other tit, please."

TWENTY-FIVE

James Burlane opened his Swiss army knife and tested the sharpness of the blade with his finger.

Kobayashi looked impassive, remembering his Jocho Yamamoto. *One may judge a person's dignity on how he looks. There is dignity in diligence and effort. There is dignity in serenity and closeness of mouth.*

Burlane said, "Linda, in *yubitsume*, a *yakuza oyabun* administers justice by severing the end of the little finger of an errant *kobun*. He is the father, and they are the children. When they misbehave, he punishes them. He can have them killed, if he pleases, or even worse, he can expel them from the gang."

Thinking of Yamamoto, Kobayashi looked thoughtful. *Remain silent. If you can manage without speaking, say nothing. When you do speak, be as succinct, logical, and clear as possible. A surprising number of people make fools of themselves by talking without thinking. These people are looked down upon.*

Burlane said, "Rene, tell *oyabun-san* he will surrender three joints this afternoon: one for Leanne Tompkins, one for Maria Reyes, and one for Linda Shive. Tell him I should take a fourth joint, for him trying to run his baseball club according to the code of Bushido. He fucked up the arms of his pitchers with all that ridiculous fighting spirit crap. Asshole."

Kobayashi, listening to Alburo's translation, was calm. This longnose had killed Kamina and Kao. He would kill him as well. So what? *The way of the samurai is death.*

Burlane said, "Tell him to hold his left hand in front of him, fingers straight."

Kobayashi held out his hand.

"Tell him beating on people and forcing them to walk around with weights on their ankles is a chickenshit thing to do. I want an apology."

Kobayashi was told. He said nothing.

Burlane sighed, and removed a digit with his knife.

Kobayashi looked unconcerned. *If one undertakes great feats, don't worry about minor failures.*

Burlane said, "Tell him fist fucking and snuff films are barbarous in the extreme. I want an apology."

Kobayashi listened impassively to Alburo's translation.

Burlane bowed again, then took a second digit.

Kobayashi kept his mind on Yamamoto: *In a fifty-fifty life-or-death crisis, settle it immediately. Choose death. There is nothing complicated about it. Just brace yourself and proceed . . .*

Burlane said, "The problem is, Kobayashi-*san* wants to die more than he wants to live. He's like Br'er Rabbit. 'Oh, please, please, massa, do whatever you like only don't throw me in that there briar patch.' If I kill him, I give him his wish."

Kobayashi looked up at Burlane. *One who chooses to live after failure will be despised as a coward and a bungler.*

Burlane looked sympathetic. "Manliness. Fighting spirit. Discipline. Isn't that what it's all about, Kobayashi-*san?*"

Kobayashi, listening to Alburo, said nothing. *A samurai must never complain, even in casual conversation. He must constantly guard against giving a hint of weakness. A slip of the tongue may reveal one's true nature.*

Burlane said, "Yeah, yeah, it's true, I know. *Gaijins* playing by *yakuza* rules can be real chickenshits." He took another of Kobayashi's Fujis from the basket and took a bite. "Mmmmmmmm. It's good, it really is." He offered Kobayashi a bite. "No? Lost your appetite? How about you, Rene? Like an apple?"

Alburo said, "I think I'll pass for now."

Kobayashi clenched his jaw. *A samurai must transcend resignation when disaster hits. He must rejoice and leap at the chance to proceed with energy and courage.*

Burlane took a third digit.

Kobayashi thought: *A perfect samurai prepares himself for death morning and evening, day in and day out.*

Linda said, "The pathetic part of it is he doesn't have the faintest idea what it is that he's supposed to have done wrong. He's in another zone."

Burlane said, "I don't give a flying fuck what zone he's in." He wiped the blood from his knife on Kobayashi's *hapi* coat and folded the blade.

He said, "Rene, I want you to tell *oyabun-san* that we don't care at all what the Japanese do to their own women. If Japanese women want to work in tit bars and sex shows and star in S and M movies and nobody in Japan objects, then fine. But the *yakuza* and their customers have violated our *gaijin ninjo* big, big time. We have to do something to stop this shit."

Kobayashi listened to Alburo, thinking: *A man who accomplishes great feats will have his faults, but what is a small screw-up to a man of great honor and dignity?*

Burlane took his .22 Ruger from his pocket. To Linda Shive, "He supervised the murder of the Filipina. In such circumstances, I believe in capital punishment. Do you have any moral or ethical objections?"

She said, "Absolutely none at all. Give it to the son-of-a-bitch. Do it!"

Burlane said, "It's his Bushido bullshit game. I just showed him how it's played in the bigs." With that, he snapped off two quick shots into Kobayashi's forehead.

Then Burlane and Alburo yanked the trousers off Kobayashi's legs and put his corpse atop the rubber *japayuki*. They spread the doll's legs wide and pinned them with the corpse's hands.

When Kobayashi and doll were properly arranged so that rigor mortis would freeze the corpse in place, Burlane set about taking pictures of the *oyabun's* final resting place. He had a half-dozen rolls of film. There would be plenty of newspapers and magazines that would love to have shots of the godfather of Takeshita-*kai* in manly action; perhaps then someone would be moved to curiosity about the *japayuki* trade.

TWENTY-SIX

On the helicopter ride north from the White House, President Olofson told Foreign Minister Masayuki Yoshida that they would be staying in Aspen cottage in Camp David, where President Dwight Eisenhower played host to Nikita Khrushchev in September 1959.

It was apparent that Yoshida-*san* was uncertain whether he should be flattered or wary. That a change in the weather of the U.S.-Japan relationship was imminent was as obvious as the turning of the leaves on the landscape below them. Yoshida had never before been invited to Camp David. He knew there had to be a reason.

As they glided along high above fields and highways and copses, President Olofson gave a running history of the Maryland landscape below them. He told of Robert E. Lee's failed attempt to crack the Union army at Antietam, and of the incredible massing of Confederate and Union armies at Gettysburg, a little more than thirty miles northeast of Camp David.

Yoshida was only half listening, wondering what the American president had on his mind, as Olofson told him about Lincoln's famous address at the Gettysburg battlefield, penned at the last moment. "Fourscore and seven years ago our forefathers set forth . . ." Olofson had a faraway look in his eye. "It was the repetition of the f's and of the 'or' sound that did it, you know. He was a lyric writer. He came by it naturally. He had an ear for language."

Yoshida said nothing.

Olofson, watching him, said, "This was Franklin Roosevelt's retreat originally. He called it Shangri-La. Ike thought that was a bit too pretentious for an old soldier like him, so he renamed it Camp David, after his grandson. He had a farm near Gettysburg."

Yoshida wondered: Did this trip to Camp David have anything to do with the rescue of Jack Shive's daughter and the murder of the *oyabun* of Takeshita-*kai?*

The helicopter hovered above the pad.

Outside, the Catoctin Mountains were a blaze of color.

The helicopter blades went *whack, whack, whack* as they sliced through the nippy November air.

Olofson and Yoshida went walking in the late afternoon along a ridge behind Camp David. It was the second week in November and time for one of the most remarkable natural sights in North America, the turning of the leaves in the Appalachian Range.

As they walked up the trail, the world a fabulous mural of yellows and golds and oranges and reds, President Harold Olofson said, "You know, Yoshida-*san,* there was much speculation in the media about my recent illness. Bugs in my guts is what it comes down to. It wasn't life-threatening, I suppose, but it sure made my life miserable."

Yoshida grimaced in commiseration.

Olofson said, "My doctors tried everything and nothing worked. Finally one day, my doctor said he thought he had found the right medicine. He gave me some kind of Latin medical term that I didn't understand. I said, 'Does it work?' He said he thought so. I said, 'What are the side effects?' He said none that could be determined. I said, 'Okay, let's try it.' " Olofson fell silent.

They walked on.

Finally, Yoshida said, "Did it work?"

Olofson smiled. "Why, yes it did, I'm pleased to report. Can you tell me the question I didn't ask?"

Yoshida looked uncertain. "I'm not sure, Mr. President."

Olofson said, "I didn't ask where it was made." He again fell silent.

The trail began to climb, and they slowed their pace.

Then Olofson said, "I didn't care if the British came up with the medicine, or the French, or the Italians. That was immaterial."

"Where was it made?"

"It was developed and marketed by a Japanese company. It cleared up my guts; that's all that mattered to me."

Yoshida cleared his throat.

They stopped before a patch of blazing yellow. Olofson said, "These are hickory trees. Famous for their yellow leaves in the fall. One of the most spectacular drives in the world this time of year is along Skyline Drive in the Shenandoah National Park in Virginia. That's along the summit of the Appalachians. The yellow of the hickories just jumps out at you."

"It's wonderful," Yoshida said. "It almost seems to glow."

"So it does," Olofson said, as they continued up the trail. "You know, Vice President Shive was curious as to how Kobayashi learned of the details of his conversation with you in Washington. He said Kobayashi knew everything he had proposed. Now how did that happen, do you suppose? How is it that a gangster winds up knowing the specifics of a confidential conversation between a Japanese foreign minister and an American vice president?"

"Japan is a small country, Mr. President. Word of something like that travels."

"It sure as hell must."

"But I implore you to please, please, not let this terrible thing color your thinking on the critical matter of trade relations between our countries, Mr. President. We sincerely regret this terrible incident."

"You know, Yoshida-*san,* in the last couple of years you Japanese have done a lot of apologizing. First it was to the United Kingdom for having used British soldiers for slave labor during the Second World War. You had to say 'I'm sorry' for having lined up rows of Chinese civilians and using them for machine-gun practice at Nanking. Then it was 'Oh yes, that wasn't good' to the Koreans, Chinese, and Filipinos, for having used their women as sex slaves to serve the troops."

"It was wrong, we know. So we said we were sorry."

They stood before a tree with bright red leaves. Yoshida blinked.

"A red maple," Olofson said.

"I was wondering," Yoshida said. He stooped and picked up a red leaf, examining it.

They continued up the trail through a blaze of yellows, golds, oranges, and reds.

Olofson said, "Then it was apologies to the Filipinos for having consumed some eighty-odd of their people on Mindanao. A little code of Bushido cannibalism there, butchering Filipinos for protein to keep the emperor's warriors fit for the good fight." Olofson sucked air between his front teeth.

Yoshida's face tightened. He said, "Kobayashi was a *yakuza oyabun*, keep in mind. They have their own, closed world, and it is nearly impossible to monitor their activities, much less penetrate their circles. You have godfathers and gangs in the United States, don't you? I have seen all three of Mr. Coppola's Mafia movies. Ohhhhhh. What's this?"

They stood before a tree with orange leaves. Olofson said, "That's a kind of maple. What's commonly called a mountain maple. We've got sugar maples, mountain maples, and sycamore trees, which I believe is a kind of maple as well. Unfortunately, you're right about the Mafia, Yoshida-*san*, although we're doing our best to put them out of business."

"The *yakuza* almost do as they please. It's very difficult to control them."

"Yes, I bet it is."

"It's a never-ending struggle."

Mmmm. Olofson looked thoughtful. He fingered his chin.

They were nearing the uncomfortable territory of confrontation. Yoshida licked his lips.

Olofson dipped into his back pocket and casually retrieved a handful of Burlane's ghastly photographs of Kamina and Kobayashi, which he gave to Yoshida. "*Oyabun-san* and his *kobun* loved cameras so much, fair is only fair. Right? He took pictures of Linda Shive. We took pictures of him. Of course you at least read about Kobayashi's associate Nobito Kao, the gentleman whose crotch was used as a target."

Yoshida's mouth opened, but he didn't say anything. Looking at the photographs, he blinked.

"These photographs are being sent to the mass media as we speak."

Yoshida made a small sound in the back of his throat.

"Embarrassing, I know," Olofson said.

They left the territory of pure color and entered a stand of evergreens speckled with trees bearing orange and red and yellow leaves. Olofson said, "The green ones are spruce and hemlock mostly."

"I was wondering," Yoshida said. He grabbed a lower branch of a spruce tree and pretended to be interested in it.

Olofson said, "Your friend Kobayashi-*san* in fact owned the Yokohama Bay Stars, and I bet you know something about *besuboru* yourself. The tape of Linda Shive he gave Jack is what we Americans call a hanging curve."

Yoshida blinked. It was unclear whether he knew or not.

"That's when you try to slip a breaking pitch by us, but you don't get the right spin on the ball, and it just hangs there, begging for the batter to jump on it and slug the shit out of it."

"I see."

Olofson picked up a stick and swung it like a baseball bat. "The ash they use for baseball bats is grown farther west, in Tennessee and Kentucky mostly. They say the use of metal bats by schoolboys has saved a lot of ash trees, but I'll never get used to that *klink* sound of hitting metal."

Yoshida brightened. The Japanese liked their baseball, and

he felt the subject was comfortable territory. "The crack of a wooden bat has a satisfying sound to it, I admit."

"The vice president sent an all-star to the plate to retrieve his daughter, I think you'll agree. Five slugs laid one on top of another in Yokohama. Linda Shive tells me she plans to write a book about what happened to her. A Japanese woman would be worried about saving face, but Linda says she's never been sure what the concept means, exactly."

The trail widened to accommodate a bench that overlooked a small valley that curved back toward Camp David.

Olofson said, "The view here is superb. Shall we sit?"

"Yes, certainly," Yoshida said. He sat.

Olofson too sat.

Yoshida, mopping his forehead with a handkerchief, said, "It's beautiful. All the color."

Olofson said nothing.

"I assure you, Mr. President, the Japanese government will do everything in our power to see that justice is done in this matter."

Olofson said, "If the *yakuza* hadn't given Jack Shive videotapes of the treatment his daughter suffered, she'd have no proof that anything had happened. Linda Shive is a headstrong, independent young woman. Vice President Shive says she's just like her mother; when she gets pissed, watch out. There's not a lot he can do to change her mind." Olofson grabbed a stick and began poking at the ground in front of him.

Yoshida pretended to enjoy the scenery.

Olofson said, "You have to watch out for these Western women, Yoshida-*san*. You take my wife, for example. *Oooooh!* She wanted to be attorney general, but I managed to ease her out of that notion. Thank God!" Olofson closed his eyes and winced. "Yes, Linda Shive wants to write a book, and her professors say she's quite a good writer. Kobayashi obviously didn't give that possibility much thought or credibility, did he? An independent, educated Western woman. Ouch!"

Yoshida stiffened.

"On the subject of trade, Vice President Shive and I are going to levy a tax to even out the price of automobiles sold here and in Japan. Screw that dumping crap, and to hell with more talk. If your cars are good enough to sell here at the same price you sell them there, well, then, as they say in Tennessee, 'Good on you.' If we sense any objection among congressional leaders, we'll have Linda talk to them in private. We too have our *giri* and *ninjo*."

Yoshida opened his mouth, then closed it.

"And fix your thieving patent laws. From now on, you give and you get. No givee, no gettee. As Kobayashi-*san* can testify from our pinch hitter, we've got talented players at every position and for every occasion. You throw beanballs at us. We throw beanballs at you."

"We . . ." Yoshida obviously didn't know what to say.

"What will you do? Commit *seppuku?*"

Yoshida's face hardened.

"If your culture is ill at ease consuming products made in other countries, perhaps your companies will be satisfied with an uncontested monopoly on your domestic market. You'll feel more comfortable that way, no more *gaijin* whining at you. You can eat your own rice and drive your own cars and use your own computers. You'll have to adjust your standard of living, but if you can't afford to buy something, you can always copy it."

"Please, Mr. President."

"Either teach yourselves to play the same game away as at home or you can play with yourselves, a practice I've been told has its champions." Olofson scratched his armpit and rose. "Shall we start back now?"

Yoshida stood too. "Certainly, Mr. President."

Olofson began walking back down the trail. "I just love these diplomatic conversations. So circumspect and civilized. Didn't get a lot of training for this sort of thing back in Idaho."

Yoshida nudged a yellow leaf with his foot.

Grinning, Olofson said, "Ordinarily, we treat the truth like *aji no moto*, don't we, Yoshida-*san?* We sprinkle it into polite horseshit in an effort to improve the flavor. The maintenance of *wa*, I believe it's called in your country."